LOOSE CANNON

Kendal Flynn

etopia
press

Etopia Press

P.O. Box 66

Medford, OR 97501

http://www.etopia-press.net

Loose Cannon

Print ISBN: 978-1-947135-15-4

Digital ISBN: 978-1-936751-08-2

First Etopia Press electronic publication: December, 2010

First Etopia Press print publication: May, 2012

~ Dedication ~

To Mom: Who always had a house full of spy thrillers for me to teethe on and an old Underwood manual typewriter for practicing my ABCs;

To Ann: Who later loaned me her IBM Selectric with the cool spinning letter ball and the automatic correction thingie;

To the Kids: Who put up with a full-time-writer-mom in frayed slippers;

And to Jack: Without whom I'd never have known enough about love to write romance.

Chapter One

The corner booth at the back of the Blind Shark Bar and Billiards was the perfect vantage point. With her back to the wall and a chipped mug of murky beer in her hand, Raeanne maintained unobstructed lines of fire between herself and all four exits: the port-holed swing-door to the kitchen and the restroom alcove beside it at her one o'clock, the fire exit on the wall at her three leading out to the alley between Stratton and 4th Street, and straight ahead, across the long, smoky room at twelve o'clock, the two sets of double glass doors propped open to the hot swarm of traffic on North Las Vegas Boulevard. The familiar clack of billiard balls beat a sharp staccato against the monotonous, electronic jingle of slot machines, and Raeanne's foot kept time. She glanced again at her watch, wiped a bead of sweat from her temple, and cursed Alex Dante to hell.

She ran her thumb over the well-worn chip in the mug handle, wondering again what he wanted. She noticed her foot tapping and stilled it. Focus and control, she remembered that much. Focus, control, and keep your shooting hand free. Judging from the size of the cockroach that scurried across the wall beside her, she might need to shoot her way out of here.

He had five more minutes, then she was gone.

A chill skittered across her skin despite the thick heat nudged around by the groaning ceiling fan. She shoved back the memory of those pale green eyes and focused on the reassuring press of the Glock .40 against her side, invisible beneath the baggy plaid shirt that hung open over her black tank top. She almost took a sip of the tepid beer, but caught herself. People came to the Blind Shark for a lot of reasons, but great beer wasn't one of them.

And rekindling the past wasn't one of them either, as far as Raeanne Springfield was concerned. Seven years ago, she'd been dumped by both the Counterintelligence Defense Agency and her partner, Alex Dante. Partner, lover, supposed best friend. Whatever.

She'd moved on.

Or so she'd thought until her phone had rung just as she was leaving the house this morning.

"I need to see you."

She'd recognized his voice instantly. She almost asked how he'd gotten her private number, but that was a no-brainer. The Great and Powerful Agency saw all. Instead, she steeled her resolve. "No."

"It's important."

"So is world peace and good dental hygiene. The answer is no. And please don't force me to change my phone number, Dante, it's extremely inconvenient."

A pause. "Please, Raeanne."

She heaved a sigh of resignation and tried to calm the adrenaline rush that had come with hearing his voice. Shouldering the phone to her ear, she zipped the bag of carrot sticks into Ryan's T-Rex lunch box. "Fine. What do you want?"

"I need to see you."

"Not until you tell me what this is about."

He hesitated only a fraction of a second, but it was enough. She knew exactly what he was going to say.

"Agency business."

Of course. *Agency business.* The almighty CODA. Why else would he be calling her after seven years?

"News flash, Dante. I'm no longer *with* the agency,

effective seven years ago. You can forward your inquiry to whoever's currently running special ops."

"Don't hang up."

She stopped with the handset halfway to the phone's base, cursing the fact that he still had that eerie ability to predict her every move.

"I know you're not happy to be talking to me, Raeanne, but this isn't about us."

Of course it wasn't. It never had been. That had always been the problem.

She didn't trust herself to speak for a long moment while she regained control of her responses. "I have a job to do, Dante. I can't just leave Senator Helmsan without a bodyguard, especially now. Some kook tried to play chicken with her on the highway yesterday. The freaks come out of the woodwork whenever new legislation is up for vote."

"The senator's covered. We have assets in place to carry out your duties."

Oh, right. What was she thinking? The agency always had *assets in place.*

"What do you want with me, Alex? I'm no longer associated in any way with CODA. In fact, I'm not even cleared to know whether or not it still exists."

"It exists. Trust me."

Trust me. There'd been a time when she'd trusted him implicitly, but there had also been a time when she'd believed in Santa and the Tooth Fairy. And now here she was, sitting in the Blind Shark, sipping skunky beer and waiting for Alex Dante to show up, just like the old days.

She scanned the room again. All four exits were still clear. The place was doing a brisk business for three in the afternoon, but none of the patrons looked in any way suspicious. Just your standard, garden-variety drunks—laughing, shooting pool, dropping change into the slot machines hoping for something better. She studied her beer a moment and wondered if the brown crust on the bottom of the mug was on the inside or the outside.

"Hello, Raeanne."

She snapped her gaze up to Alex Dante's light green eyes, bold within their rim of dark lashes and beneath the ledge of his dark brows. Jaguar eyes, she'd always thought. Predatory.

"You've gotten careless, Raven," he said. "I could have shot you dead a hundred times in the last ten minutes and you'd have never seen it coming."

Apprehension and desire coursed through her at the sound of her old code name dripping off his tongue. And that voice of his, deep and rich, like sex and chocolate and cognac all together.

"I saw you," she lied.

His smirk told her he wasn't buying it. She held her gaze firmly on his, keeping her expression neutral. Trying not to let herself look at his body.

She couldn't help it.

He hadn't changed a bit, damn him. Darker tan, maybe, but other than that, he was just the same. Six feet of lean muscle under a shock of close-cropped dark hair, which despite her prayers, hadn't thinned a bit. His faded Levi's hugged the same strong thighs and rode the same low arc across his hips. Damn, but the man knew how to fill a pair of jeans. Behind the blue T-shirt, his hard, tight abdominals hadn't grown the least bit soft. She remembered those abs, how they felt under her hands and against her cheek, with the patch of crisp dark hair trailing down to...

"Aren't you going to ask me to join you?"

She jerked her gaze back up to his face. "Suit yourself."

The sleeves of his blue T-shirt stretched taut over his hard, round biceps and showed off the strong cords of muscle ridging his forearms. He carried a black denim jacket draped over his left arm and hand—that was nothing new—and he left it that way as he slid in beside her, rather than across the booth from her.

"You should have taken the table next to us," he said, surveying the room. "That bank of slot machines is partially blocking the doorway to the restrooms."

She glanced at it again. "I can see the doorway fine."

"Then explain how I made it all the way to your table without being seen."

He was sitting too close. She inched toward the wall. "Guess I didn't expect you to swim up through the sewer pipes. Although evidently I should have."

The heat of his gaze seared a path down her body then burned its way back up to her paint-splotched Red Sox cap, the one that used to be his. She knew he recognized it even though he said nothing. The desire to look away was almost irresistible, but she did, in fact, resist.

"Interesting outfit," he finally said.

"Just trying to blend in."

"Still packing the Glock?"

"Still got the expert rating to go with it, too." She nodded at the casual fall of denim over his left forearm. "Still hiding your weapon under your jacket, I see. God knows you can't conceal anything with a T-shirt *that* tight."

He smiled slightly, but it held no joy. "I like things where I can keep a hand on them. Prevent them from wandering off."

She gave him a sniff of annoyance. "How 'bout you tell me what's going on? Senator Helmsan's expecting me back soon."

"I told you, the senator's covered. The agency's taking no chances with her life."

Raeanne's eyes narrowed. "So that's what this is about? Who's trying to kill the senator?"

"Now Raeanne…"

"Don't 'Now Raeanne' me. You just said the agency was taking no chances with her life. That means you have reason to believe her life is in danger. And I want to know what that reason is. Now."

He gave her a long look with that intense, green gaze of his. She refused to look away, and she refused to acknowledge the heat pooling in her groin. *Keep it professional. "Agency business," remember?*

"The senator's fine, Raeanne. It's you who's in danger."

A crash from across the room drew her gaze away from Alex. Instinctively, her right hand slid inside her shirt to her holster.

Over by the bar, a cocktail waitress stooped to pick up the broken pieces of the glass she'd dropped while the bartender called her several uncomplimentary names, not quietly.

Raeanne put her hand back on the table. "Who wants me dead and why?"

Alex studied the bartender a moment longer, then looked back at Raeanne.

Outside, a car horn brayed, loud through the wide, plate glass doors that stood open to the heat and exhaust fumes. A sleek white Mercedes crawled past, tailgated by an impatient driver shouting expletives from his open window.

"Remember the December Ice mission?" Alex asked.

Raeanne's heart lurched in her chest again. Russian Mafia, organization called the Ice Syndicate. Traded old soviet military equipment to warlords in Africa for diamonds and used them, instead of the unstable ruble, to finance their drug operation.

It was right after December Ice that Alex had made it perfectly clear they would never have a "someday." Standing her up, not returning her calls for a week, then changing his phone number... "Yeah, I remember. What about it?"

"They're back."

The blood drained from her face and left her cold. "That's impossible. Kovalenko and Petrov are dead. You killed them yourself."

"Kovalenko is dead, but Petrov apparently survived. He's

pulled the syndicate back together, and this time they're not bothering with African warlords. They're playing with Al-Qaeda, Hamas, and anyone else who's shopping for post-Soviet weapons, specifically nuclear."

Raeanne took a long swallow of warm beer. "So how does that involve me? Petrov saw you kill Kovalenko and half the syndicate, but last I knew, my cover hadn't been compromised." She gripped the clammy handle of her beer mug and scanned the room again. Fear took her breath for a moment, cold and sharp like a blade between the ribs. If the syndicate knew where she was, then neither she, nor Ryan, was safe.

"He saw you. On TV with the senator. Hell, the whole world saw you, Rae." Alex picked the mug out of her hand and drank deeply, then put it down with a look of disappointment, at her or the beer she couldn't tell.

She could feel the heat of his thigh against hers, even though they weren't quite touching. He was right. She hadn't exactly kept a low profile over the last few years, but somehow, the past had seemed so far away.

Petrov was alive...

She'd screwed up. She should have taken the agency up on its offer when they relieved her of duty, should have let them give her a new name and relocate her to West Nowhere, Minnesota. But she hadn't. She'd used some connections to land a security detail with Senator Helmsan, and had thought that would somehow keep her safe. And now she'd led Petrov straight to her door. He wouldn't give a red-hot damn that she was just an ordinary mom who drove a minivan and chauffeured her son to Cub Scouts and Little League, and not some agency droid who changed her address every year and kept grappling hooks and body armor in the trunk of her car.

And then there was the senator and her son, Tommy.

"I'll have to resign my position with Senator Helmsan until the situation is contained. I don't want her involved."

"She already is," Alex said. "That's how they found you in the first place. She's sponsoring a nice little piece of import legislation that's going to be a real nuisance to the syndicate's global trade activities. It was during their preparations to strong-arm her that they realized who her bodyguard was."

"What do they want from her?"

"They want her to pull the bill. They made it very clear this morning that when Congress reconvenes next week, she's to make sure her legislation doesn't get any farther than the trash can on the Senate floor."

"Have they physically threatened her?"

"Other than that game of chicken yesterday that you mentioned?"

Raeanne looked into his cool green eyes, wishing she could find some reason to walk away. How had things spun so out of control without her even noticing?

He laid a hand across hers. "Don't worry about the senator. We've already taken her to a safe location, and we're watching some of her more vocal supporters to make sure they're not targeted as well. You're the last loose end."

Raeanne pulled her hand out from under his and used it to lift her mug. The last thing she needed was Alex feeling her hands shake. "So what makes you so sure they're after me?"

One of the old-fashioned Jokers Wild machines by the restroom doors blared its winners jingle over the metallic downpour of quarters. Alex glanced over at it momentarily, then turned back to her with that look she'd seen a million times.

"Don't you dare tell me it's *agency business,* or I walk right now."

"You know I can't discuss classified information."

"Look, Dante, you just told me I'm a target. Either you tell me what you know, or I walk, simple as that."

Alex gave her the other look, the one that said he knew he was outmaneuvered and hated it. "If you walk, I'm instructed to take you into custody."

"I guess you could try."

His dark brows drew together. "Why do you always have to be so damned difficult?"

She maintained eye contact and waited.

"Fine. We have a mole inside their operation in Azerbaijan. Our source tells us that Petrov has made you a primary target."

"Facts, Dante. I want facts."

"You *want* to get me arrested, don't you?"

She waited.

He let out a breath. "Sources say the Ice Syndicate planed to take you out at the press conference for the bill next week in Washington, at which time, they also planned to snatch the boy from home as an insurance policy to make sure the senator did as she was told."

"That's crazy. They'll never get past her security."

"That was before Petrov saw you on TV walking beside the senator. Our source says Petrov became enraged." He gave her a long, cold look. "The words 'freaking psychotic' were used."

She took a deep breath to settle her nerves. "*You* shot Petrov. You killed Kovalenko and brought the entire organization down. Does your source have a good explanation for why they'd waste time targeting me when you're the one who put them out of business?"

But she already knew the answer. She'd known the minute she'd heard Petrov's name.

It had nothing to do with business. For Petrov, it was personal.

"I don't know, Rae. Maybe it was that really long phrase in Russian that translates roughly to: 'I want that cheating whore's head mounted on the wall'?" A muscle twitched at Alex's jaw for a moment, his trademark sign of annoyance. "You were his pride and joy, Raeanne. A couple of .45's to the chest was probably nothing compared to finding out that your love affair was just a ruse." His pale eyes froze her to the spot, cold as green, glacial ice. "In fact, I can tell you from personal experience that it's no comparison at all."

She let his words hang there a moment. "What are you talking about? I wasn't the one who changed my phone number."

He opened his mouth to reply, but she wasn't going to let him go there. Not now. "Thanks for the tip, Alex. I owe you one." She nudged him to let her out of the seat, but he didn't move. "Please, I'm not trying to be difficult, but I have some very important things to take care of, given the circumstances."

He looked up at her with a strangled expression on his face that told her exactly what he was working up to.

"Forget it, Dante, I'm not going to any safe house like some cowering child. Now, please. Get out of my way."

"Raeanne…"

"Oh, it's Raeanne, now, is it? No more *Raven* now that you want me to come along all peaceful, like a good little civilian?"

"I know you resent being protected, Rae, but I don't want to see you hurt."

She took a deep breath and forced her muscles to relax, even though her heart was tearing through her chest like a Mack truck. "What about Ryan? Did you pick him up already and whisk him away to the safe house without even telling me?" She glanced at her watch. 3:52. Ryan rode home with Tommy Helmsan's nanny. If they'd already picked up the Senator, then obviously Tommy and Ryan were with her. At least there was that.

"Ryan? You mean Tommy? We took him out of school this morning. He's with his mother."

A cold foreboding settled over her, making her hesitate. "Not Tommy—Ryan. Didn't you pick up Ryan?"

"No. Who's Ryan?"

Her hands went cold as ice. "Ryan's my son. He goes to school with Tommy Helmsan."

Alex stared uncomprehendingly back at her as if she were speaking a foreign language.

"Alex, tell me CODA picked up my son when they picked up Tommy Helmsan."

A dozen emotions flickered across Alex's face before he finally settled on dismay. "I'm sorry. No. We have no record of you even having a son."

Raeanne swallowed a roil of nausea. She had to have misheard him. His expression, though, was clear. "How could you get Tommy and not Ryan? They're practically joined at the hip. The Helmsans' nanny drives both boys to and from school every day of the week." Then it hit her. Hard. "If you picked up Tommy at school instead of the nanny, then who picked up my son?"

Alex stared at her for a moment, without an answer.

"Damn it, Dante, where is my son? Still in the schoolyard waiting for Petrov to come get him?" She squeezed out of the booth over him, and he followed her toward the front of the room.

Out on the street, the white Mercedes crawled by once more. Then it stopped just outside the open glass doors. The front and back windows slid down and two men appeared — the driver, wearing aviator shades and a goatee, and a passenger behind him, fat and completely bald with small round glasses. The barrels of two MP5 submachine guns poked out of the windows and pointed straight at Raeanne.

"Get down!" Alex yelled. He dropped the denim jacket concealing his Smith & Wesson and tossed over a cocktail table. A wave of beer and glassware crashed to the grimy linoleum, stunning the place into a momentary hush.

Raeanne dived behind the table. Alex went down beside her and covered her with his body. In one fluid motion, she drew her Glock and took aim.

The chatter of automatic weapons ripped through the air. Plate glass doors exploded in a ringing crash and bullets bit into the wall beside them. Rounds tore into the padded booths, filling the air with a snowstorm of yellow foam. People screamed and dove for cover, some running, some dropping to the floor where they stood. In front of Raeanne, the thick wooden tabletop shuddered but held against the barrage of 9mm fire.

The guns fell silent; then came the angry screech of tires. Alex poked his head out from behind the table and raised his pistol. Raeanne came around the other side, holding her own gun in both hands.

She got the passenger window in her sights as the rear end of the white Mercedes fishtailed sideways, but a fleeing patron ran across her line of fire. She jerked her weapon up with a curse and watched the car disappear.

Her heart thundered in her chest. Death hadn't walked so close for a long, long time.

"I need to find my son."

Alex scanned the room briefly. "Back door."

The bartender yelled a few incoherent obscenities, but Raeanne ignored him. She made for the fire exit, keeping as low as possible.

Ahead of her, Alex threw his weight onto the handle and pushed open the door. The harsh clang of the fire alarm blared over the shouting of the patrons, then warbled to silence as he fired a round into the cables. He stuck his head out into the alley and glanced left and right, while Raeanne spun to cover him from possible fire from inside the bar.

Just like she'd done so many times, so long ago. The sense of déjà vu was so powerful it almost broke her concentration. But not quite. Somewhere in her mind she had reached that calm place, the place where she separated from the human element and simply did her job.

Nothing like incoming fire to put you back in business.

"Clear," Alex said and slipped out the fire door into the alley.

She stayed a step behind him through the narrow alley, her ears still ringing from the roar of gunfire, but her hands were steady on the pebbled grip of the Glock. The air reeked of old garbage and vomit and ammonia. Something in a bag beside the Dumpster had drawn flies, loads of them, humming around it in a pulsing black cloud.

"Follow me." Alex started running, weaving through mounds of discarded junk. From behind them came the distant wail of sirens.

Raeanne glanced backward, expecting to see a police cruiser. Instead, the white Mercedes appeared at the mouth of the alley. One of the submachine guns slid its muzzle from the rear window.

"Behind you!" she yelled.

Alex spun back and raised his .45. Gunshots exploded around them — everyone's — echoing along the narrow alley. The barrel of the submachine gun jerked, then dropped from sight. Raeanne aimed and fired again, and the pistol jumped in her hand. Her shot blew out the driver's side mirror as the car fishtailed away from the alley entrance.

She knelt to locate the spent shell casings, found them, and swept the hot brass gingerly into the breast pocket of her plaid shirt.

Alex grabbed her arm and pulled her to her feet. "Hurry up. We need to get out of here before the police show up if we expect to get your son."

A jolt of adrenaline pulled her out of the calm place and twisted in her gut. This was nothing like the old days. This time, she had a son.

* * *

Alex glanced around as they stepped out of the alley just

past the pedestrian-only section of Fremont Street. No white Mercedes. Downtown traffic was heavy in the late afternoon rush hour, the sidewalks thronged with foot traffic, locals and tourists both. Ahead of them, the row of classic old casinos glittered like rhinestones under their canopy — The Golden Nugget, the 4 Queens, the Fremont, their lights throbbing in sparkling bands of gold and white amid the more colorful lights around them. This was the part of the city Alex loved, or had, until they'd buried it all under that ridiculous light show "experience." Why did people always have to change things?

"The car's over here," he said, slipping the gun into the back of his jeans and nodding toward the primer-spotted, '69 GTO parked a block ahead.

"God, you still have that thing?" Raeanne said, keeping low as she trotted behind the wall of parked cars.

"Why wouldn't I?" Alex opened the door, slid behind the wheel, and started the engine. It rumbled to life with the deep baritone of big cylinders as Raeanne yanked open her door and hopped in.

"Because you might want a car made in this lifetime? And a weapon, too. Ever heard of a Glock, Alex?"

"Nothing wrong with the Smith." He waited for a break in traffic, then buried the accelerator. Tires squealed and the car leapt away from the curb.

"Jesus, Dante." Raeanne's hand shot out to grab the side of the door. Two blocks ahead, the white Mercedes screamed around the corner and shot toward them. Alex gunned it. He steered the GTO onto the center line and came at them head on.

"Hold on." He put the car into a hard turn and slipped past the sedan's bumper with inches to spare. Behind him horns blared, but a quick check of the rear-view showed the Mercedes turning and coming back for another charge.

He weaved between two cars, then floored it.

Raeanne's head snapped back on her neck. "I see your

driving hasn't improved with time," she said through gritted teeth, fumbling to fasten her lap belt and hold on to her weapon at the same time. "I can't believe you haven't wrapped yourself around a phone pole by now."

"I got us away from those goons, didn't I?"

She glanced back over her shoulder. "Not yet, they're still on us."

Alex put the car into another sharp turn, making his tires scream and leaving black arcs on the pavement. Behind them, a submachine gun chattered. The rear window blew in with a crash and the tinkle of raining glass.

"Get down!" He swerved again and glanced over to check on Raeanne. She'd ducked down in her seat, covered with diamonds of safety glass that glittered green all over the inside of the car, but she didn't appear hurt. "You okay?"

"Fine," she said, brushing glass off her gun arm.

An incredible sense of relief filled him at the sound of her voice, terse but unhurt. "Stay down until I lose them."

She lifted her head and turned in her seat to look behind her. She must not have liked something she saw, because she raised her pistol and fired off several shots.

He steered the GTO across a side street, then swung back onto the main road. Somewhere, not far in the distance, he could hear the wail of sirens.

"Do *not* get pulled over," Raeanne said. "We don't need any more delays."

"Don't worry, we won't get caught." Alex glanced in the rearview. "Not by the police, anyway."

The white Mercedes was coming up behind them. The MP5 nosed out the window and fired at them again. A few rounds thumped home into the trunk.

"You know," he said, "those guys are definitely starting to rub me the wrong way."

He pushed the car faster. Horns blared and cars swerved to get out of their path. He took the next corner with a screech and the road opened into a less populated section of town.

The stark beauty of the desert landscape rose abruptly past the city limits, the red mountains jutting bare and scorched in the distance. He cut onto an empty road. The car slid a little, but he steered it out of the skid and continued without slowing, raising great clouds of dust behind. A few seconds later, the sedan appeared in the rear view. It tried the same maneuver but spun in a wild circle and fetched up against a telephone pole.

Alex didn't slow down. "Anyone getting out of that car?"

Raeanne swiveled to look back. "Not yet."

"Good." Part of him wanted to turn back to confirm the kill, but he didn't. His orders were to get Raeanne — and now her son — to safety.

Her son.

Few things in this life shocked him anymore, but that revelation had made his gut clench. Where the hell had she gotten a kid? Well, the usual place, he imagined, but...who? What man had she loved enough to have a child with? He remembered her little vanishing act back after December Ice, and the advice the former CODA director, Abe King, had given him in his jaded, Patton-esque grumble. *Women are fickle, Major Dante. They can't take the heat. Yesterday she wanted a marine with a big gun, today she wants an oral surgeon with a Porsche. You got shafted. Get over it.* That had been just before Abe gave him command of the op in Afghanistan. His first operation without Raeanne beside him.

A surge of discomfort raised a sweat on his skin and made his blood surge faster in his veins. He'd never really thought about kids, but he'd always had this vague, half-formed assumption that someday he and Rae...

Ah, to hell with it.

He braked hard and skidded into an angry U-turn to take them back to the main road he'd just passed.

"You really ought to put shoulder belts in this thing."

Raeanne slid the magazine out of her pistol and checked her remaining rounds, then popped it back in and wiped her palms on the thighs of her faded jeans. She pulled her phone out of her belt clip and pressed an autodial key.

Who was she calling? Dr. Porsche?

Alex bit down the ire. Abe was right; he got shafted. But he was over it. Seven years was too long to carry a torch for someone who didn't even have the guts to tell him to his face she was leaving.

Raeanne snapped the phone shut and clipped it back at her waist.

"Who was that?" he asked.

"The Helmsan's nanny. She didn't pick up."

The nanny. He cursed himself for the swell of relief he felt at that. "She's probably with the senator and her son."

Raeanne nodded, but didn't say anything as she stared out the window. Her fingers absently toyed with the frayed edges of a small hole in the denim above her knee. Alex glanced at the road and then back at her. She'd always loved her jeans like that, faded to pale, sky blue and frayed around the edges of the pockets and the top of the waistband where it hugged her hips.

"Keep your eyes on the road, Flame."

He turned back to the cars ahead of him. *Flame.* She'd always called him that, even off the job. Even in the grocery store. Even in bed.

Flame. His code name was Phoenix now. No one called him Flame.

"They must have followed you to the Blind Shark," he said, more for something to say than anything else.

She turned to glare at him. "You could have warned me this morning that people would be shooting at me, instead of giving me the cloak-and-dagger routine."

"Well, I didn't think you needed to be told something as basic as *don't let the bad guys make you.*"

She said nothing for a moment, only glanced back in the side mirror and then fixed her gaze on the road. "Like I expected Petrov to rise from the dead after seven years."

The blood sank to his stomach. "Seven years must be the statute of limitations for jilted lovers."

It was a cheap shot, and he knew it, but seeing her had dredged up all the muck from the bottom that he'd thought had settled: the paralyzing fear that something had happened to her, then the anger and pain and disbelief when he'd found her Dear John letter. Then the emptiness, the all-consuming nothing that had pressed in on him and made it hard to breathe for months after Abe had told him she'd resigned and had married the oral surgeon with the Porsche.

She gave him a look fit to frost the desert, and the tears swimming before her eyes glittered like ice. "If you had told me this morning what was going on, I wouldn't have sent Ryan to school to be left out for Petrov."

Chapter Two

"**H**ow long until we reach the school?" Alex followed her terse directions away from the city and into less congested neighborhoods. How had the agency not known she had a child? They'd known everything else she'd done. They'd tracked her for three years after she resigned—for "personal reasons," her dossier said—until Abe King retired and Joe Richardson had taken over as director and had sealed her files. But the data was sketchy, as if she'd been trailed on and off with no coherent plan. Her file said she'd gone back to college, gotten an eighteen-month certificate, and had become a dental hygienist in St. Paul, Minnesota. Which seemed a step down for someone with a degree in law enforcement who'd been plucked out of FBI intelligence training, but apparently she'd had enough of honor and discipline. She'd divorced Mr. Porsche, had several—okay, a lot of—relationships, if you call two dates a relationship, most of them overlapping and involving such elegant venues as the Come Along Inn on a Tuesday night between 10:46 and 11:27 p.m.

Thinking about it again got his blood pressure all spun up.

Yeah, her dossier was full of interesting fun-facts. But not a word about a son.

"We're almost there," she said. "Take your next right."

He snatched a sidelong glance at her as he turned. Her thick, dark ponytail poked out of the back of that damn Red Sox cap she'd commandeered from him the first time she'd been to his apartment. God, that had to have been fifteen years ago. The hair caressed her neck, making his fingers want to follow suit.

The buildings grew farther apart and the properties grew larger, more nicely landscaped, more affluent looking. Just where he'd expect to find the ritzy private school of a senator's kid.

"It's up here on the right," she said.

The large brick building that housed White Oak Academy looked oddly out of place in the desert city, as if it had been lifted off an Ivy League campus back East. It was a far cry from the L.A. war zone he'd attended as a child. The beautifully landscaped grounds took up the small block, bordered on each side by a small parking lot and a side street. Both lots were empty. No surprise, as it was long past dismissal.

"I don't see him," Raeanne said, her voice deceptively free of emotion.

Alex scanned the grounds as best he could with one eye on the road. This was a bad tactical situation. Too many zones of possible attack, not enough cover. They had to move fast— get in, get the kid, and get out as quickly as they could.

If the kid was still there.

"Is there a playground around back? Or sports fields? Maybe he's there."

"There's a playground. He likes the swings. Turn here."

Alex passed the White Oak Academy building and turned down the side street.

"Maybe one of his friends' parents gave him a ride." He tried to inject his voice with relaxed certainty but wasn't sure he succeeded.

"Maybe."

To their right, the huge brick building stretched on. Behind it lay the playground and soccer fields. Everything looked deserted. Alex pulled to the curb, and Raeanne was out of the car before he'd taken the key from the ignition. He slid out and trotted to catch up.

Across the yard, a collection of playground equipment huddled in the shadow of the main building. A huge wooden play structure hunched dark and forbidding between a tangle of monkey bars and several brightly colored, plastic playhouses, motionless in the gathering twilight. The swings swayed slightly in the breeze, but there was no little boy among them.

Motion from the wooden structure. Alex drew his .45, then saw something red move from within. The red thing appeared at the mouth of a dark hole in the wood, then slid down a short metal slide and thumped to earth, bright as a beacon against the dull gray backdrop of sand and weathered planks. A child's backpack. A second later, two legs appeared from the hole, and the rest of Ryan Springfield slid out and landed in the dirt, raising a cloud of dust.

Raeanne cupped her hands to her mouth. "Ryan! Over here!"

A spark of tenderness caught Alex in the throat at the sight of the boy, so small against the wooden towers and ladders, his shirttails flapping out of dark uniform pants and his striped necktie askew. A breeze ruffled the boy's coal-dark hair, and his head jerked up at the sound of Raeanne's voice.

Alex lowered the Smith and tucked it behind his waist.

"Mom!" The boy's voice rose and fell on a sob. He snatched up the backpack and began running awkwardly toward them, struggling under the jouncing weight of the red monstrosity that looked almost twice his size. "Mom!"

Behind the play area, on the opposite side street, a white Mercedes with a crumpled front quarter pulled to the curb.

"Raeanne…"

The car slowed, inching along the edge of the grass. Finally, with a squeal of tires, it hopped the curb and pulled up onto the lawn, tearing up sod as it sped across the ball field toward them.

"No!" Raeanne slowed only a second, then took off at a full sprint toward the boy.

Alex yanked the pistol from behind his back and sped toward the oncoming car.

"Ryan, run!" Raeanne screamed. Her long legs tore up the ground. Somehow, her gun was already in her hand.

The white Mercedes got to the boy before she did.

The car cut across his path and slid to a stop, spitting turf from its tires. Both front doors flew open.

"Ryan, *run*! Get away from the car!" Alex shouted.

The boy froze. The man with the goatee jumped out from behind the wheel and clamped his arm around Ryan's neck.

"*Mommy!*"

Alex pushed himself faster. The second man, the fat bald one, stepped out of the passenger side, raised a pistol, and pointed it at Raeanne.

Close enough now, Alex leaped for Raeanne and tackled her as the first shots rent the air. He covered her with his body, his pistol up and aimed.

"Get off me!" she yelled. She struggled to get up, but he kept her down and covered. A bullet struck the ground near his shoulder and kicked up a geyser of dirt. Another bullet whined past his ear.

The goateed man dragged the boy back to the car, shoved him into the back seat, then jumped back inside. The car started forward. The bald man paused a second longer and aimed another shot at Alex.

The bullet razored into Alex's left bicep. The impact jerked his arm and he lost his grip on his weapon.

Fury blazed to life within him. He grabbed up the gun and aimed at the bald man who was trotting after the rolling sedan. Too close to the boy to risk it.

Three more gunshots, this time from beside him. Raeanne. Her shots took the bald man in the chest just as he was trying to get in the car. He recoiled into the side of the moving vehicle, then slid off the back and onto the ground. The white Mercedes sped off, the open door flopping like a broken wing, leaving the bald man bleeding on the grass.

Alex ran for him. He glanced back at Raeanne, still in her shooting stance, sighting the car as it tore across the lawn, bounced down the curb onto the side street, and disappeared down the road. Then she spun her aim to the man on the ground. She marched to where he lay and kicked him soundly in the ribs. Nothing.

"Where did they take him?" she roared.

Still nothing.

Tears had channeled tracks down her dusty cheeks. She knelt beside the man, holding her gun on him with one hand and pressing her other against his carotid artery. A few seconds later, she stood and holstered her gun.

She turned to Alex with a look of such profound emptiness that it left him without words.

Finally, he said, "We might be able to catch them if we hurry."

"No." She turned to look back toward the dead man. The agony in her voice was a hundred times more intense than the pain in his arm. "They'll kill him. We should wait until they make their demands." She turned back again and took a deep breath that didn't completely steady her voice. "They've won, Alex. They have my little boy."

The rush went out of him, and he cursed bitterly. How had he fucked this up so completely? How could the agency have not known about her son?

He went toward her, and with every footfall, a bolt of pain shot up his arm. But it was nothing compared to the pain he felt at the sight of her dark, vacant eyes.

"We'll get him back." He poured every ounce of determination that he had into his voice. "I swear it, Raeanne. I'll get him back."

Raeanne looked at him for a long moment, her eyes wide

and dark and slightly unfocused, as if she were looking past him at something he couldn't see. Her whole body trembled. He stepped closer and gingerly wrapped her in his good arm. She let out a long, deep breath, then buried her face in his shoulder and wept.

* * *

Raeanne stared out the car window as Alex drove. Everything was a blur. A colorless, empty blur. All that stood out was the image of her son the moment he'd been stolen away, his wide, terrified eyes as that bastard's arm closed around his neck and began dragging him toward the car. She tried to force herself to see his face just moments before that, when the joy had been shining in his eyes at seeing her, but the memory was too fragile. Like porcelain, it slipped from her grasp and shattered at her feet with the sound of Ryan's scream.

For the third time, she flipped through the wallet she'd pulled from the dead man's pocket. Two hundred twelve dollars in small bills. Arizona driver's license, probably fake. Visa, MasterCard, American Express, definitely fake. There was no way his name was Steve Peters. Sergei Petrenko, maybe. Nothing else to indicate where they'd taken Ryan.

She was dimly aware of Alex's voice, but she was too wrapped up in her own thoughts to realize he was speaking to her.

Finally, she felt his cool hand cover hers.

"Rae?"

"I'm sorry, what?" He had blood on his shirt. "Are you shot?"

"Just a graze. I said I'll get him back, Rae. I promise you."

She saw pain in his eyes, pain for her loss, and she had to look away. She scanned through the radio stations, but there was nothing good on.

"We should notify somebody," she said. "I don't want kids to show up for school tomorrow and find a dead man in the soccer field."

"The agency will take care of it. I'll pull over as soon as I find a good spot and call in."

Raeanne put the wallet back on the seat and took up the other item they'd found on the dead man. A cell phone. She flipped it open and pulled up the phonebook, but there were no numbers stored. None in the sent calls list, either. There was, however, a single number stored in incoming calls.

"Jackpot," she said.

"What?"

"Stored number, last incoming call." She looked up to find herself in an unfamiliar section of the city. "Where are we going?"

"A place we keep down on Hyacinth Street. We'll be safe there for a while. It's clean; there's food, clothes, whatever you need."

"Enough .40 caliber rounds to make lace of Petrov for taking my son?"

Alex gave her a wry half smile. "More than enough."

She couldn't keep up the façade of cold deliberation, so she just nodded then looked quickly out the window. She looked at the number on the display and copied it onto a notepad pilfered from Alex's glove box. While she wrote, the dead man's phone twittered in her hand like an electronic finch.

Alex snatched it from her before she could react.

"Hello?"

She watched his face, her heart beating rapidly.

"Sorry, he's unable to come to the phone right now, he's dead. Who's this?" Alex listened a moment, then his face went dark. He looked at her and mouthed, *Petrov.*

She grabbed the phone from his hands. "Where's my son, you bastard?"

A soft chuckle came through the phone. "Ah, Krista, my darling. Or do you go by Raeanne these days? How nice to hear your voice again, my beloved." Petrov's tenor still held a moderate Russian accent, schooled in British English. Memories of that voice hit her like a physical weight, like a fist to the stomach. *Krista, my darling...* How she'd loathed the sound of that voice, like acid over her nerves, and the pale ghost of a man who owned it. White-blond hair half gone gray, limpid gray eyes the color of dingy laundry, set too close together behind colorless steel-rimmed glasses, and always, that look of cold calculation, like a cobra ready to strike. But she'd done her job, and December Ice had been a success. Until now.

"No more games, Petrov. I want my son."

"Please, my dear. Such anger is unbecoming in a woman. I assure you, the boy is quite safe. For now."

"What do you want?"

"You have become quite a thorn in our side, my beloved. And now you have retired one of my best employees. I should be very cross with you, if you were not so beautiful."

"I hope he burns in hell."

Laughter. "Yes, I'm sure you do. And if there is a hell, he's probably quite crisp by now. But we have more important things to discuss."

"What do you want?" she repeated.

"What do I want?" the voice purred. "There are many things that I *want*. Unfortunately, I must insist upon business before pleasure. The people protecting you have a certain senator we would like to do business with."

"Go on."

"If she will withdraw her legislation, I shall be happy to let this handsome lad go free. Then, I would like the senator to put her support behind a bill we ourselves have crafted. No media, no tricks. I want this new legislation introduced when Congress reconvenes on Wednesday. No later."

"What is this bill of yours?"

"Just a little something to encourage free enterprise between our respective economies. If the senator does not comply, then your son... Ah, well, small boys can be so accident-prone, no?"

"Where is he? How do I know he's all right?"

Muffled sounds came over the phone, then at last, a small, tenuous voice. "Mommy?"

Raeanne's heart raced, sending a cold rush of blood through her veins. Her throat tightened, and when she spoke, she nearly choked on a sob. "I'm here, baby."

More muffled noises, then the faint sound of Ryan's voice from the background, quickly silenced.

"As you can hear, the boy is fine," Petrov said. "I expect the good Senator shall do as we require on Wednesday. You shall find a copy of our bill on her desk at her office."

"Why should I trust you?"

Another low chuckle. "Come now, my beloved, what choice do you have?"

Raeanne seethed, her blood thrumming in her ears while she tried to think of some way to gain the upper hand. But she couldn't. The upper hand belonged to Petrov.

"Besides," he said, "I believe it is you who has proved unworthy of a man's trust, is that not so, *Raven*? I believe it was your partner who almost killed me. Rumor has it *he* was your lover as well as I."

"You were never my lover. You were a target."

"So it seems. How cruel, the hand of fate. But never mind. For the time being, money is more important than vengeance, so we must all play nicely. Rest assured, though, my beloved — I shall have satisfaction."

"You name the time and place, and I'll be there."

More laughter. "I shall be in touch."

"Wait a minute," she said.

He didn't speak, but he didn't hang up.

"I'm sorry my partner shot you in the chest."

"Oh, are you?"

"I am. Because I would have taken the head shot."

Petrov laughed again, and the line went dead.

She wanted to scream with rage and frustration and the awful, drowning sense of powerlessness that was whipping her blood into a frenzy, but she only closed the phone and set it down on the seat, beside the dead man's wallet. Her hands were shaking, and she found her jaw clenched so tightly her teeth hurt.

Alex's voice was soft and smooth, like warm cognac. "Don't give up, Rae. I swear to you, we'll get him back."

She turned her attention out the window to try to distract herself from the tears pressing against the backs of her eyes.

"And just to let you know," he said, reaching out to squeeze her hand, "I did take the head shot. I just didn't make it. I had to take what I could get."

He pulled over not far from Freedom Park. The air had grown colder. The sky loomed low overhead, darkening toward sunset. He let go of her hand, and it suddenly felt very cold.

"What are you doing?" she asked.

"Calling in." He leaned over her and popped open the glove compartment. He took out a satellite phone and punched in several sets of numbers.

"Is that secure?" Raeanne asked.

He looked up a moment and gave her a small smile. "We've got a pretty complex relay."

Raeanne heard the voice pick up at the other end. "West End Supply Company." Whoever the agency had playing receptionist at the com desk, she sounded like a 12-year-old.

"Heidi," Alex said, "I've got Raeanne. We just left the scene of two engagements, one at the Blind Shark downtown, and the second at the White Oak Academy. Need a clean-up crew at the White Oak soccer field, ASAP."

"Copy."

"Also, we've got ourselves an additional objective. Male, age seven. Caucasian, dark hair, wearing a white dress shirt and blue pants, Ryan...?" He looked at Raeanne with an eyebrow raised.

"Springfield."

"Springfield," he repeated. "Abducted by targets from White Oak Academy less than a half hour ago. Targets driving white Mercedes S600 sedan, Nevada plate number 284...shit..."

"XTC," Raeanne added.

"Two-eight-four, X-ray, Tango, Charlie. Destination unconfirmed. Targets heavily armed. Tell Mom we'll be home soon."

"Copy," the voice said, and the line went dead.

Alex turned off the sat phone and sighed.

"Do you think we have a chance?" Raeanne asked.

He smiled, picked up her hand again, and gave it a squeeze. "We've got a man on the inside, a woman, actually, ex-CIA. She's a good operative. She'll find out where they've got Ryan in no time."

"I wish I believed that."

"We'll get him back, Raeanne, I swear it."

Raeanne tried to return his smile, but it just wouldn't come. Instead, a sudden wash of memory made her pull her hand away.

How had things gone so wrong? One minute, she'd been enjoying a relatively peaceful life, and the next she'd gone back in time to find herself knee-deep in some black op that was probably going to get Ryan killed by one of the most ruthless men she'd ever had the misfortune to meet. And then there was Alex, with those intense, ice green eyes that had haunted her sleep for so long that she had begun to think she'd see them forever. Alex, sitting here holding her hand, shattering the peace she'd worked to hard to find after he'd left her, and thrusting her back to those days of loss and desolation and grief.

Why had he just up and left her? Abe King had told her he'd requested a transfer and wouldn't say anything more, then had locked her down when she'd tried to probe further. She'd pulled every string she had inside CODA and out, even a few unsavory ones from assets on the ground, but no one knew a thing. Not even her connections at the CIA could find a trace of him. He'd covered his tracks like he'd never existed.

In all fairness, he hadn't known she was pregnant when he lit out. But he would have if he hadn't stood her up at the Blind Shark that day, the fucking coward. If he hadn't moved in the middle of the night and changed his phone number and put in for a transfer to God knew where without even telling her. What kind of chicken-shit move was that? Not even a note? An e-mail? A damn *text* message?

H8 U, dont follow me. AD

So what was she supposed to do now? How was she supposed to tell him after all this time that Ryan was his son?

Chapter Three

"You've got to be kidding me," Raeanne said, looking up toward the rusted bottom rung of the fire escape ladder two feet above her head.

Alex chuckled, glad she was feeling something other than pain. "I'd take you in the front door, but where's the fun in that? Up you go." He grabbed her by the waist and tried to boost her up, but she didn't jump. Instead, she planted her feet and turned those stubborn eyes back on him.

"I can reach it, you know. I'm not helpless. And you're wounded." She spun away, swatting him in the face with the dark ponytail sprouting from the back of her baseball cap. She bent her knees and leapt, grasping the bottom rung easily, then swung her feet up to hook her knees around it. From there she grabbed the next rung and pulled herself up, hand over hand.

"Tis just a flesh wound. And I'd forgotten you were a monkey." He watched her pull herself easily to the landing and admired the agile strength of her.

"That's funny," she called down. "I haven't forgotten you were an ass."

He smiled. She was feeling better. If being the butt of her jokes could erase the empty desolation he'd seen earlier in her eyes, he'd consider it a small price to pay. He leapt for the ladder and forced himself not to wince as he pulled himself up.

"Are you sure this is a safe enough neighborhood for a safe house?" she asked, looking down to the alley below.

The sounds of city traffic around them — blaring horns, the deep bass of booming car stereos, a siren off in the distance — all melded together into a sound so familiar to Alex that he almost didn't hear it at all. "It's perfectly safe."

He climbed the stairs and met her on the second floor landing. It wasn't the best neighborhood in Vegas; in fact, it wasn't very good at all, but petty thieves and common criminals were no match for the agency's brand of security. He located the electronic locking mechanism along the underside of the bulletproof Lexan window, entered the alphanumeric code, and heard the lock slide free. He lifted the sash and drew his weapon.

"Right," Raeanne whispered. "People always enter safe places with their weapons drawn."

Alex motioned for silence, then ducked his head and entered the dark gap of the open window.

He heard her climb in behind him. They were in the smaller of the two bedrooms, and he had the overwhelming urge to ask her to wait while he secured the apartment, but he knew it wouldn't do any good and he wasn't in the mood for an argument. He crept along quietly, ignoring the throb of pain from his arm and listening hard for any sound that might indicate they weren't alone. A footstep. A breath. The soft ratcheting of a gun being cocked. But all that greeted him was dark silence.

At the far end of the room, he flipped on the light, and the harsh white glare made him blink.

The bedroom appeared empty. It was sparsely furnished, with only a twin size captain's bed, a bureau that no one ever kept anything in, a nightstand that usually held a couple of ancient magazines, and a hideous orange shag rug. The closet was stocked with miscellaneous bedding, but was otherwise empty as well. Alex secured the window once more, then motioned silently for Raeanne to take the kitchen at the left end of the hall. Cautiously, with his weapon raised in both hands, he started toward the rooms to the right.

The master bedroom was similarly empty and similarly Spartan. Another captain's bed, a chest of drawers, a small round table, and two chairs. Another closet, this one locked. He flipped up the false doorknob to reveal the electronic keypad, then entered the access code and heard the lock click open.

The agency spooks who kept the place up may not have known squat about interior decorating, but Alex smiled as he always did when he got a peek at their true genius. The double-width closet was lined with rows and rows of shelves, which housed everything from a variety of shampoos, soaps, and deodorants, both masculine and feminine; to towels, blankets, and bed linens; to several cases of assorted-caliber rounds, a few sets of lock picks, a digital key card scrambler, night sticks, hand cuffs, pepper spray, and two Tasers. Kevlar vests, gas masks, and other assorted riot gear hung from the right-hand end of the rod, between the row of brightly colored terry cloth bathrobes and the cabinet housing the firearms. The topmost shelf held several notebook computers and assorted peripherals; a huge medical kit—which he hoped was fully stocked; a box of assorted office supplies, binoculars and night vision gear; digital surveillance equipment, two portable GPS units, and three crocheted granny-square afghans.

He heaved a sigh of carnal pleasure. God, how he loved CODA.

He grabbed a gun cleaning kit and a box each of .45 and .40 caliber rounds. Raeanne had always been full of smart-aleck comments about the real reason he liked big, powerful gadgets, but she'd never been able to come up with a satisfactory answer for why she lugged around seven different tubes of beige lipstick.

Before relocking the closet, he helped himself to the best of all the safe house's amenities: two Butterfinger bars. And a penlight.

At the end of the hall was the living room, as lovely and as empty as the rest of the place, and on the far wall hulked the front door. Alex snapped on the penlight and checked the adhesive filaments marking the hinges, lock, and top and bottom jambs. The nearly invisible seals were all unbroken; no one had forced entry. Normally, he'd have removed them so that they could use the door for the duration of their stay, but he had a nagging feeling they wouldn't be staying very long.

A moment later he walked back into the kitchen, where Raeanne was wincing at its avocado green and harvest gold mushroom-print wallpaper.

"Back rooms are clear," he said.

"Kitchen and bathroom are clear too. But I think the wallpaper's on acid." She put her pistol back into her holster and leaned against the counter. "I didn't realize wall paper glue could last fifty years."

"Yeah, well, they keep the important stuff fresh." He tossed her the box of ammo and a Butterfinger.

"Thanks." A grin slowly spread over her face. Alex thought it was one of the most beautiful things he had ever seen.

But it didn't last. A moment later, the smile flickered out like a candle and left her expression dark. She left the candy untouched and wandered to the window to peek out through the thick, gold drapes. Alex watched her for a long moment, watched the desolate look in her eyes as she gazed out into the night.

He debated whether or not to go to her, to comfort her, but decided against it. She'd never been the type to want comforting; she'd always preferred to do her brooding alone. Besides, she'd made it perfectly clear seven years ago that she was no longer interested in whatever he had to offer.

He let out a long, tense breath. He wasn't going to think about that. He'd spent long enough wondering where she'd gone, wondering if she was ever coming back, and eventually he'd had to just take Abe's advice and face the facts. She'd left him. Simple as that. Good thing Abe had given him the op in Afghanistan to get his shit together, otherwise he probably would have tracked her to friggin' Minnesota and done something stupid.

He was a fool to let himself dwell on feelings that had taken him so long to box up and put away. This op was strictly business.

But it wasn't. Her child's life was on the line.

Anger and guilt surged through his veins, icy hot like Freon. He'd failed. He'd been assigned to protect her, and instead he'd let her son get snatched right out from underneath him.

How the hell had they not known she had a son?

He watched a slow, fat tear roll down her cheek, watched her swipe it away. He'd get her boy back, no matter what he had to do to guarantee it.

"I'm going to go lie down," she said. "It's been a long day."

"Good idea. Take the small bedroom. Let me know if you need anything."

She turned from the window and headed silently for the hallway, trailing a scent as she passed in front of him that jarred loose every memory he'd forced to the back of his mind. Every nerve in his body came instantly alive as he remembered her — every curve, every taste, every motion, each small sound and each ragged moan as she climaxed around him. How the hell could she still smell exactly the same after seven years? Didn't she ever try a new brand of soap?

He noticed that his heart was pounding as he watched her lithe dancer's body disappear down the hall and into her room, and he felt a small stab of ridiculous disappointment when she closed the door behind her.

What the hell was he thinking? The last thing he wanted was to get mixed up with all that again.

He leaned back in his chair and tried to think of something else.

How the hell was he supposed to think when Raeanne was right there in the next room, after all this time? When her scent still lingered faintly in the air around him?

The sick irony of it astounded him. For years he'd hoped and prayed and bargained for this with whatever higher powers might be listening. For the chance to see her one more time. To stand beside her, to be able to reach out and touch her.

Well, here she was. And all it took to get her here was her little boy's life.

Be careful what you wish for…

Ah, to hell with it.

With a deep sigh of resignation, he did what he always did when he felt conflicting desires. He opened the cleaning kit and began to strip down his gun.

This was going to be a really long assignment.

* * *

Raeanne turned over once more, trying unsuccessfully to relax, but every time she closed her eyes, she saw Ryan's big green eyes wide with terror as Petrov's thugs dragged him into the Mercedes and sped off. She got up and went out to the living room, where, maybe, if she were very lucky, some mind-numbing TV would rot those very brain cells like she'd always been told.

Alex was in the shower. She grabbed a can of diet ginger ale from the fridge and flopped down into the saggy plaid couch, glad to be alone. Alex Dante had the annoying ability to make things just a little too close for comfort.

She glanced around the room. This place sure hadn't been in use back when she'd been with the agency. Where had they found such ugly furniture? She poked through a stack of old magazines on the coffee table. Yeah, she remembered that hair-do. The last time she'd seen that on a living person was at Girl Scout camp. She tossed the magazines down and wondered how much she could get for them on eBay.

He'd left a gun cleaning kit on the end table. She decided instead to clean her gun. This was the first time she'd fired it outside of the shooting range in…seven years. It was the first time she'd ever fired it in anger.

Something told her she should feel bad about that, but she just couldn't work up enough energy to care. She had her Glock stripped down and was looking for the right brush to ream out the barrel when Petrov's cell phone twittered from the end table. Her heart leapt in her chest and a surge of adrenaline iced her veins.

"Alex?" she called, even though she knew he couldn't possibly hear her from the shower at the other end of the apartment.

Another twitter. She put down her gun and snatched up the phone. "What do you want, Petrov?"

"Good evening, my beloved. I trust you are resting well after such an eventful day."

She forced the ice in her veins to freeze the emotion out of her voice. "Where's my son?"

"Ah, Raeanne—it seems so strange to call you that, but never mind. Your son is precisely the reason I've called. I've decided to take you up on your offer to name the time and place for a meeting."

Her heart turned over. "Good. Where?"

"I was thinking perhaps dinner. Wednesday evening, after the senator takes care of her end of the bargain. The Blue Lagoon restaurant in Washington, say, eight p.m.? I shall have a table reserved under your name. A table for two. No, make that…three. Does this sound satisfactory?"

Raeanne's palms broke out in a clammy sweat, making the tiny phone slick as a live fish in her hand. "I'll be there."

"Come alone. If my associates find the least indication you're being followed, then I will, unfortunately, be forced to dine alone."

"Don't worry, Petrov. This is just between you and me."

"Excellent." His lilting accent boiled over her nerves like raw acid. "Wear something red. You always looked ravishing in red."

The line went dead.

"The only thing red will be your blood on the floor," she said and dropped the phone onto the table.

She looked toward the hallway, toward the sound of the shower running. Alex would never agree to let her meet with Petrov without backup, and if Petrov smelled CODA, Ryan would die. She'd seen Petrov kill more people than she cared to count, without a flicker of remorse in those cold, reptilian eyes. She let out a heavy sigh and finished reaming out the barrel of her weapon. This dinner was a set up, that much was certain, but today was only Friday. She had until Wednesday to come up with a way to turn the tables on Dmitriy Petrov.

She'd have to think faster to come up with a way around Alex Dante.

She picked up a bullet from her stripped-down weapon and spun it in trembling fingers. Her hands had been still as stone when she'd been with CODA, but that was a long time ago. She was older now. Softer. Providing security to a senator had its rigors, but it wasn't like working black ops in the world's most war-torn regions for an organization that technically didn't exist. She willed her heart rate to slow while she fingered the round. Cool brass jacket, smooth as a lover's caress. Hollow point for maximum stopping power once it entered the body. "Table for three" had better mean Petrov was bringing Ryan, because if anything happened to her son, God help her, she would put that bullet through Petrov's evil, murderous skull.

If she were still capable of such a thing. Seven years was a long time. What if she wasn't strong enough or fast enough or steady enough anymore? What if she wound up getting Ryan killed?

She quickly reassembled her pistol and packed away the cleaning kit. She'd have to be good enough; she had no choice. Someone had to get Ryan back, and she sure as hell couldn't trust CODA to do it. She knew them too well for that. CODA didn't make mistakes. If there was no mention of Ryan in her files, it was because someone had made sure there wasn't.

The shower went silent. A few moments later, Alex walked into the living room, carrying the scent of soap and some fruity shampoo. He'd changed into a clean white T-shirt—from one of the bedrooms, most likely, the place was a regular Goodwill—which was too tight for him across the chest. His well-trained pectorals strained at the cotton fabric, daring her to look at them. She didn't intend to, but she couldn't help it.

He'd field-dressed his wound, almost as well as she would have done, but even interrupted by the band of gauze, his biceps still flexed admirably as he moved. She refused to acknowledge the heat that burned inside her at the sight of him. She wasn't here for Alex.

"So what's our next step?" she asked.

He settled himself beside her on the saggy couch. One of the springs *thwonged* under his weight. He didn't seem to notice.

"I need to check in with the main office." He put his feet up on the coffee table and reached for the secure phone that rested upon the end table beside him. In sharp contrast to the authentic retro décor—that is, the old junk they'd dumped here rather than pay to dispose of—the phone and the scrambler attached to the side of it were sleek and high-end. He dialed, and a few moments later he was connected. "Heidi, put me through to Richardson."

Raeanne took a deep breath to calm herself.

"I have Raeanne here," Alex said. "Let me put you on speaker phone."

"Hello, Raeanne," came the deep, gravelly baritone.

Joe Richardson. Her heart lurched with nostalgia at the sound of that voice. "Hey Joe. So you're the Big Boss now, huh? It's been a long time."

"Yes, it has," Richardson said. "How are you holding up?"

"I'm alive."

Alex leaned back on the couch, staring grimly at the phone. "There was a very costly error of omission in Raeanne's dossier."

"So I heard," Richardson said. "Raeanne, I'm terribly sorry. There's nothing I can say that will make up for it, but I want you to know how awful I feel. We've launched a full investigation into this situation. Please know that we're doing everything in our power to get your boy back safe and sound."

She bit back the words she wanted to say and said instead, "I know you are. Thank you."

"Have they tried to contact you?"

"Not intentionally," Alex answered. "Petrov called the dead man's cell phone, and Raeanne got her chance to speak her mind. He made some veiled threats of getting satisfaction that lead Raeanne to believe he will kill the boy as revenge for December Ice."

Silence. Raeanne kept hers as well.

"So what's your plan for getting Ryan back?" she finally asked. "Alex mentioned you have an operative on the inside that may be able to learn something."

Alex rolled his eyes. "Aw, hell, Rae."

Richardson sighed. "I'm sure he also mentioned that was classified information."

Raeanne smiled. "Come on, Joe, it's not like I'd believe you were running a black op without someone inside. Besides, I can't help you if you don't keep me informed."

Another moment of silence. "I'm sorry, Raeanne. You

know I can't allow you to be involved. This is agency business."

She hesitated, disbelief momentarily stealing her words. "But Ryan's my son. That makes it my business."

"Raeanne, listen to me—"

"No, Joe, you listen to me. I'm not some civilian you can stuff into a safe house until you get things figured out. You know me better than that. I won't sit back and watch soap operas and wait for you to find my son."

There was silence from the line. "Don't threaten me, Raeanne. You know how deeply I admire you, but whether you like it or not, you *are* a civilian. This is non-negotiable. You will stay in that safe house until we find your son, or I will have you picked up and thrown in jail for your own safety and the integrity of this operation. Do I make myself clear?"

She cast a glance at Alex, but he was studying his fingernails. So he stood with the agency. Fine. Let him. She looked back at the phone and curbed the impulse to throw it against the wall. "Whatever."

She looked at Alex again, but he still wouldn't look at her.

"What do you want me to do?" he asked Richardson, as if ignoring her would make the tension in the air go away.

"Sit tight for now. We'll be in touch when we locate Petrov and the boy. In the mean time, do not let Raeanne out of that apartment."

She sat calmly beside him, refusing to show the anger seething through her. She wanted so badly to do something—punch something, shoot something, she didn't know what. But instead, she took several deep breaths, leaned back into the sunken couch cushions, and crossed her leg slowly over her knee.

That settled it then. If Richardson wanted to throw her in jail, he'd have to catch her first.

Chapter Four

Alex turned on the old television and adjusted the rabbit ears until the snowy picture stabilized on the screen. The phone might have been state of the art, but the console television was almost as old as he was.

"…Authorities have released no information on the identity of the man shot at White Oak Academy earlier today," said the slightly green-complected reporter, "but, sources say the man may have been part of an organized crime syndicate with roots in the former Soviet Union. Police have not released the name of the boy believed to have been abducted from the school grounds by members of the Russian crime syndicate, but authorities are searching for the boy's mother, who disappeared sometime prior to the shooting and is believed to be somehow connected. Back to you, Ted."

"Questioning about the shooting? What do they think a kidnapped boy's poor, despondent, civilian mother would know about such things?" Raeanne grinned her evil, Cheshire cat grin at him from the voluminous folds of a fluffy, red terrycloth robe and finished her bowl of canned stew. "This is delicious by the way. You're a downright epicure."

"Don't be a smart aleck. The last thing we need is the media speculating about your involvement."

She put the empty bowl down on the coffee table and tapped her chin thoughtfully with one finger. "Hmm, let's see… A missing senator, her missing bodyguard, and the bodyguard's missing child. I doubt even the bumbling CODA could miss the connection there."

Alex sighed heavily and ate another cracker. He decided he liked her better weak and distraught. And quiet. "What I want to know is how they found out about the Ice Syndicate at all. Agency people would never divulge that kind of information to the press."

Raeanne gave him one of her looks. "First the screw up that got Ryan kidnapped and now this. And you wonder why I don't trust CODA to get my boy back?"

"What about me, Raeanne? I promised you I'd get him back. Don't you even trust me?"

She just sniffed at him and turned back to the TV.

He realized how ridiculous that had sounded. Of course she didn't trust him. Not after the last few hours.

He'd had to take her weapon, of course, and she hadn't liked that one bit. Neither had she liked giving him her clothes. He'd listened to the sharp side of her tongue for hours after that indignity, and years of field ops with ex-Marines, -Navy Seals, and -CIA had honed that tongue to a razor edge. But he'd be damned if she were going to sneak out while he was in the john. Or worse, force him to let her go at gunpoint, which part of him thought was pure paranoia, and another part was pretty sure she'd eventually try, if she could. It was her son, after all, and lately she'd borne a striking resemblance in temperament to the big German Shepherd dog he'd had growing up. Winnie, her name was, and she'd been Man's Best Friend. Until she whelped. Then God help anyone who got too close to those pups.

He glanced over at Raeanne, and she gave him an ultra-saccharine smile.

Yep, definitely glad he'd taken her gun.

He got up and grabbed the empty bowls and took them into the kitchen. While he washed them, he tried to decide what to do about her. He knew he couldn't leave her unprotected—or unguarded, whichever—but he was not happy with Richardson's dictate that he leave the tracking of the boy to other agents. He had to agree with Raeanne, even though he understood the logic of "lost objectivity," that doing something felt infinitely better than doing nothing.

Besides, he'd promised her he'd get her son back, and he wasn't about to break a promise.

But orders were orders, and despite Raeanne's strength and determination, Richardson was right. She'd been out of the business for seven years, and most of Petrov's troops had grown up dodging mines in post-Soviet war zones for the last twenty years. She was out of her league. She'd be in no shape for the demands of the job, physically or mentally, and to pretend otherwise would only get everyone, including her and her son, killed.

For her own sake, and for the sake of the mission, he had to keep her contained.

But it didn't mean he had to like it. And it didn't mean he had to break his promise.

As he headed back down the hall, he saw her rubbing her neck, trying to work out the kinks. The robe gaped a little, and Alex found himself stopping in his tracks before leaving the cover of the hall. The curve of one round breast was just barely visible, and all his resolve to maintain his hard-line stance melted into a puddle at his feet. He felt like a fool, watching her from afar like a hormonal teenager, or worse, like some kind of peeper, but he couldn't prevent the stray thought that begged the red terry cloth to drop just one more inch.

Thoroughly disgusted with himself, he cleared his throat and barged into the room.

She had her face turned up to the ceiling and her eyes closed, but when he stomped in, she jerked around to face him. She noticed her open robe and just as quickly snatched it shut. "Jeez, warn me next time you decide to sneak up on me after you leave me with no clothes, thank you very much."

"Sneak up on you?" Was she for real? He almost stomped through the floor trying to make enough noise to announce his entry. He had absolutely no reason to feel guilty, none at all.

She had her feet propped up on the coffee table, and she gathered the robe more tightly over her legs, just in case. "You could at least have let me have some pajamas. It's not like I would've run through the city in pajamas."

Despite her attempts to cover as much of her skin as possible, the robe only came to just above her knees, and her long, toned calves were still bare. Bare and tapering gently to those delicate ankles, crossed one over the other.

"Quit looking at my legs, Dante."

He remembered well the feel of those legs, smooth, silky skin over tight, strong curves, and warm. She was always so warm.

"Is there a heating pad in this place?" she said, reaching back to knead her shoulders again. "My back is killing me." She arched her back to reach her shoulders, and the robe again gaped open.

Alex sat beside her on the couch. It had been an exhausting day, mentally and physically, and he couldn't blame her for the tension that made her so snappy. He couldn't help the surge of tenderness that forced his hands out to squeeze the tense muscles at her neck. "Sorry, no heating pad that I'm aware of, but I can help you rub the kinks out."

* * *

Raeanne sighed softly as Alex's hands kneaded her shoulders. *Step into my parlor, said the spider to the fly.* She sighed again and let her lips turn up in a small smile. Men were so predictable. Show a little cleavage and they came trotting right up with their brains in neutral.

If CODA wasn't sharing their plans to get Ryan, then she was on her own. God knew if they even had any plans to extract him, but she refused to let her thoughts follow that line of reasoning. Part of her hated doing this to Alex, but she couldn't let herself forget that he and CODA were responsible for Ryan's kidnapping in the first place. Whatever they were up to, they'd done enough. She couldn't sit and wait around for Petrov to deliver her son to the agency in a body bag.

She needed her clothes, her weapon, and Petrov's cell phone if she was going to make contact and arrange a meeting with the SOB, but they were locked in Alex's room. She'd toyed with a dozen scenarios, but could think of only one solution: she had to get into Alex's room while he slept. And the only way to do that was to be invited in.

Rather like Dracula.

Alex slowly rubbed the muscles in her neck, his long fingers moving with deftness and strength. But there was also tenderness, and Raeanne had to force down the guilt. Whatever CODA was up to, she couldn't believe Alex would knowingly risk the life of a child. She closed her eyes and let herself feel the soothing pressure of his hands as they sought out the aches and kneaded them away.

She lost herself in the sensations. He worked his hands up and down her back, tracing the muscles along her spine, across her shoulder blades, around her arms. His warm breath caressed the skin on the back of her neck and made her heart beat faster.

No. No, she didn't want to feel *this*. This wasn't part of the plan.

"What happened to us?" he asked softly.

Every muscle jolted awake. That question wasn't part of the plan, either. All her fears and secrets, all her anger and pain and feelings of betrayal came crashing back into the forefront of her mind and she drew away from his touch.

Alex sat back and watched her with those intense, green eyes, looking more predatory than ever.

"This isn't the time or the place," she said.

"When will be the time? It's been seven years."

She tried to think of something to say, but couldn't.

"I had no way to contact you after you left," he said.

"Please. You knew where I was."

"I'm not a stalker, Rae. You wanted out, you got out. But you could have saved me the trouble of checking with police and hospitals for a week, thinking you were dead in a ditch."

"Are you kidding me? Who sat in the stupid Blind Shark for two hours waiting for *whom*? Who called *whom* for a week until the number came up disconnected? Yeah. And you had no way to contact me."

"What the hell are you talking about?"

"Oh my God. You are not sitting here pretending you have no idea what I'm talking about."

"No, I'm not pretending anything. I loved you, Raeanne."

"Uh-huh."

He was silent a moment. "But that was a long time ago, right?" His voice took on a hard edge of barely restrained bitterness. "Never mind. This is pointless. Forget I asked."

She stood up, moved to the window, and drew the ugly drape aside to stare off into the night. Why was he doing this? Beyond the window, the city was a sea of brilliant lights, neon, arc-sodium, white, yellow, and orange, brightening the darkness. In the distance, the parti-colored lights of the Strip glittered and danced like a river of spilled jewels.

He came up softly to stand behind her. So close. Her breath caught in her throat. She wanted him close, yearned to have his strong hands touch her, comfort her, but at the same time she ached for him to keep his distance. Losing her job, then losing him had hurt so much, she didn't think she could face that kind of pain again.

"I'm sorry," he whispered. "You're right, it's not the time. You have enough on your mind right now." His hand fell lightly, tentatively, upon her shoulder, as if waiting to see if she would throw it off.

She wanted to. God, she wanted to, but she just couldn't make herself move. She could feel the pressure of his hand through the fabric of her robe, heating her skin.

"You shouldn't stand by the window," he continued, still speaking softly. She could feel his breath again, close, on the back of her neck. Goosebumps formed on her skin and she almost shivered. But he didn't move to shut the curtains. His hand slid across her shoulder and down her back, tracing a path along her spine as delicately as a leaf borne along a current of water. She leaned back into his muscular chest and rested her head against him. It felt so good to touch him, to have him touching her.

His hand cradled her elbow and turned her gently toward him. And then he kissed her. Softly, questioningly. Her lips answered and opened to him. And a moment later, the soft delicacy disappeared. He pulled her into his chest and his mouth devoured hers with unrestrained passion.

She kissed him back just as fiercely, striving to lose herself in the contact, in the bliss of the hard, strong reality of him. Her hand reached out and caressed the broad, hard muscle of his good arm. She could feel the eagerness of his erection against her body, and her own body responded in kind. She'd spent so many nights wanting just this, to be back in the arms that had loved her so well.

He broke away.

The harsh white light of the room flooded her with a dose of reality. The open curtain seemed suddenly bare, and the city lights glared like a thousand staring, taunting eyes.

"I'm sorry," he said. "I can't do this."

Confusion rose to fury. "What, pretend you still have feelings for me?"

"I'm not here to seduce you, I'm here to protect you. And I won't be distracted from my job."

Something inside her crashed and burned. His job? Oh, right, Agency business. It was impossible to keep the bitterness from her words. "We can't have that, can we."

She yanked the curtain closed and shut out the night. She wanted to slap herself for allowing herself to feel those things for him again, for allowing her body to override her will, but the realization of her failure served to fuel her resolve. She had a job to do, too. She wasn't here to rekindle some doomed romance with Alex Dante. She was here to get her son back. And she wouldn't be distracted from her job, either.

But her job required freedom. If her will had sold out to the needs of her body, then his would too, she'd make sure of it. She turned back to Alex, pulled him tight against her, and kissed him with everything she possessed.

* * *

Alex hesitated a second, startled, standing back stiffly from her grasp. Every alarm bell in his head was going off, but he couldn't figure out why. She deepened her kiss, then slid a hand down his back to find the hard curve of his buttocks. Her lips dragged a hot trail from his mouth to the sensitive spot at the base of his ear.

His body shrieked to life. Without his consent, the pent-up desire that he'd been fighting since he'd first spotted her across the Blind Shark came raging up, forcing a groan from his lips. She took her hands from his body and stepped back. His lips tried to follow, but she pressed him back with her hands. Smiling, she shifted her shoulders, looking vaguely feline. The red robe slid off and puddled at her feet.

Alex lost the ability to breathe.

She closed the distance between them and pressed her body against his. Of their own accord, his hands came up to caress the silken skin of her back.

Again, she wrapped her arms around his neck and nuzzled his ear, just like she used to. That had always been his weakness. "Stop playing the martyr, Alex," she whispered.

"Forget the damned Agency for five minutes and just let yourself be human."

Forget the damned agency…

His passion congealed in him like cold grease.

He grabbed her shoulders and stiff-armed her away from him. The cold grease in his veins caught fire and fueled a hot, burning anger. "Nice try, Raven, but you seem to forget I'm the one who taught you those tactics." He pushed her away, probably a bit harder than he should have, and bent to pick up her discarded robe. He gave her one more good look, up and down. She stood there tall and regal in her nakedness, unashamed, with one hand cocked on the curve of her hip, and glared daggers at him.

He gave her one of her own self-satisfied grins. "Now go to bed like a good little civilian, and if you behave yourself and stay put, I might give you your robe back in the morning."

Without waiting for a response, he tossed her robe ever his shoulder, turned on his heel, and headed for his bedroom — the one with all the supplies — ignoring the string of curses that dogged him down the hall.

This was going to be a really, really long assignment.

Chapter Five

Alex helped himself to a box of .45 caliber ACP rounds from the supply closet in his room and stuffed them into his duffel bag. He'd been up most of the night, a combination of keeping one ear open for anything Raeanne might have tried, and thinking about Raeanne, period. Raeanne, sleeping right across the hall. Naked. Angry. Scared as hell for her son and too damned proud to admit it.

The ache to hold her had hummed in his chest until sleep finally took him, somewhere around dawn. And even now, after a few hours of sleep, a shower, and half a pot of strong, black coffee, his mind still wouldn't let go of the memory of how she'd felt in his arms, pressed against his body—the softness of her skin, the inviting curves of her, that sneaky little brain of hers trying to seduce him into letting her go.

Or maybe her plan had been to seduce him to distraction so she could break one of the safe house's hideous lamps over his head and escape while he was out cold. He smiled and tucked one of the portable GPS units into his bag, just in case. If he were a betting man, he'd put money on the lamp.

But the biggest impediment to sleep had been the questions. Why had she resigned from the agency and left him behind? Was it because of Ryan? The timing added up. Was it because of the boy's father? Who was he? It really wasn't any of his business, but...

Oh, the hell it wasn't his business. He'd shared everything

he'd ever had with her, had worked with her, had loved her. It damn well was his business when she disappeared into thin air to have some other man's baby.

And it had to be someone else's. If the boy were his, there's no way she would have kept that from him.

Yeah, so he was jealous. So what? That didn't make him stupid. Regardless of her tactics, he was well aware that part of her hadn't been playacting last night. He knew her, better than he knew himself, it seemed. Time could change ideas and opinions, but not the substance of a person. After all these years, he could still read her eyes.

There was a knock at his door. He turned to see her, wrapped in a gold floral bedspread, standing in the doorway like a disheveled pixie.

He couldn't help the wide grin that assaulted his face. "Good morning, Sunshine."

"Good morning, Warden. May I please have some clothes? I'd like to try making something for breakfast, but the sleeves on this thing are a fire hazard."

"There are frozen waffles in the freezer. No cooking required. But I'll give you some clothes, anyway." He turned to her and pointed toward the bureau. "You'll find a bunch of stuff in there."

"Thanks," she said. He could tell from her expression that she hadn't expected him to comply. Actually, she looked as though she wasn't a hundred percent sure he was really Alex and not an alien.

"Make it quick, though. We're going to see the senator. Richardson called with new orders."

"Me too?" She paused with the top drawer open.

"You don't think I'd leave you here alone, do you?"

That petulant look of hers seated itself across her face "I get paid to take care of a U.S. Senator, Dante. I think I can take care of myself for a couple of hours. Especially in this bunker."

Alex grabbed an MP5 from the firearm cabinet, an extra

magazine, and enough rounds for a bad day. Then he tossed her a stick of deodorant, a mini bottle of shampoo and another of conditioner and secured the closet. "I'm more concerned with your whereabouts than your safety. I'm not letting you out of my sight."

"I guess it's better than staying here another day," she said, rifling through the drawer. "Although I think I'd rather wear my dirty clothes. Or maybe my bedspread. I am *not* going out in public wearing what's in this drawer."

"Maybe if you're good we'll do laundry later." If we're lucky, he added to himself. But in the back of his mind, he didn't really believe they'd be doing anything as mundane as laundry for quite some time. "Now get a move on. We have a date with Senator Helmsan."

A half hour later, Alex paced the kitchen waiting for Raeanne to finish in the shower.

The strangeness of it all churned his thoughts into mush. He never thought he'd ever be doing that again, waiting for Raeanne to get ready to go somewhere. So many pieces of his past, so many memories, which he thought he'd successfully banished from his mind, had clawed their way back to the forefront in the last twenty-four hours. But he couldn't let himself fall victim to the seduction of memory. None of this was real. Just because Raeanne was here, didn't mean she was *here*. She was still as gone as she'd been the last seven years.

But it was hard to remember that with the strains of her off-key voice wafting out on clouds of steam from the shower, just like in the old days. Damned woman never could carry a tune. It was about all he could do to keep the fillings in his mouth when she started in with her morning concerto. Today it was Itsy Bitsy Teeny Weenie Yellow Polka Dot Bikini. Damn her and her infernal squawking and the yellow polka-dotted images of her that were belly dancing before his eyes.

Without changing his pace or his expression, he slung the duffel bag over his shoulder and decided to go wait for her outside. Where it was safe.

The air was cool, almost cold. Alex leaned back against the hood of the GTO and crossed his arms over his chest. He'd spent a few minutes looking around for his denim jacket, then remembered he'd left it in the Blind Shark during yesterday's excitement, which didn't improve his mood any. He looked up toward the bathroom window of the little apartment, where Raeanne was, please God, making some progress toward finishing up her feminine bathroom ritual. For a woman who could go weeks in the field without running water, she could be the ultimate high-maintenance female when she wanted to be. The worst part about it was, since he had spent weeks in the field with her, he knew that she was perfectly capable of three-minute showers in cold water while simultaneously washing her hair and brushing her teeth. This high-maintenance thing was pure spite.

Women were evil.

His eyes scanned the street for the fiftieth time. Normal traffic, no repeat vehicles. His holster sat snug against the small of his back, conspicuous, but that couldn't be helped. The .45 wasn't easy to conceal in the best of circumstances, and access to the weapon had to be top priority. He glanced at the steamy bathroom window again. He should have never given her the hair conditioner.

"Ready to go?" a voice whispered from behind.

He spun toward the sound, his hand going for his holster. It was empty.

"You've gotten careless, Flame," Raeanne said. "I could have shot you dead a hundred times in the last ten minutes and you'd never have seen it coming." Her eyes danced with fiendish mirth as she handed him back his weapon.

He couldn't help it; he laughed out loud. "Touché," he said and gave her ponytail a yank. "It's about time. I thought I'd be eligible for Medicare by the time you finished in there." He walked around the car to open her door for her. She'd found a pale yellow blouse with padded shoulders, which seemed a little too tight on her and was missing a couple of buttons so that it plunged a good deal lower than her normal preference. But he wasn't about to complain. She'd gained considerable cleavage in the last seven years, one of the changes he decided he liked. She was still in great shape, but she obviously was no longer as psychotic about keeping her body fat percentage down in the negative numbers. And he liked where that extra little padding had wound up, peeking out from the vee of that really ugly shirt. He offered a silent thank-you to whoever was responsible for stocking the clothing at the safe house.

"Whoever supplies the clothes at this place should be shot," she said.

"I was just thinking the same thing."

"I can't believe I'm going out in public in shoulder pads. My mother once put a blouse like this out at a yard sale and couldn't give it away. I think it was mine from the sixth grade. I think this might even be it."

"Yeah, well, it's free," he said and was rewarded with her laughter.

"Yeah, well, you get what you pay for." She threw him a brown zippered cardigan, a la Mr. Rogers. "Here. So you have somewhere to conceal your weapon. It's not like you can hide much in the muscle shirts you've taken to wearing. I think Ryan's shirts are bigger than—" The smile died on her lips.

He paused in his motion to unlock the door and instead laid a hand on her shoulder. "We'll get him back, Rae. He's got the best team in the world fighting on his side."

She nodded, then smiled a little. "I know. Just being a neurotic mother." But the look of loss and fear still peeked through her eyes.

"Just wait 'til I get the bastards in my sights. You're gonna be a happy mother hugging her little boy, you hear me?"

"I know." But the conviction in her voice sounded just a

tad forced.

A couple of minutes later, Alex headed northbound on I-15 toward the location where Senator Helmsan and her son had been secreted away. With any luck they could arrange to make it look as if the Syndicate's requests had been followed, which was the first step in getting Raeanne's son back.

The boy was never far from his thoughts. And neither were the unanswered questions about Raeanne's abrupt disappearance. The only thing that eluded him was a good way to bring it up.

"So... Ryan's about seven?"

"He turned seven last month." She glanced at him briefly, then turned back to stare out the window.

August... He'd gone over the math a dozen times while lying sleepless in bed the night before, and August was exactly the month he didn't want to hear. He kept toying with the idea that maybe the boy was his, but that was nothing more than a pipe dream getting the best of him late at night. She'd always been more than careful about that kind of thing. He'd thought maybe the boy had been conceived after she'd left the agency, just after December Ice. But unless he'd been severely premature, an August birthday put the numbers too far askew for that.

His jaw clenched. Whoever the boy's father was, his relationship with Raeanne had obviously overlapped Alex's own. Being dumped was bad enough, but being two-timed was infinitely worse.

But at least he had his answer.

Now all he had to do was find the bastard and feed him his heart. The SOB obviously hadn't been man enough for a woman like Raeanne Springfield.

Hell, obviously he hadn't been, either.

The desire to hear it from her own lips became overwhelming, and he found what he hoped was a good opening. "Maybe we should contact the boy's father to let him know what's happened."

Raeanne didn't look at him, but he could feel the coldness emanating from her like frost from an iceberg. So it was a touchy subject was it? He knew he was risking all the tenuous headway he'd made with her since yesterday afternoon, but then again, what did it matter? She'd made her choice and it wasn't him.

"He doesn't have a father."

Alex turned to her, then back to the road. "Coward didn't stick around, huh?"

"I didn't stick around. I don't know who it was. Could have been any number of people."

Alex turned to her with disbelief. So it was true, what her dossier said about her relationships with every available male west of the Rockies.

She shrugged slightly and kept her focus on the scenery blurring past her window. "What can I say? I dated a lot after I left the agency."

Her words struck him like a slap. Then...something in her voice, or her body language... "You're lying," he said.

She glanced over at him and raised one eyebrow. "Am I?" She turned back to the window again, cool as ice, and Alex's certainty evaporated into mist.

He could think of nothing to say. For a long time the only sound came from the radio, turned low, and the deep growl of the big engine under the hood. The silence between them was stifling. He could still smell the flowery shampoo she'd used that morning, and it made him want to touch her hair, which made him want to rip out his own.

She was lying, he was sure of it.

Or maybe it was just his refusal to believe what he didn't want to believe—that the woman he loved was really gone.

"Guess you can't blame a guy for wanting to stay warm in those Minnesota winters," he said.

She turned to him, a look of confusion on her face.

"Minnesota?"

Jackpot.

He concentrated on guiding the GTO off the freeway and onto another side street, trying not to let the exultance show on his face. Raeanne would never sleep with a platoon of random men; she found most of them weak and spoiled, and compared to her, most of them were. And she sure as hell had never lived in Minnesota. He knew there'd been something wrong with the agency not knowing about her son, and he was beginning to suspect there was a lot more wrong with her file than that. After this was finished, he was going to figure out why.

He doubled back and reentered the freeway, now heading south. Certain he hadn't been followed, he took another off-ramp and drove a while until he came to an upper-class neighborhood. He circled the block before parking in a small lot by a children's play area, where minivans and SUVs sat in a line, waiting for parents who pushed their children on swings or romped with them in the grass. They got out and walked a short distance down the road, then Alex stopped in front of a large, well-maintained ranch house, indistinguishable from any of a dozen others on the street.

"Nice place," he said, just to say something.

"Very."

There was a Lexus parked in the driveway, probably McHugh's. Alex walked to the front door and knocked. He rested a hand on the grip of his pistol, just in case.

A shadow appeared in the peephole, then buzzed them in.

Kyle McHugh's face blossomed into stunned joy. "Raeanne! Where the hell have you been?" He slipped his pistol back into his shoulder holster and wrapped her in a fierce hug.

She hugged him back just as tightly. "Oh my God! I haven't seen you in ages!"

Pulling away, Kyle glanced behind them, then ushered them quickly inside.

"The senator has been asking for you since yesterday. You'd better go and let her see that you're still in one piece." He stepped back and motioned them inside.

Alex followed Raeanne into the living room. The house was decorated in that uncomfortable, magazine-cover way that always bothered him, with a huge open floor plan done up in shades of cream and black. Tommy Helmsan sat on the tan and black oriental rug, sorting piles of trading cards and chattering to his mother. On the tan leather couch behind him, Senator Diane Helmsan perched like a falcon waiting to be loosed.

She was much more stunning in person than on television, beautiful in that classic, Jackie O sort of way, but with a sharpness to her features that belied her conservative dress. Mid-forties, dark hair cut blunt at her chin and turned slightly under, she exuded poise and sophistication, but with an undercurrent of steel. The proverbial iron hand in the velvet glove. Alex found himself liking her immediately.

Diane gave Raeanne a smile and arched one perfectly plucked eyebrow at her. "So there's my lost bodyguard. You take one day off and all hell breaks loose." She let her gaze wander to the door, then back to Raeanne's face. "Where's Ryan?"

Raeanne stiffened. Alex put a hand on the small of her back to reassure her. Evidently Richardson hadn't chosen to disclose any information about the boy. He glanced at Kyle and saw only questions in his eyes, too.

"Ryan has been kidnapped," he said, "We need your help."

Diane blanched, then she stood and rushed to hug Raeanne. "Oh, Rae, what happened," she said, pulling back to hold Raeanne at arm's length.

Raeanne glanced at Alex for help.

Diane would know nothing of CODA, most of the intelligence community didn't even know of their existence. They were probably identifying themselves as FBI, or maybe some subset of Homeland Security, depending on how they were trying to play it off. And he knew Raeanne would never have mentioned her history with them.

He cleared his throat and frowned. "They've decided to use your bodyguard to get to you," he said. "When they didn't succeed in snatching your child, they went for hers."

"Wait a minute," Kyle said. "Who's Ryan?"

Raeanne turned to him and said softly, "My son."

His face went as stark as Diane's had. "You have a son?" Then he turned to Alex. "Did we know that?"

"That seems to be the question of the hour." Alex guided Raeanne to a leather wing chair, but she resisted his direction to sit. Instead, she curled up on the rug beside Tommy.

The boy looked up at her with youthful trepidation. "Is Ryan okay, Miss Rae?"

Raeanne pushed his sandy bangs out of his face, then let her hand drift around his shoulders to pull him into a hug. "So far, Tommy. You see these people who are taking care of you and your mom? Well, they're the best in the world at saving people from bad guys. In a few days, you and your mom and Ryan and I will all be home, safe and sound, okay?" The slight catch in her voice was probably only audible to someone trained in interrogation, but it told Alex, quite plainly, that while Raeanne was doing her best to convince everyone that things were okay, she didn't believe it for a minute.

"We'll get him, Rae," he said. Raeanne turned her big hazel eyes to him, haunted eyes, and in them he read her certainty that he was wrong. His heart twisted in his chest for the hundredth time over the last two days. But he would prove to her that he was right. "I'll get your son back. I promise you that."

Raeanne's eyes went cold, the passion waning, replaced with the lifeless acceptance of defeat. "You're blurring the line, Dante. You can't make a personal crusade out of your objective. That's the quickest way to get yourself, and your objective, killed."

Alex stared into her cold gaze, refusing to look away, refusing to take her rebuke. She was right, of course; a mission had to stay professional. But this was no ordinary mission.

This mission was FUBAR to the power of ten.

She refused to look at him. Instead, she turned and smiled down at Tommy. "Ooh, you brought your Pokémon cards. Wanna play?"

Alex watched Raeanne scoot across from Tommy and start dealing out cards as if she didn't have a care in the world. His heart constricted in his chest, with tenderness and longing.

"And we didn't hear about this why?" McHugh said under his voice, edging up next to him.

"Someone screwed up, that's why." He motioned for them to step away from Raeanne and Tommy, through the wide archway leading into the dining room, where he pulled up a chair and seated himself at the table. "First of all, there's no reason in hell we could have missed something as obvious as a kid. Then yesterday, we had a run in with Petrov's goons, and someone leaked the identity of the kill to the press. No one outside CODA could have known he was a member of the Ice Syndicate, or that they're even still in existence."

McHugh's eyes narrowed. "Are you suggesting there's a leak inside the agency?

Alex shrugged.

McHugh just stiffened his jaw. "Have you spoken to Richardson about this?"

"Not yet, I'm still trying to figure things out. But right now, I'm not taking any more chances. I promised Raeanne I'd get her boy back, and I mean to do it."

"So what are you planning to do with Rae in the meantime?"

"That's where you come in." He gave McHugh a long, pointed look.

"Oh no." McHugh took a step backward. "No way. The

last thing I want is to be picking pieces of my ass off the floor. Besides, I already have my hands full with the senator and Tommy."

Alex grinned. "Don't tell me you're afraid of her? She's been out of the business for seven years."

"I'm not afraid of her," McHugh said.

Alex raised one eyebrow. *"Bluck bluck..."*

"Okay, fine. I'll take her. But if Richardson finds out, I'm not going to cover for you."

"I wouldn't ask you to."

"So what's your plan?"

"Petrov has dictated terms for the boy's release. Instead of just pulling the bill, he now wants the senator to introduce some crackpot legislation of his own."

"Done," Diane Helmsan said from the archway.

Alex turned to her and slid out a chair for her to join them. "There's more, Senator. They want it introduced by Wednesday."

Her eyebrows rose into her wispy bangs. "Wednesday? Are they crazy?"

"Apparently. Doesn't mean they're not serious, though."

"What kind of bill are they proposing?"

"We don't know. They've left a package on your desk in your office. But you can bet it will somehow enable them to transport their illegal weapons through the US. Perhaps even to and from Al-Qaeda operatives living within the border."

McHugh frowned. "When are they going to release the boy?"

"Unknown."

Diane Helmsan cleared her throat, drawing the attention of everyone in the room. "Then we'll simply have to appear to give them what they want until such time as your people can apprehend them. I'll call some of my colleagues on the senate finance committee and tell them to stall the bill for further debate. Then I'll have my assistant make some calls to the press and leak that the bill is dead. That should at least buy us some time."

Alex smiled. "I'm impressed by your quick grasp of the essentials, Senator."

"Oh, please. If they think this is so tough, they ought to try dealing with some of the conservatives on the Senate Finance Committee." The senator's precisely lined lips were set firm. "One of you will have to take me to my office so I can pick up their supposed legislation and get a few files that I'll need."

"I'm sorry, Senator, but we can't let you leave the safe house."

She opened her mouth to argue, but Alex cut her off. "They've already broken into your office once, to drop off the package to begin with. What's to stop them from doing it again in order to get you, too? We can't risk putting you in harm's way."

"Then how will I get the files that I need? I'm good, but I'm not clairvoyant."

"Make a list of what you need and I'll collect it when I go to retrieve their package."

She opened her mouth, then closed it and smiled. "Forgive me, but quite a bit of that material is confidential."

Alex smiled at her. "Ma'am, no offense, but my clearance exceeds yours by several levels. I'll need directions and any keys or combinations that may be necessary."

"I have keys," Raeanne said, walking in and pulling up a chair beside the senator. "And I know where we're going. We can discuss things on the way."

Alex felt his blood begin to course more quickly through his veins. This was where things were about to get sticky.

"Alex...?" Raeanne prompted, raising a brow at him.

Here it comes. "Raeanne, you have to stay here."

"What?"

"I'm sorry. I know how much you want to help, but..."

"Damn you, Alex Dante, you lied to me!"

"No, I didn't, I told you—"

"You told me Richardson had given new orders and that I could come."

"I told you we were coming *here* and that you could come. I didn't say one word about the senator's office or anywhere else."

"But you purposely let me believe I was going to be allowed to participate in this operation!" She glanced at the faces around the table, but McHugh wouldn't meet her eyes. "So you could drop me here and make Kyle babysit me like a child, is that it?"

Alex let a long, hard sigh pass his lips. "I'm sorry, Raeanne. Orders are orders. And as you so astutely pointed out, blurring the line between personal and professional is the quickest way to get both you and your objective killed."

She fumed at him, wordlessly, then smiled. "So tell me, Dante. Just how do you plan to get to Diane's office if you don't know the address?"

He raised an eyebrow and called her bluff. "I can have the location in less than three minutes. And you know it."

Raeanne's glare would've curdled milk. "Oh yeah? And the alarm code? And the password to her computer?"

Diane stood and discretely attempted to leave the room.

"Hold it, Senator," Alex said, stopping her in her tracks. He turned back to Raeanne. "The good Senator will not impede our attempts to save your son by playing childish games. She will tell me exactly what I need to know to get into her office and access her files."

Diane Helmsan laughed daintily. "Mr....Dante, is it?"

He turned again to her and stiffly offered her his hand. "It's Major, actually. Alex Dante. U. S. Marine Corps. Retired."

"Major Dante," Diane said, smoothing his ruffled feathers with her smooth alto. "It's quite clear you have everything well in hand. I have every confidence that you and your team will bring this situation to a successful conclusion."

"Thank you, Senator."

She smiled at him. "But with all due respect, you don't seriously think you're going to dissuade Raeanne from participating, do you?"

"Dissuasion isn't necessary, Senator. She's a civilian under my protection, and as far as this room goes, I'm the ranking officer."

"Get over yourself, Dante. I'm under no one's protection but my own. If you think for one minute that I'm going to allow you to pursue any of this without me, you're nuts."

"See?" The senator added. "She's quite stubborn. Trust me, Major Dante, I've worked with her for many years. Once her mind is made up, there is very little you can do to change it."

"Tell me about it." He ran a frustrated hand through his cropped dark hair. "She's so stubborn I'd swear she was half goat."

"Nah, she's cuter than a goat," McHugh said with a grin, which earned him a scathing look from Alex. "Well, she is," he continued. "And then there's Dante, who's just as stubborn, only with him there's a definite resemblance to the goat. Around the eyes, especially."

"I'm going with you," Raeanne said. "You need me. I was the best damn officer this agency ever had."

"The operative word being *was*."

"You mean, like how I *was* able to take down that man at the school? Or like how I *was* able to get his phone and find Petrov's number? Or maybe how I *was* able to disarm you this morning on the sidewalk, before you'd even realized I was out of the shower?"

Alex stared her down with the look that normally had men *sir-yes-sir*-ing him to death. But she stared him right back, waiting for him to make the next move, her hazel eyes boring into his like lasers and a thin white line forming around her lips from the force of pressing them together. And as he looked at her, he knew he was checkmated. She *was* one of the best agents CODA ever had, and even seven years retired, she was still the only living person who'd ever successfully disarmed him.

In more ways than one.

Besides, he'd seen last night how desperate she was under her cool façade and how far she'd go to do what she thought she had to in order to save her son. And he just couldn't find the strength to tell her no.

He gave her his hardest stare. "You realize that by asking me to do this, you're asking me to disobey a direct order."

"Yep."

"And you realize you're asking me to allow you to put your life and the lives of the rest of my team in danger, as well as the life of your own son."

"I realize *you* believe that."

"And you don't?"

She took a deep breath. "No, I don't. I believe you've made an error in assessing the situation. I believe that unless we play by Petrov's rules—which you know include revenge against me personally—that you will fail and my son will be killed."

He glared at her, wondering where his sanity had gone. "Fine. But you will adhere to strict field protocol at all times. If you so much as breathe without asking me for permission, I swear I will let Richardson throw you in jail."

"Yes, sir." Just a hint of relief showed through her dark, determined gaze.

Alex pulled his car keys from his pocket and heaved a sigh of resignation. "What are you waiting for then? Get the keys and a list of the files we need, and let's get a move on. We're burning daylight." He turned to McHugh, who had wisely attempted to blend into the upholstery. "And one word from you to Richardson about this and you'll be with me in the brig until you're a very old man."

Kyle stood up and headed into the kitchen. "Me? I didn't hear anything. I was too busy doing my job guarding the senator and getting something to eat."

Alex looked through the archway into the living room where Raeanne stood huddled with Diane over her briefcase. He had to be crazy. When this assignment was over, he was going to get good and drunk and take a very long vacation. That's if he was still alive.

Chapter Six

The senator's office was one of many off East Washington Street, set in a modern glass and concrete structure overlooking the park. Raeanne's face stared back at her from the square black pools of glass as she gazed out the GTO's open window. They circled the building, scouting for potential trouble. There was nothing out of place. But it just didn't feel right.

"Looks clean to me," Alex said.

"Yeah," Raeanne said. "That's what worries me."

They hadn't been followed; they both agreed on that. And neither were there any signs of enemy presence along the perimeter of the parking lot and building. No cars. No people. Not even a stray dog. But still, Raeanne felt that odd sensation of wanting to look back over her shoulder. She had her Glock in her hand and the MP5 Alex had brought from the safe house beside her, and short of having a sniper posted in an adjacent building, they were about as good as they were going to get.

"At least we have some heavier firepower this time," she said, gesturing toward the submachine gun.

Alex parked his car in the lot to the left of the building and cut the engine. "That's staying here."

"What good is it going to do us in the car?"

"What good is it going to do us along a city sidewalk? You want someone to see us and call the cops?"

"No one's going to call the cops. Throw your ugly sweater

over it or something—it's only twenty yards to the door."

"And what if there's someone inside? One look at that thing and they'll have the cops there in five seconds." He pulled two spare .45 magazines out of his duffel bag and shoved one down each of his front pockets.

Raeanne sighed and rolled up her window. "I want in on record that I strongly disagree."

"Sorry, kid, I give the orders around here, remember? You're just the uninvited guest that won't go home."

She turned to object, then saw his taunting grin. "Okay, fine," she said. "It's your show. But if I end up fighting off half a dozen, combat-armed Russians with just a handgun, I won't hesitate to say 'I told you so.'"

"You never do."

"Because I'm usually right." The building was locked as usual after business hours. She slid the keycard through the reader and the light turned from red to green. The wide, tinted-glass door unlocked with a click, but before she could enter, Alex grabbed her shoulder and took the lead, pistol in hand.

She let his macho "me first" routine slide. He'd always been like that, thinking he could actually protect her by being in front. As if hostiles never tried to shoot you in the back. But at least he'd let her come. She'd won that battle, and if there was one thing she'd learned over the years, it was to choose one's battles carefully.

Motherhood had taught her that.

She followed Alex in and turned to clear the right-hand side of the room. She moved quietly across the black marble floor to the reception area, furnished with dark, polished wood and clear glass that combined moneyed tradition with cutting-edge design. Directly ahead was the front desk, behind which a floor-to-ceiling abstract painting hung amid a jungle of hanging plants. To the left, a small fountain sat dark and still, beyond which a bank of elevators led up to the building's top floors. To the right, a wide corridor branched off to the first floor office suites. The faint drone of a vacuum cleaner somewhere farther inside was the only sound that spoiled the building's quiet dignity.

Alex stalked toward the front desk. Raeanne put her hand on his shoulder to stop him for a moment. Something wasn't right. She turned to stare out the tinted windows into the parking lot but saw nothing. No motion at all. Not so much as a breeze.

"What?" Alex mouthed silently.

She shook her head to indicate nothing was wrong, then signaled him to go on.

He nodded and continued his careful approach to the receptionist desk. He thrust his pistol over the front desk, aimed down at any possible threat hiding beneath. Raeanne covered him, sweeping the rest of the room.

Nothing.

Overstuffed wing chairs. A low marble-topped table full of magazines. A few potted plants. Behind the front desk, a stack of papers avalanched out of an in box. One of those spiky-haired troll dolls hung suspended from a suction cup on the side of the computer monitor, while an abstract screensaver made random looping patterns on the screen that angled inward.

The vacuum cleaner stopped. Raeanne spun in the direction of the sound, toward the corridor off to the right. The shortest route to Diane's second floor office. Alex moved out ahead of her, his gun pointed downward, but ready. Just inside the corridor, to the right, was the door marked Stairs. Alex flung open the door, pivoting to cover the open area within, then lowered his weapon and quietly closed the door.

At the end of the hall, a large gray trash can stood slung about with spray bottles and rags. A thin, gray-haired man in a baggy janitor's uniform walked into sight and dumped a wastepaper basket from one of the offices into the trash can.

He sang a country song to himself, a bit too loudly and not quite on key, accompanied by some inaudible music on his headphones. Raeanne tucked away the pistol just as Alex did the same. There was no need to draw attention to themselves, just two ordinary business people stopping off for some overtime on a Saturday morning.

The janitor was too distracted to see them approach until Alex stepped around the trash can and into his line of sight. The old man jumped, then slid the earphones off his wispy white head.

"You folks gave me quite a start." He grinned, showing nicotine-yellow teeth. Earl, his name was, according to the embroidered name patch on his blue work shirt. He seemed harmless enough—just an old man, slightly stooped, with thin arms and filmy, faded blue eyes. "Didn't hear you come in."

"Is anybody else in the building?" Raeanne asked.

"What? No, no. You folks are the only people I've seen all day."

Alex peered into the man's garbage can, but didn't react. Obviously not a threat. "Thanks," he said. "We'll be in and out in a short while." He snapped his fingers and started briskly down the corridor. "Come along, Jane. I want you to start taking notes as soon as we set up the conference call." He turned the corner at the end, not waiting for her to catch up.

"Of course, sir," Raeanne answered dutifully, then offered a smile to the janitor and trotted after Alex.

She rounded the corner, and Alex was waiting for her. "Nice one, Mr. Thespian," she quipped. "But if you snap your fingers at me again, you're a dead man walking."

"Liked that, huh? Let's see, we're on the east side of the building?" He stood a moment, getting his bearings. "Three entrances total, front and back doors this way and…that way, and that puts the service entrance…down there."

"Correct." Raeanne gave him a saucy grin. "I might let you live, after all."

"You know, you've been awfully feisty since we left the senator's safe house. Funny how your mood improves when you get your way."

She pressed the elevator's call button harder than she needed to. "Let's just go."

Diane's office suite was exquisitely decorated with more dark wood and gorgeous antiques, as polished and sophisticated as Diane herself. Raeanne entered the code to disarm the security system, then moved silently across the blood-red Persian rug of the small sitting area to the two inner offices.

"I'll take Diane's computer," she said, "and you take the file cabinet in the assistant's office."

"Since when did you take control of this mission?" Alex asked, but he went into the other office without further complaint.

He was always complaining about something, Raeanne thought, and she felt a tug of nostalgia for how easy it was, even after this long, to fall back into their old routine. It struck her then, like a dart, fast and deep, how much she'd missed their easy banter. How much she missed…him.

She watched him enter the other office, pull the handwritten list from his pocket, and begin to search through the file drawers. God, he looked just the same. The smooth grace of his movements had never failed to fascinate her, and nothing had changed. He still possessed that loose agility, like a huge cat, equally ready at any moment to either lunge at a threat or collapse into a puddle of languid laziness—relaxed, sensual…

No. Get to work.

On Diane's desk lay the manila envelope, courtesy of their Russian friends. Her heart flip-flopped again, this time with dread at the reminder of Ryan's situation and Petrov's invitation to dinner in DC The desire to tell Alex about it and gain his assistance, and the need to follow Petrov's directions to the letter to prevent him from harming Ryan, twisted together in a knot of tense confusion. Petrov intended to kill her, that much was clear. But she was willing to play it his way if there was a chance he'd free Ryan.

She shoved the thoughts away, pulled up the heavy leather swivel chair and booted up Diane's computer. She needed a plan, maybe several, which would enable her to free her son. Her own life was secondary. She'd rather not leave her son an orphan, but it was better than leaving him a corpse.

Fifteen minutes later, she popped the CD containing everything on Diane's list out of the drive. Congressmen who owed her favors. Lobbyists who'd crossed the line. Media contacts and their pet crusades and whatever dirt she'd found on them to keep them useful. Petrov was in for a surprise. Diane Helmsan was nobody's bitch.

Alex had collected the hard copy files she'd requested, and appeared at the office door, stuffing them into the duffel bag. "You about ready?"

"Yep. Got everything we need." She shut down the computer and the monitor went black. She turned and glanced out the large plate glass windows framing the eastern wall, but the parking lot remained empty. For the first time, she began to feel a small blossom of hope. Soon they'd get Diane off to Washington to start politicking about the new bill, and by Wednesday night, she'd be at the Blue Lagoon collecting her son. As far as a plan went, she'd have plenty of time to come up with one between now and then. At least for now, things were moving; she was doing something, and that made her feel more in control than she had since Alex Dante had imploded back into her life.

Through the window, she saw a white Mercedes Benz glide into the parking lot.

She froze.

"Dammit, they're here," Alex said from behind her.

It was very quiet. The blood rushed through her body as

her heart began to thump faster against her chest. "Yeah, well, so am I." She drew her pistol from her shoulder holster and flipped off the safety.

Five men got out of the car. Four she'd never seen before. The last, carrying a large black duffel bag, wore aviator shades and a goatee.

Alex grabbed the CD and shoved it into his duffel bag. He zipped it shut, slung it over his shoulder, and drew his weapon from the holster at his back.

Two of the men hurried around the rear of the building, the other three toward the front.

"The two in the back will have to split their attention between the back door and the service entrance." Alex whispered. "Which one's closer?"

Raeanne chambered a round and followed him into the corridor. "Either one, from here, but we'd have to risk the elevator. The stairs will take us to the front lobby."

"No back stairs?"

"Nope."

"Damn."

"Personally, I'd rather have three targets lined up ahead of me than be a sitting duck in an elevator."

"No argument here. Front door it is."

The corridor was clear. They flew to the end of the hallway and wrapped around the corner. As she passed the elevator, Raeanne expected the chime to sound and the doors to slide open to reveal Goatee and his two henchmen with assault rifles. But the elevator remained still.

The stairwell was quiet, as well. They ran as stealthily as they could past the beige cement walls and tubular steel rails, down to the first floor, then flattened themselves against either side of the doorframe leading out into the main corridor. The heavy door latch *thunked* loudly as Alex pumped it open a crack and scanned the hallway. He motioned her to follow, and she stepped out after him into the hall.

The corridor was empty, but the lobby wasn't. They pressed themselves to the opposite wall, but it wasn't much cover.

"This stinks," Raeanne whispered, her hand growing sweaty on the grip of her Glock. Being closest to the corner, she inched herself to the edge and peeked into the front reception area. The janitor stood next to Goatee and his two lackeys: a tall, blond mountain with a crew cut and a dark sport coat that didn't quite fit his bulk, and a smaller man, dark-haired and weasel-faced, in a starched white dress shirt and blue tie that didn't make him look any less feral. Unless they had fake key cards, the janitor must have let them in.

Goatee set the duffel bag upon the low coffee table in the reception area and pulled out two MP5's, passing one to each of his henchmen. Blondie headed off in the direction of the elevators and out of her narrow field of view. The janitor watched them nervously, but not nervously enough. He didn't appear alarmed by the sudden appearance of automatic weapons.

"He's working for them," she whispered. Alex nodded once, then turned his attention back to the party out front.

Goatee addressed the janitor with a heavy Moscow accent. "Which direction did they go?"

"Down the hall and to the left. Took the elevator, so they must'a went up. Don't know what floor, though."

"Are they still up there?'

"Haven't seen 'em come down. Front door's the only one unlocked on the weekends, otherwise they'll set off the alarms."

Weasel pulled the bolt on the submachine gun, and the mechanical click-clack echoed through the empty building.

"What about my money?" the old man said, rubbing his hands on the thighs of his blue work pants. "The fella I spoke to said I'd get enough to retire if I called you as soon as—"

A three-round burst of gunfire cut off whatever else he

was going to say.

Raeanne glanced at Alex. "They shot the old man!" she hissed.

"This is not going to work," Alex whispered. "We need to find another exit."

They hurried back down the hall, making no noise. Behind them, Raeanne heard footsteps across the marble floor of the lobby. At the corner, she slipped passed the janitor's trash can into the open door marked Maintenance, with Alex right behind.

The room lay in semi-darkness, lit only by the light from the hall. It was scantily furnished, almost empty save for several remnants of old office furniture and skeletal steel shelves full of cleaning products and miscellaneous supplies. They crouched behind a metal secretarial desk across from the door, and Raeanne tried not to breathe like a freight train.

It was hot as hell back there, too. A line of sweat formed on her top lip and made her itch to wipe it off. But she kept still. She couldn't see much, just a patch of floor by the doorway, visible through a small hole in the side of the desk where it had once been bolted to another piece of furniture. From Alex's position behind her, he was probably blind.

Feet entered her small circle of vision. Legs in dark trousers, the muzzle of a submachine gun. The weasel-faced one.

He paused in the open doorway. Raeanne's breath caught in her throat and her grip tightened on her pistol. "One in the door," she barely whispered.

Alex tapped her arm twice—*okay.*

A moment later, the feet continued on.

"Where's the other one?" he whispered.

"Unknown."

His breath was warm on her neck. "How close is the nearest exit?"

"Other side of the building, back door."

He stood slowly. "Then we'd better get a move on."

Raeanne stood too. She kept her voice soft. "You go high; I'll go low."

"Yeah, I'll go—"

Footsteps, the swish of a nylon windbreaker, coming up the hall.

Alex pushed her back down behind the desk and crouched beside her, his arm bumping the side. The jolt made a hollow sound against the metal.

Another Russian in a dark windbreaker stopped in the doorway and looked in.

Where the hell did this one come from? She hadn't gotten completely down behind the desk, but she couldn't risk the motion to duck lower. Through the assorted boxes and bottles of cleaners on the desktop, she could see the man standing still, scanning the room.

Her gun was ready in her right hand. *Keep going,* she silently coaxed, her thigh muscles starting to burn in their half crouch. She didn't want to have to shoot him. The sound of gunfire would draw the rest of them like flies.

The man's walkie-talkie crackled in unintelligible Russian. Alex tensed beside her, ready to spring.

The man answered in Russian, something that sounded like "all clear." He lowered the walkie-talkie and moved away.

Raeanne let out a long sigh, but the relief turned to frustration. He was heading toward the back of the building. The direction they'd planned to go to reach the rear exit.

"They're all over the damn place," Alex said, standing and moving toward the door.

"You want to follow him to the back, or try the front again?"

"Front door. Hopefully they've all scattered, looking for us."

Outside the maintenance office, the corridor was clear. Alex moved against the far wall. Raeanne followed, her palms sweaty against the textured pistol grip and the rough wallpaper. At the end of the corridor, the lobby was silent.

Raeanne hoped the silence meant emptiness. She pressed herself flat to the wall and peered around the corner into the reception area. And straight into the pale blue eyes of Blondie, not a foot away.

"They're here!" he yelled in Russian into his walkie-talkie. "Front door!"

He raised the submachine gun and opened fire. Raeanne jerked her head and dropped low. From above her, Alex got one wild shot off before an answering shot forced him to the carpet beside her. The 9mm slugs of the submachine gun chewed into the opposite wall, raining plaster chips around them.

Raeanne rolled away from the wall. More bullets shaved off the corner and left a gaping hole in the drywall where her head had just been.

Alex rolled to his feet and pulled her up. "Stairs!"

More gunfire followed, perforating a line across the metal fire door to the stairwell.

Alex pivoted and ran back down the hall "Back door!"

Raeanne dogged his steps. She sprinted around the corner and ran down the next hall. Alex pulled up short, spun around, and raised his gun. The throaty boom of his .45 filled the air as he fired three rounds to cover their passage and slow their pursuers. They turned another corner by the elevator and raced toward the back of the building.

The way was not direct. Raeanne led Alex through several twists of corridor, praying she wouldn't plow headfirst into one of the Russians. Finally, just ahead, the corridor ended and was crossed by another, forming a T. Around the corner to the right and ten yards down was the back door.

She rounded the corner and skidded to a halt on the low-pile carpeting. The Russian in the windbreaker and one other stood just inside the doorway. They both held pistols.

Both pistols swung up.

Everyone opened fire at once. Raeanne's .40 rang out in counterpoint to the Russian's larger caliber weapons, and then she leapt back to the cover of the corner. She felt the push of air against her bare legs as she dove and the hum of a round as it passed her head.

The man in the windbreaker jerked backward as a round took him in the shoulder.

Raeanne hit the carpet and rolled, timing it perfectly and coming up in a crouch, safely behind the wall, beside Alex.

"White panties, eh?" He was pressed against the wall, watching her with that Cheshire Cat grin of his.

She turned to him, speechless for a moment. "I almost bought it out there and all you can do is look up my skirt?"

"Sometimes life just up and offers you a little beauty," he said and winked at her. "How many were out there?"

"Two. Both with pistols. I nicked one." She pressed back against the wall, her heart sprinting and her breath harsh in her throat. "I'm freaking exhausted. I'm having flashbacks of Kosovo."

Alex inched ahead for a glance around the corner. Submachine gun fire rattled in response. He quickly ducked back behind the corner.

"They've got more than pistols," he said.

"They must have picked up company." Raeanne popped a fresh magazine into her Glock and dropped the empty into her skirt pocket.

"And me without my Howitzer."

She peered around the corner, trying not to stick her head out. "I told you we shouldn't have left the MP5 in the car."

"Figures you chose that moment to actually listen to me. You badgered me to get your way on everything else."

"I'm going to go see what I can see out there. Cover me."

"No way, you're not going to —"

"Three, two, go!" she said. Without waiting for his

agreement, she poked her head around the corner and took aim.

Alex leapt up and fired three blind shots around the corner to cover her. "I hate when you do that!"

By the door, the uninjured Russian stood with Weasel, assisting their downed partner. They turned at the sound of Alex's shots and tried to take cover. Alex's rounds went over their heads, but they bought time for Raeanne. She fired three quick shots. All three took the unknown Russian in the chest before he even raised his weapon. He staggered backward, firing a stray round as he fell.

"One down," she called to Alex, wherever he'd ended up.

Three shots sang out from behind. Not Alex's — these were from a submachine gun.

"Damn, they've caught up," Alex said. "Move!"

Raeanne crouched low and ran down the opposite corridor, away from the two remaining Russians guarding the back door. She leapt for the corner ahead and halfway around it, fired three more shots. Weasel went down, spraying a barrage into the ceiling as he fell.

"Another one down," Raeanne called.

Alex came up beside her around the opposite corner. He popped his clip and slipped another one in, his arm muscles bunching like constricting pythons. Yesterday's wound had reopened and stained his sleeve red, but it was minor. A scattering of brass casings clustered around his shoes, but she didn't know if they were his or her own. The air was thick with the acrid stench of burned gunpowder. "We can't stay here," he said. She could barely hear him over the ringing in her ears from the gunfire. "This is my last clip."

"Mine too," she said, willing her heartbeat to slow. "My arms are killing me. I'm going to ache for a week."

"Hey," he said, dropping his cavalier grin and giving her shoulder a squeeze. "Nice shooting back there."

She looked up into his vibrant, light green eyes, noted the

concern knitted into the dark brows, but also the smile tugging at the corners of his mouth. "Thanks," she said, then took a deep breath and tried not to let his praise make her smile too broadly. Instead, she turned back to the hallway around them.

"I'm not happy with our position, though," he said.

"Really? I thought you loved being outnumbered, outgunned, and surrounded."

"Well, yeah, but only when I know the terrain. Right now, I feel like a rat in a maze."

"I'll get us out," Raeanne said. "Don't you worry." She turned and launched a savage kick at a closed office door. Another kick and it buckled around the latch, but didn't give.

"Allow me," Alex said, taking her arm as she wound up for another assault. He stepped forward and threw a kick that sent the door crashing back into the wall.

"Sure, after I got it started for you."

Inside was an office laid out just like Diane's, only with cheesier paintings and plastic plants. Raeanne hopped onto the chair near the wall and reached up. The drop-ceiling panels, set in removable two-foot squares, were just out of her reach. "Give me a hand," she said.

Alex jumped up beside her and pushed the panel up and over. "Tell me you have a plan." He laced his fingers together to give her a leg up.

"Of course," she lied and placed her foot in his hand so he could give her a boost. She caught the edge of the ceiling joist, where it met the wall, and pulled herself up high enough to see. Inside there were long bundles of wrapped wire for the fluorescents, slim water pipes for the sprinklers stretching every which way like metal spider legs, and dull aluminum a/c ducts. She pulled herself the rest of the way up, supporting her weight on the joist. "And no looking up my skirt this time."

She heard him murmur something about legs.

"You'd better hurry up and climb in before our friends

find us," she said. "And stay on the wall. I don't need you falling through the ceiling panels."

A moment later, Alex jumped and pulled himself up beside her. "You sure this is a weight-bearing wall?"

"No."

"Great." He slid the ceiling panel back in place, leaving them in total darkness.

Chapter Seven

Raeanne crawled forward in the dark across the top edge of the wall. If she remembered correctly, all she had to do was cross over to the adjacent office, whose door opened into the hallway where the back door was located. That, and avoid slipping off the wall beam and falling through the flimsy, three-quarter-inch ceiling panels, right into the lap of the enemy.

A moment later the door burst open in the office below and hit the wall with an angry bang.

"Crap," came Alex's voice behind her.

She kept on crawling. Alex bumped her foot with his hands. Below them, the wall creaked in protest.

Muffled conversation drifted up from below, followed by frantic Russian chatter over the walkie-talkies. Finally, silence. She froze in place, straining to hear what was happening. Alex plowed into her legs and teetered along the four-inch beam.

He caught himself. Raeanne let out a long breath but remained silent. From the location of the sound beneath her, she was almost over the wall to the other office. Just a few more feet.

Gunfire erupted around them, ripping up through the ceiling panels and shooting up crazy, narrow beacons of light. Sparks exploded like fireworks from one of the fluorescents. A section of bullet-riddled paneling fell down and sent up a geyser of light from below.

She crawled faster. The metallic clacking of a clip being changed and a slide worked echoed from below her.

Almost there. Another foot and she'd be over the adjacent wall into the next office, and she could kick a panel out of her way and jump down. One more foot. The longest twelve inches ever.

She heard more chattering in Russian down below and then the sound of furniture being moved. She and Alex both turned to look back just as the one she'd shot in the shoulder stuck his head up through the hole in the paneling.

Alex shot him. The muzzle flash blazed like a momentary bonfire in the semidark, leaving its afterimage dancing in front of her eyes. Her ears rang from the sound. The man toppled back, dead before he could even scream.

Raeanne rushed for the crossbeam that indicated her goal, the wall to the next office. She reached it and felt her knee slip out from under her.

She went down. The ceiling gave in with a rending crash as ceiling panels and their flimsy aluminum supports tore out and collapsed beneath her. She left her stomach eight feet above her and tumbled down in a hail of plastic, paneling, and dust. She hit something on the way down; a piece of furniture caught her in the ribs. Her head cracked against the hard concrete beneath the thin industrial carpeting, and she bit her tongue.

Alex grabbed one of the sprinkler pipes, which snapped under his weight. A cold spray of water rained down upon them, soaking everything as he landed beside her, somehow managing to keep his feet.

Raeanne pushed herself up and snatched her pistol. Her head hurt like hell where she'd cracked it against the floor, and the ferric tang of blood coated her mouth. But at least they were in the right office.

"Hurry, Rae." Alex pulled her up by her arm. She barely heard him over the ringing in her ears. The ribs on her right side ached, but didn't feel broken, and her right elbow stung with rug burn. Her left calf was smeared with blood — whose, she didn't know — and it was starting to wash down her leg in a wet red smear, thanks to the sprinklers. She let Alex pull her forward and staggered after him, through the door and into the corridor.

"*Astana vitsa!*" she heard in Russian behind her. *Halt!*

She turned and stared directly into the muzzle of Goatee's gun. Eternity stared back from the small, black hole.

The gunshot was close and deafeningly loud. She stood still, hand against the wall, unable to raise her own weapon. Unable to move.

She watched Goatee slide slowly down the wall to the floor. She wondered why he was falling, then belatedly realized she was still standing.

"About time you let me take one," Alex said. He wrapped her in one strong arm and propelled her toward the door. She sagged against him for a moment, trying, but not quite able, to catch her balance as he pulled her along. Her legs felt like they belonged to someone else.

Blondie appeared from the cross-hall and fired wildly. Alex shot back, but the gunman jerked back behind the corner.

"Go!" Alex yelled, pushing her toward the door. The building's alarm began hooting as she slammed into the push bar and the door opened out from beneath her. She lost her footing, but then found herself upright and running, propelled by Alex's hand on her back. He sprinted beside her, his long legs flexing in his jeans like engine pistons.

Her head felt strange, too small and too tight as if it were about to burst. Somehow, the pavement in front of her wasn't where it should be, and her feet seemed to hit it out of synch with her steps. Alex's arm was bleeding where she gripped it, but it was hard and powerful and she knew it was the only thing keeping her on her feet.

Alex. As he ran beside her, his face was carved into rock-hard determination, and she decided that there wasn't a more perfect man in the world. He was the most powerful, stunning thing she had ever seen. And she loved him more than her own life.

No, something about that wasn't right. She didn't love him anymore.

Yes, she did. She always had. She always would. At that moment, she didn't have the strength to try to deny it.

Or to remain upright.

Her knees buckled. She thought absurdly as she went down that this was no time to be drooling over a man.

Alex wrapped his arm around her and heaved her up before she met the pavement. They were at the car. Her vision was starting to narrow, closing in to black dots around the periphery.

Gunshots behind them. Alex pushing her through the car door. More motion, Alex reaching over to shake her awake. She tried to sit up, and the motion of the car sent her sprawling sideways into him. Something behind her pushed her head down between her knees, the old vinyl of the car's seat pressing uncomfortably against her face and smelling like oil and dirty plastic.

"Breathe," Alex said.

Breathe. She knew what that meant. She just needed to remember what, that's all.

Finally, the spots began to clear, and the grogginess left her. She saw the MP5 on the floor under Alex's ugly brown sweater. The MP5. At least she remembered what that was for.

The car tires shrieked as Alex spun the GTO around in a hard turn and barreled toward the parking lot exit. She sat up and rolled down her window, then pulled the submachine gun off the floor, flipped the switch to full auto, and pointed it at the white Mercedes. Her vision wasn't as clear as it should have been, but she did her best to empty the 30-round clip into the tires and engine block.

"Put that thing down before you hurt somebody!"

She turned and gave Alex a patronizing look. "Uh, that would be the point, Alex." She flipped off the switch and pulled the weapon inside while Alex spun out of the parking lot and onto the street. Men. So overprotective.

Exhausted, giddily in love with the man next to her, she leaned her head back against the seat and tried to remember how to say "See ya, losers!" in Russian.

* * *

Alex glanced briefly at Raeanne with his other eye on the road. This wasn't good. The last thing they needed right now was for Raeanne to be laid up, healing a concussion. She was conscious, which was good, and she'd been answering his questions without hesitation, but that didn't mean she was fine. Sometimes the problems didn't appear immediately, and this wasn't her first bash to the head. Concussions generally weren't life threatening, but repeated beatings to the brain were another matter. She needed to see a doctor, just in case.

Of course, concussion or no, she'd throttle him the minute he got her anywhere near a hospital.

The question was, should he get throttled at Lake Mead, the closest civilian hospital, or the US Army hospital about a mile away? Either way there would be questions about the goose egg on the back of her head, not to mention the blood on the both of them, but at least he knew how to talk to military personnel. And if the questions got too pointed, Richardson would be able to pull more strings with the Army than with the Vegas police.

Decision made, he continued in the direction he was heading and hoped to hell Raeanne was too groggy to notice.

"What are we doing here?" she asked when he pulled into a parking space outside the emergency room entrance. So much for groggy.

"I want to get that concussion checked out. I don't want you blacking out on me halfway through this mission."

She sat up straighter and narrowed her eyes at him. "Baloney. You just don't want me on this mission. Well, it's not going to work, Dante. I'm not going to let you ditch me in some hospital while those bastards have my son."

"I have no intention of ditching you, I just want to make sure you're okay."

"Jeez, Dante, you've been drilling me with trivia questions since we got in the car. Have I seemed confused to you? I'm fine. Really."

Alex looked at her and grinned. Checkmate. "Then if you're sure you're fine, you've got nothing to be afraid of, have you? They'll just flash a penlight in your eyes and tell me to wake you up every couple of hours tonight, and tomorrow you'll be good to go. Right?"

The look she gave him was definitely not one of her warmest.

"Besides," he said, "we made a deal. You agreed to follow orders if I let you tag along."

She let out a long, groaning sigh. "You know, Dante, sometimes you're a real pain in the ass."

"Give me that weapon," he said. "We really don't need any more complications today." He grabbed the MP5, re-wrapped it in the gray sweatshirt, and deposited it in the trunk.

"Like the police getting curious about a wrecked car with no windshields and bullet-sized Swiss cheese detailing."

Alex gave her a look. "Be good and let's get this over with, okay?"

* * *

Twenty minutes later, the doctor snapped off his penlight and turned to Alex. "She's got a concussion, all right. Pretty good one, too. Given what you said about it not being her first, I'm going to order a CAT scan to make sure there's nothing else going on that will come back to haunt us later on."

Raeanne cleared her throat. "Pardon me for speaking without being spoken to, Doctor, but I do have enough digits in my IQ to discuss my own healthcare options, thank you."

The doctor turned and gave her a pointed look. "I have no doubt of that, *Mrs. Dante*."

So he wasn't buying it. No surprise. Alex contained his frustrated sigh and kept quiet.

"A nurse will be in shortly to get you prepped for the scan," he said. "Major, I'd like a few words with you outside, if I may."

Alex watched him step past the curtained exam area and tried to figure out who he reminded him of. He was a tough-looking SOB, that much he knew. His cropped hair was a few steps past salt and pepper, but the arms that pressed taut against the sleeves of his green scrub shirt were hard and defined. His dark eyes, sharp and hawklike, were familiar as all hell, but he just couldn't place them. He glanced down at the nametag. *Mills, Daniel.* A Captain. With an alphabet soup of medical designations. Didn't ring a bell.

Raeanne sighed loudly and hopped off the gurney.

"Please, Raeanne, not now," Alex said. "They're already suspicious, and we don't need to be held up answering questions."

She sighed and tugged at the neck of the paper gown billowing around her like a giant paper towel. "Fine. I'll keep quiet. But just cut the Broadway routine with the *honey* and *sweetie* stuff. I'm NOT your wife."

"If you want them to treat you without keeping us here all day asking questions, you'd better pretend you are. Or have you decided you no longer want to help me find Ryan?"

Her voice dropped to a low, venomous register. "I should hate you for even suggesting that."

"Then remember where you are. You've made yourself a part of this mission, and like it or not, I am in command here. Now get a grip. You're a professional. Or you used to be."

The cold emanating from her eyes was almost palpable. "You're a bastard."

"Agreed. But as long as you're part of this team, it's your job to support me, bastard or not, to the best of your ability. If you find that you can no longer, in good conscience, do so, I will be happy to take you back to the safe house."

She glared at him another moment, then froze her expression into neutral. "Then you'd better go see what the doctor wants, *honey*. It's probably important."

Alex looked at her another moment, his emotions tangling around his heart. He knew how much she resented this, what she saw as his attempt to control the situation, but that was his job. She was in no condition to control anything, and he knew how much *that* frustrated her, too. He wanted to reach out and plant a small kiss on her forehead, or touch her hand, or something, but instead, he gave her a half smile and followed the doctor into the corridor.

* * *

Mills had stopped to wait for him a short distance down the hall. "Would you like a cup of coffee, Major?" He led them back toward the admissions area, where a coffee machine stood in the hall beside several other vending machines.

"Oh-oh, that's not a good sign," Alex said with a grin. "Is this going to take a long time?"

"Depends. Can you give straight answers?"

"Depends. Can you ask un-classified questions?"

"Who's the woman? She's obviously not your wife."

"She is my wife."

"Then you'd better have some coffee. This is gonna take a while."

Back in Mills' office, with the door closed and a paper cup of something black that almost smelled like coffee burning his hand, Alex did his best to appear casual. Inside, he was silently berating himself for not choosing the civilian hospital.

"So who is she?" Mills asked.

"I told you, she's my wife. I apologize for her attitude. She's not exactly thrilled with me at the moment. And the concussion's probably making her more agitated than normal. She's usually very sweet."

"I'll bet. What I want to know is who she is. I admit that these days, I spend most of my time bandaging up ankles of old officers who forget they're no longer twenty-five and picking foreign objects out of kids' noses, but I've seen my share of action, Major. I can still recognize combat wounded when I see them."

"Combat? In downtown Las Vegas? Fighting the One-Armed Bandit, I suppose?"

"Don't play games with me, Major. I know you jarheads like to think we Army grunts are stupid, but some of us can actually read. And even a new recruit can recognize a sidearm in a shoulder holster. A very dirty sidearm, at that. The nurse confiscated it. Security, you understand."

"She has a permit. It's all very legal."

"I'm sure she does. Someone in her line of work would have to. A woman who obviously spends a great deal of time keeping her body in peak physical condition, who comes in reeking of gunpowder and combat sweat, with a bullet wound in her calf and a lump the size of my fist on the back of her head, toting a sidearm that's been fired repeatedly — very repeatedly — and very recently… Or maybe she pours lattes for a living."

"Cities can be dangerous places. There are criminals all over, even in coffeehouses. Sometimes things get ugly."

"I imagine so. Especially for a lady who travels with a retired marine who's just as dirty and still has what appear to be two large caliber handgun clips in his front pockets. Spent clips, I'd guess."

Alex smiled. "They're packs of bubblegum. I'm trying to quit smoking."

Mills took another sip of his coffee and sat back farther in his chair. "Funny. There was all that in the news recently. About Senator Helmsan and her bodyguard and the kidnapped boy. And now I get a pretty little brunette through my ER that could be either a professional athlete, or—oh, I don't know, a professional bodyguard, maybe? To a senator, perhaps? Either way, I know a soldier when I see one, pretty little thing or no. Not a cop, or FBI, either—they love to flash their IDs around. That makes you folks either CIA or NSA, or maybe some bastard offspring of Homeland Security. But whoever you folks are, she sure as hell isn't your wife."

"You missed your calling, Doc. You should be writing paramilitary thrillers."

"Yeah, I guess you're right," Mills said. "Guess she's just your basic criminal, since she's not carrying any ID or a permit for the weapon. I suppose we'll just let the police deal with it."

Alex sighed. "Okay, Doc. You win."

Mills just looked at him, one brow inquisitively raised.

"Let's just say you're smarter than your average grunt."

"But you're still not going to tell me anything."

"I would," Alex said with a grin, "but then I'd have to kill you."

Mills put his coffee down with a sigh. "Walked right into that one."

"What about the gunshot wound to her calf?" Alex asked.

"Superficial."

"And the concussion?"

"She took a good hit to the head. I'm not expecting the CAT scan to show anything overly troublesome, but you never know. She shows signs of some minor subdural bleeding, and that needs to be dealt with. But I have a feeling no matter what

I say, a week of bed rest won't be on her agenda."

"Well, you finally got one answer right. Keeping her in one place is like herding cats."

Mills finally smiled. Almost. "I'll bet."

"So are you going to yank my chain and make me waste my time on the phone, getting someone higher up than both of us to order you to stand down, or are you going to patch her up and let us go and do our jobs?"

"Depends."

"On what?"

"On whether you think she'll stay in bed a few days, or if I'll have to admit her and strap her down to keep her from hurting herself."

"Once she hears that, you'll have to strap her down to keep her from hurting *you*."

"Then you'd better make your calls. Because until someone higher than both of us tell me to stand down, I'm admitting her until at least Wednesday."

Alex let out a long, tired sigh. Forget herding cats; Richardson was going to have kittens.

* * *

"You did *what*?"

Alex let out the breath he'd been holding and switched his cell phone to the other ear. One kitten down, another half dozen or so to go. "I allowed Raeanne to accompany me to the senator's office to retrieve the Ice Syndicate's documents."

"I told you specifically that I did not want her involved in this mission."

Alex stood outside the hospital's ER entrance, watching the traffic speed along East Sahara Ave. Around him, the concrete buildings trapped the smell of exhaust and the sounds of distant engines. "I'm aware of that, and I apologize. But you may as well wait to hear the rest before you commence lecturing."

Silence. A soft exhalation of breath. If he knew his boss, Richardson was probably sitting at his desk, raking his hand through his silver hair and staring at the floor, as if trying to find patience there.

"Go on," Richardson finally said.

"We retrieved the documents. That's the good news. The bad news is that we had company."

"Petrov?"

"No, just his henchmen. About a half dozen of them, and a lot of gunfire. Several kills, including one civilian—their kill, not ours—but nothing confirmed. Raeanne's at the Army hospital with a concussion. Not too serious, they don't think, but they're doing a CAT scan now. The doctor wants her admitted 'til Wednesday."

Another soft exhale.

"I need you to make some calls."

"Are they suspicious?"

"He thinks we're CIA. He's also got it figured out that she'll just hurt herself unless she's strapped down."

Richardson was silent another moment. Probably pushing out another kitten. "Give me his name."

"Mills, Daniel. Captain, US Army. I need you to call him off so I can take Raeanne back to the safe house this afternoon. But don't get him screwed. It was my fault. I should have cleaned her up before I brought her in. I wasn't thinking."

"I told you having her involved was going to cost everyone their objectivity."

"Yes, sir."

Another sigh from Richardson. "Until further notice, I want her at the safe house with McHugh. I'll send Briggs over there to assist." He sighed once more. "And you are to avoid all contact with her until this mission is completed."

"Yes, sir," Alex said again.

"Until then, I want you back on your original target. And

that means tracking Petrov, not playing house with Raeanne Springfield. Do I make myself clear?"

"Crystal." He pressed the off button and stared out at the heat shimmer off in the distance. Avoid all contact with her. Like that was going to be in any way possible.

* * *

Raeanne leaned back into the pillows and closed her eyes. If only she could sleep for just a few minutes. She thought she'd drifted off during the CAT scan, and now, laying here half-upright in the gurney back in the curtained room in the ER, she felt like she'd just run a marathon. She slid down a little lower, turned slightly onto her side, and gave in to the seduction of sleep...

"Get dressed, Mrs. Dante. Time to go home."

She opened her eyes and stared into the stern, but not unattractive, face of Dr. Mills.

He dropped her holster onto her lap and crossed his arms. "Seems whoever your husband is, he wasn't kidding when he said he had friends in high places."

Raeanne gazed at him a moment, trying to make sense of his words. "What do you mean?"

"It means you're being discharged. Not because you're in any shape to be, but because some suits in Washington seem to think they know how to treat a head injury better than I do."

"Oh, crap." Raeanne closed her eyes. Why couldn't they have waited a couple hours so she could have just gotten some sleep?

"So that's that. They want you out of here, so you're out of here. But that doesn't change your condition. You need to rest. I know you people like to think you're superheroes, but you're not going to help your little boy if you pass out in the middle of your op."

Raeanne's eyes jerked open. "What little boy?" she said,

trying to cover her reaction, but she knew she'd already tipped her hand.

Mills' expression went grim. "I know who you are. I know your injuries have something to do with retrieving your son."

Raeanne couldn't help the tears that sprung unannounced to her eyes.

He pulled the vinyl stool closer to the bed, sat down, and pulled a tissue from the box on the supply cart beside her. "Here."

She took it. What was wrong with her? Covert operations didn't remain covert for long if everyone knew what was going on.

The concussion. Confusion, lack of judgment... He was right. She felt foggy as hell.

"You feeling okay?" he asked.

"Yeah," she said, "I'm fine. Just tired."

"They won't let me keep you here, even though I think you need to be in bed a few days. There is a small area of bleeding in your brain. It's nothing to fret over, but you do need to let it heal up. And that won't happen running around exchanging fire with bad guys."

She looked up at him, surprised once again.

"I've been in this business a lot of years, Mrs. Dante; I've seen my share of combat injuries."

Unsure of what to say, Raeanne said nothing.

"Do me a favor," Mills said. "Don't be a hero. You're in no shape for combat. More trauma to the head could cause you some real problems."

"I'm fine. Really."

"You're not fine. That grogginess could cause you to do something that will get your son hurt. Or you, or someone on your team."

"I have no choice," she said, her words barely making a whisper from a throat tight with tears. She sat up and slipped the holster over her shoulder.

"Yes, you do. Let your team handle it."

"The people who have my son want *me* to handle it."

In a blur of dizzying motion and green surgical scrubs, Mills had her Glock out of the holster and pointed at her face. "You don't look ready to handle anything to me."

She raised her eyes from the small black hole to Mills' sharp, dark eyes. He sighted her over the muzzle of the gun a moment, then lowered the weapon and handed it back to her.

"I can handle it," Raeanne said through gritted teeth. "I just need some sleep. I'll be fine." Tears burned the backs of her eyes as she rammed the gun back into her holster, but she refused to cry in front of him. She refused.

"Don't be a fool," he said, reaching into his pocket and holding out her remaining three rounds. "Whoever they are, they'll kill you, and probably your son, too. Let your team handle it. Let Dante handle it. He's a good man."

She took the bullets from his hand. "And how would you know that?"

"I told you, I've been in this business a long time. I know a good soldier when I see one. Dante's a professional."

Raeanne let out a small sigh. "I know," she said, then turned to glare into Mills' strong, commanding face. "But so am I."

* * *

Raeanne awoke to a warm ray of early morning sunshine slanting through the window and onto her pillow. She immediately lay still and assessed the condition of her head. No headache, no unusual sensations at all. Just hunger, but that was nothing new. She sat up and swung her legs over the side of the bed. No dizziness.

And no reason to stay cooped up in this foolish safe house when her son was waiting for her to rescue him.

She got up and grabbed her clothes from the chair beside

the bed. Her own clothes. As far as safe houses went, this one was a heck of a lot more accommodating than the dump on Hyacinth. In addition to the garment delivery service, the folks here evidently preferred contemporary décor. But that was to be expected, she supposed. She tried to imagine a U.S. senator climbing up a fire escape in a silk suit and heels with her Prada handbag dangling from her elbow. Or worse, doing it in the Salvation Army cast-offs borrowed from the bedroom bureaus. The agency would be run out of town on a rail.

Here she had her own connected bathroom, and she took advantage of the hot water, soft towels, and salon shampoo. Combing her wet hair back from her face, she wished she had her gun, but they'd confiscated it, and she couldn't risk getting caught trying to retrieve it. She'd just have to stay out of trouble long enough to get home and get her spare.

The bedroom was on the first floor, and the double hung window unlocked from the inside. Admittedly, it was still Agency-issue, made of bulletproof Lexan instead of regular glass, but she trailed her fingers below the sill and around the frame and it didn't seem to be equipped with any of the James Bond extras. Evidently, the agency's better safe houses were more concerned with keeping the bad guys out than keeping the good guys in. Which, she decided wryly as she slid her legs over the sill and slipped out onto the damp grass, was their first mistake.

Chapter Eight

Alex reassembled the MP5 and set it on the scarred coffee table of the Hyacinth Street apartment. He'd cleaned each of the rifles and submachine guns in the firearm cabinet and was about to start in on the handguns, when the phone rang. The secure phone.

Richardson.

He grabbed the receiver and hoped all those kittens had come out okay.

"This is Dante."

"Dante, it's McHugh. We've got a problem."

Not Richardson. And there was only one kind of problem McHugh would be calling him with first thing in the morning.

Raeanne.

"Goddamn it, I told you to keep an eye on her!"

"I'm sorry," McHugh said, "I have no idea what happened. One minute she was singing in the shower, the next she was just gone."

He'd spent a half hour trying to impress upon both McHugh and Briggs just how slippery their long-lost little Raeanne could be. But apparently, "slippery" meant different things to different people. He shouldered the phone to his ear and popped the magazine back into the MP5. "I'll find her."

McHugh's voice hesitated. "We haven't alerted Richardson yet. I wanted to tell you first."

"Fine, I'll call him. He's already pissed at me anyway."

Alex brought the submachine gun to his eye and took aim at the atrocious painting on the far wall, wishing it were Petrov in his sights instead of that ugly matador with the swirling cape. "I'll be in touch."

He laid the gun down on the coffee table and dug through the pile of miscellaneous equipment on the floor beside him. He grabbed the two shoulder holsters and strapped them on. His Smith, freshly cleaned, gleamed up at him from the end table, and he shoved it into the holster tucked against his left side. To the holster on his right, he added one of the spare .45s, the one he'd just been about to strip down. It would have to wait until tonight, now. He had a cold, nauseating suspicion it would need it even more by day's end.

* * *

A half hour later, the cabbie pulled up in front of Raeanne's large contemporary in Green Valley. She couldn't remember being happier to be home.

"I'm so sorry; I'm just so ditzy sometimes." She cocked her head at an angle and gave him her cute-but-stupid grin. "Ran out of the house this morning without my purse. My wallet's just inside—be back in a sec, okay?"

Without waiting for an answer, she hopped out of the cab and trotted jauntily up her driveway, swishing hips and ponytail, and through the arbor gate to the back yard. She'd left her wallet in the trunk of her car when she'd gone to meet Alex, and her keys in the little magnetic box hidden in the wheel well, but she knew better than to go get them. The agency would have someone waiting for her. She retrieved the spare key from the under the plastic chameleon that stalked the rock garden, then climbed the two steps to the kitchen door.

It was already unlocked.

A frisson of fear licked its way up her spine. She never left the house unlocked. Her pulse rate shot up. Silently, she stood aside and pushed the door open with her foot.

The kitchen was quiet as death. On the wall just inside the door, the light on the alarm panel was out entirely. Not disarmed — disconnected.

She glanced in to the left. Nothing but empty counters. Nothing to the right.

She stepped silently into the kitchen, wishing like hell she had her weapon. She peered over the center island. Nothing. Without taking her eyes off the open space leading to the dining room, she moved as softly as possible across the tile floor to the counter and pulled her checkbook out of the drawer.

She moved quickly back outside and down the driveway to the curb, where the cabbie was just getting out of the car. The last thing she wanted was for him to start making a scene. If anyone were in the house, they probably knew she was there by now.

"You take checks?" she asked, flipping her checkbook open and scribbling an amount on the line. She tore it off and handed it to him. "Keep the change."

The cabbie just glared at her, very subtly shaking his head as he got back into the cab and shifted into drive. She watched him pull away, waiting until his brake lights disappeared around the corner before she turned and looked back at the house.

The darkened windows seemed to be watching her, like eyes. Watching her. Waiting for her.

What on earth had possessed her to leave the safe house without her weapon? She should have tried harder. The damned Ice Syndicate would have known she'd go home eventually. After their little demonstration at Diane's office, she was a complete fool to have thought she'd be coming home to an empty house.

Maybe Dr. Mills had been right, after all. Maybe she

wasn't functioning at peak performance.

She put the idea out of her mind. Petrov wanted her at his dinner table in DC on Wednesday night, and peak or not, she had to be there. If she wanted Ryan back alive.

Again, she slipped into the kitchen, soft as a breeze, searching to the left and right before stepping into the dining room. The place was completely silent. The thick Berber carpeting swallowed her footfalls as she made her way into the great room. Just as it would swallow the steps of her intruder.

She kept her eyes moving, searching for signs of trouble. The open floor plan provided few corners to hide behind. The room was sparsely furnished with only a few groupings of spare, mission-style furniture, broken only by austere potted cactus and foliage plants against the creamy white walls, leaving scant cover to hide behind. The gauzy curtains created no shadows or recesses. The room contained only pale, warm sunshine and the faint scent of lemon furniture polish.

Still, the alarms clamored in her head, warning of ambush.

Through another archway stretched the hall to the bedrooms. Darker. Less open.

God, she could do without any more hallways. The memory fired a rush of adrenaline through her blood. Her head spun a moment, then regained its equilibrium. Her spare gun was in her bedroom closet, assuming none of Petrov's thugs had found it and had it trained on her at this very moment.

Her room was at the far end of the hall. Of course.

She moved silently toward the first door on the left. Guest room. Keeping back out of the line of fire, she pushed the door open. Bed, dresser, bathroom door, all silent. She wasn't going to clear the room completely without a weapon, so closing it off until she got her spare gun was the best she could do. Pausing only enough to get a clear visual, she moved in and grabbed the knob, then quickly but soundlessly pulled the door shut. One down.

The guestroom across the hall was also silent, seemingly empty, and she closed it off as well. If there were any hidden threats of attack from behind those two doors, hopefully she'd hear them before she saw them.

She sealed off the bathroom, then proceeded across the hall. Ryan's room.

She hesitated in the doorway, unable to cross the threshold. Tears pressed against the backs of her eyes and her throat tightened with the sob she fought back. Everything was where he'd left it the other morning — was it just two days ago? His bed was still unmade, his Pokémon cards still on the floor where he'd been arranging them according to some logic of his own as she'd called for him to hurry up. Just before Alex had called and turned her whole world on its ear.

She pulled the door shut on the memory and walked softly to her own door at the end of the hall. Alex Dante. Why couldn't he have just stayed away?

She peered into the master suite, normally her refuge, feeling lost and adrift instead of relaxed and welcome. The silence gave it a strange, alien quality, as if it belonged to someone else. Without Ryan, the house was unnaturally still. Tomblike.

Seeing nothing, hearing nothing except the whisper of her own breath, she stepped across the doorway and headed immediately for her closet and the safe, familiarity of her spare gun.

"About time, Raeanne. I was getting tired of waiting."

* * *

She jumped with a satisfying little squeal and spun toward him with one hand to her chest and a look of startled panic in her wide eyes. Alex smiled. The look on her face was almost worth the sleep he'd lost worrying about her.

"Damn you, Dante, you nearly gave me a heart attack!"

He did his best to look nonchalant, reclined against the pillows in her wide, overstuffed reading chair in the little window alcove. The bright, morning sunlight bathed his face in decadent warmth, and with his feet up on the big, square ottoman, he sank back into the cushions like some desert prince, ready to be fed grapes. To his right, the MP5 stood propped against the thick, rolled arm of the chair, and two .45s nestled in their holsters at his sides. "Funny, I could say the same about you."

"What are you talking about?"

"Your concussion, your little disappearing act from the safe house. I got no sleep at all last night, worrying what kind of stunt you'd pull and whether you'd end up dying from some kind of brain hemorrhage. Or from another run-in with Petrov's lap dogs."

She huffed out a breath and rolled her eyes as she turned back to the closet and pulled a metal fire box off the top shelf. A second later, she had a 9mm in her hands and had popped out the magazine to check its contents. "It's really nice, this faith you have in me after I saved your ass like eleven times yesterday."

"You heard the good doctor. You need to rest."

"I need a lot of things, Alex."

"So do I." He felt the fire stir within him again. The fear for her safety. The empathy for her loss. The absolute inability to follow orders and have no contact with her. Truth was, he needed her as much as he'd been telling himself she needed him. Probably more. After seeing her again, after spending the last few days face to face with the memories he'd so successfully packed up and stored away, he could as easily avoid contact with her as cut off his right arm.

Especially after sitting there in her bedroom, looking at the picture on her bureau. The picture of him. Of them. The two of them sitting by the fountain outside the Paris Hotel. She'd always kept that picture on her bureau, right there in the same spot; he couldn't believe she still had it. It did something to him, said something her snarky remarks and bad attitude couldn't cover up.

She hadn't forgotten. She'd never stopped caring.

Maybe she'd never stopped loving him.

He glanced again at the bureau. The photo was gone.

No, it was still there, laying flat. She must have turned it face down with that eerie sleight-of-hand she possessed that would have made her a terrific pickpocket if she hadn't become a spook.

He smiled a triumphant smile to himself. He'd seen the photo. She could give him all the attitude she wanted, but she couldn't fool him now.

He knew she'd never been to friggin' Minnesota. Everything else in her file was probably complete fiction, as well. What he didn't know was why.

She shrugged into a shoulder holster, snapped in the gun, and placed the metal fire box back upon the shelf. She turned back to him and gazed into his eyes, her expression desolate, devoid of all feeling whatsoever. "I'm not going back to the safe house," she said. "You might as well know that now. I don't want to have to do something that will turn us into enemies, or get one of us hurt—probably me in all likelihood, given the way my head feels right now. But I will. I'm giving you fair warning. I *will* use force against you if you try to take me back to the safe house."

Alex had to swallow the emotion thickening in his throat. "I'm not here to take you back."

"Then why are you here?" She gestured toward the MP5 with her eyes. "So I can say hello to your little friend?"

He grinned at her. Why *was* he there? Because he loved her? Because he'd existed in a lonely, desolate vacuum for the last seven years without her, and he wasn't going back to that, regardless of what Richardson would do to him for disobeying orders?

"Because you need me," he said. "I'm here to help you get Ryan back, like I've promised you a dozen times."

* * *

Raeanne glared at him, trying to read the look in his eyes. He *looked* sincere. And that was what bothered her. The last thing she needed was Alex Dante tagging along after her, plying her with chicken soup and bed rest like a mother hen and getting himself noticed by Petrov, now that she was so close to getting Ryan back. Petrov's instructions had been perfectly clear. One whiff of agency backup, and Ryan would die. And Petrov never made idle threats. She'd seen more than enough examples of that during December Ice.

"Does anyone know you're here?" she asked. "Anyone from the agency?"

"No. This isn't agency business."

"Then whose business is it?"

"Mine."

She turned back to the closet and hauled out a small carry-on suitcase, then strode past him to the bureau. Mechanically, she began pulling clothes out of the drawers. She had to get rid of him. "So you're going maverick. You're going to risk getting yourself fired, or thrown in jail, most likely... Which one of us is suffering from the head injury, again?"

"Me, apparently. If I were sane, I'd just take you in, let Richardson lock you up for your own protection, and proceed with the operation as planned."

"Then why don't you?"

"Hell if I know."

She let her eyes linger a moment on his, trying to fight the magnetic pull of them, pulling her back into the past, back into the time when looking into those eyes was as natural as breathing and reading what was behind them like knowing her own soul. Her heart clenched with the wanting of things to be different. To be the way they used to be.

But they weren't. He'd never wanted the things she'd wanted, and what they did have, he'd tossed away without a backward glance. Without even saying goodbye.

With the weight of that knowledge dragging at her like an undertow, she turned back to the closet.

"Besides," he said, his voice soft and low with emotion. "It's my fault you're in this situation in the first place. We should have known about Ryan. We should never have allowed this to happen."

"It's not your fault CODA can't keep their records straight."

"I'm the commanding officer. Whatever mistakes were made are ultimately my responsibility."

Responsibility. She paused with her hand on a hanger and felt her heart clench tighter. Damn him. Damn him and his overdeveloped sense of *responsibility*. Nothing was ever a matter of personal desire with him; everything was always a matter of some damned point of honor.

Nothing had changed. Nothing would ever change. Alex Dante wasn't a man, he was a CODA operative. Any doubts she might have had about that tumbled away like dry leaves before the storm.

She began pulling garments off the hangers and tossing them onto the bed. "Go away, Alex. I don't want your help."

He laughed then, and she turned to glare at him.

"You don't get it, do you?" he said.

"Get what?"

"You think you have a choice? The only choice you have is whether I allow *you* to help *me*, or whether I let Richardson toss your butt in jail until I'm finished."

"I thought you weren't following Richardson's orders anymore."

"I'm improvising. The mission is still a go, and I'm still the CO. I've just decided to quit swimming upstream, and I'm allowing you to tag along. Unless you tick me off sufficiently to make me take back everything I've just said and deliver you to Richardson myself. Bound and gagged, if necessary."

"Why do you have to turn everything into an ultimatum?" Her hands had begun to shake, and she couldn't still them. "Why don't you pack up your little arsenal and get back to work before Richardson finds out you've lost your mind."

"Okay. If you go back to the safe house with McHugh and Briggs."

She took a deep breath, let it out, and then pulled her red cocktail dress off the hanger. Damn Petrov and his persistent fetish for women in red. "I told you, I can't do that."

"Then your only other choice is to work *with* me, instead of against me."

She turned to him, but he wasn't looking at her. He was looking at the carry-on bag and at the pile of clothes on her bed as if he'd just that moment noticed what she was doing. Then his eyes traveled to the skimpy red dress in her hand.

"Interesting choice of wardrobe. The last time I saw you in a red dress, you were dancing with Petrov at your bogus engagement party."

She shoved the dress into the suitcase and forced it down. "Really? I don't remember."

"Where are you going Raeanne?"

She took a deep breath. She had to regain control of this situation. "Why, with you of course. Isn't that what you've been suggesting for the last ten minutes?"

* * *

She was full of baloney.

He forced his face to retain its bland expression of calm, forced his hands to remain relaxed on the rolled arms of the overstuffed chair. He kept his breathing slow and regular as she zipped her suitcase shut and pulled out the handle.

"You ready to go, Commander, or are you going to fall asleep in that chair?"

He stood, grabbed the MP5, and invited her to proceed him through the door with a gallant sweep of his arm. He knew better than to let her out of his sight for a minute, especially when she was wearing her sidearm.

"So where are we off to?" she asked as she keyed in the alarm code. Nothing happened. She gave him a look from beneath a furrowed brow. "That's right, you killed my alarm. I hope you intend to fix it."

"I'll send someone to reconnect it once we get back to the safe house on Hyacinth."

She stopped and gave him a dark look. "I told you I wasn't going back to any safe house."

"Wrong," he said, taking her elbow and leading her across the gravel yard to the other side of the house, where the GTO was waiting patiently between the house and the decorative concrete wall at the property line. "You said you wouldn't go back to the safe house on West Passage Drive with McHugh and Briggs. I happen to be using the Hyacinth Street house as my base, so that means you are too. If you're still interested in being my partner."

He let go of her elbow to unlock her car door and heard her snort of derision.

"Your partner. Right."

"My partner. Right. As long as you keep your mouth shut and your head down and do what I tell you, like you did for every other CO when you were with the agency." He opened her door and she slid inside, then leaned across the seat to unlock the driver's side door for him.

That small action stopped him with his hand on the door handle, the motion of closing her door forgotten. It slapped him in the face like a wave of cold water. No one other than Raeanne had ever done that for him, before or since, and with that single, small gesture, the last seven years fell away. Once again, he was back in those dark, aimless days after her disappearance, forced to face every waking moment knowing she was gone.

She wasn't getting away again.

He opened the door, tossed the MP5 in the back, and slid into the car.

"Tell me again why you're doing this?" she asked.

"What do you mean?" He started the engine and backed the GTO out of the side yard, around the back of the house, and through the narrow strip of gravel around the garage with inches to spare to the driveway.

"Why are you suddenly risking your entire career to help me. The real reason."

He sighed and turned the car onto the street. What was he supposed to say? That he loved her and couldn't deny her something like this? Or that he had a vague, uncomfortable feeling in his gut about CODA's involvement in the whole thing, why her files had been altered, why any information they'd had about the boy had disappeared? She'd never believe him. If Abe had told him she'd run off with someone else, *get over it*, God only knows what he'd said to her.

No wonder she'd been so hostile toward him. She probably thought he was…just like he'd thought she was.

God damn it, if CODA had orchestrated the whole separation between them…

Would Abe really have done that? Why?

She rolled down her window. "Aren't you going to answer my question?"

"I'm sorry?"

"Why you're helping me?" Her eyes held a mixture of suspicion and hope, disillusionment and the desperate desire to believe.

"I made a promise to get your son back, and I intend to keep it." Regardless of what he learned in the process.

Chapter Nine

So beautiful…

Alex stole another glance at Raeanne's sleeping face, barely visible beneath the arm she'd slung over her eyes as she sprawled out on the hideous plaid couch. Beautiful, yes, but deadly too. Sitting there watching the gentle rise and fall of her breasts as she slept, he felt a sudden, uncomfortable kinship with the male black widow.

Damn woman was going to be the death of him. He really should have let Richardson lock her up. For her own good and everyone else's. She was far too involved to have anything remotely resembling objectivity. Hell, if she did, there would be something wrong with her. But be that as it may, the field was no place for an enraged mamma bear out to protect her young. Patience and strategy and the ability to delay gratification were the last things she'd possess once she got her first whiff of Petrov.

And then there was the problem of what she was doing to him right now. He suppressed the urge to trace his finger along her lips, not wanting to wake her, not wanting to have to admit how badly he wanted to kiss her. Patience and strategy and the ability to delay gratification weren't something he had in abundance right now, either. Not with her laying there a foot away.

He flipped off the lamp and headed down the hall to the safe house's equally hideous kitchen, stared absently into the refrigerator for a moment until he realized he wasn't hungry, then drifted back down the hall to the living room. The poorly sprung wing chair squeaked under his weight as he sat and tried to concentrate on the television. He wished he had a beer. Or a can of soda. Anything except more coffee. He wasn't going to be able to sleep tonight as it was, never mind adding a gallon of caffeine to the mix.

He needed something to do. He'd checked in with Richardson and had assured him that Raeanne was resting quietly at the safe house. He'd just conveniently failed to mention which one. He'd checked in with McHugh. Three times. Yes, the senator was fine. Yes, she was burning the midnight oil to get her new proposals into the right hands before they left for Washington in the morning. No, Richardson hadn't asked about Raeanne's whereabouts.

He'd cleaned the bathroom. He'd cleaned and oiled every firearm in the place — again — had loaded every magazine and had reorganized the supply closet twice. Damned if he wasn't ready to start knitting one of those grandma afghans.

The television was turned to an old Audrey Hepburn movie, and for a second, the doe-eyed smile reminded him of Raeanne. He turned to look at her again, to see her tousled dark hair falling around her face in a disorganized tumble, longer now, a few inches past her shoulders. His fingers ached to brush a stray lock of hair from her cheek. He could imagine how that hair would feel — no, he remembered how it felt. Silken soft. Soft, like her skin. Soft like her lips.

He turned back to the TV, but the yearning pain in his chest didn't disappear.

Abruptly, he stood and headed back to the kitchen. He had to get out of there. Otherwise, he would wake her. He would wake her, and then he would kiss her, and then everything would go to hell.

* * *

Raeanne awoke to the dim flicker of TV and something scratchy and mildewy-smelling against her face. For a moment, she wasn't sure where she was, but then it came back. The safe house.

The concussion.

Petrov.

Then, like a fist to the gut: Ryan.

And finally, softer, but not any more comfortable: Alex.

She sat up and felt the blood rush out of her head, leaving her momentarily dizzy. She could hear him moving around in the kitchen. What was she going to do about Alex Dante?

Nothing. He was a means to an end. He'd promised to help her get Ryan back, and his robotic sense of honor wouldn't let him quit until he did just that.

But it was his method that confused her, why he was deliberately disobeying Richardson's direct orders to keep his promise. Alex Dante refusing to follow a direct order was like the sun refusing to ri—

"You're awake."

She leapt off the couch, her hand going immediately for the holster that wasn't there. What she found instead was Alex's hand, reaching out to steady her.

It was warm, and his fingers were strong and firm under hers.

She dropped them like she expected them to bite. "Jeez, Alex, will you quit sneaking up on me? I'm beginning to think you're trying to drown me in my own adrenaline."

"Sorry," he said, but she could hear the grin in his voice that said he wasn't sorry at all. "Just making sure you were okay."

"I'm fine." She let out the breath that had caught in her throat at the feeling of his hand under hers. He wasn't supposed to feel that warm.

He was standing too close.

"Is there anything to eat in this godforsaken pit?" she

asked.

"There's some Chinese left. I even saved you the last fortune cookie." He just stood there, not stepping back out of her personal space.

For some reason, her heart started to race. "Thanks, but no thanks. I need real food. Meat. Red meat. Lots of it."

"Well, oh carnivorous princess, I might be able to cook us up a little something." Standing backlit by the lamp on the end table, tall and broad and dark, he looked like some kind of Hollywood action hero. All he needed was the assault rifle and crisscrossed bandoliers.

She cleared her throat.

He smiled, the skin around his vivid green eyes crinkling with amusement. "Come on."

Something compelled her to follow. "Since when do you cook anything besides MREs and ramen noodles?"

In the kitchen, he began opening cupboards and looking through them as if he really did know what he was looking at. "I'll have you know that I have more handy homemaker skills than I know what to do with."

"I'll bet."

He paused with his hand on a cupboard door. "Really. I cook, I clean, I even make julienne fries."

She watched him, and her mind finally came fully awake. "You said we had Chinese in the fridge?"

He turned back to her. "Yeah. Change your mind?"

"No. I just…when did we go for takeout?"

He closed the cabinet and gave her a searching look. "Last night. You don't remember?"

She searched her memory but found nothing there.

"Honest," he said. "You had the Peking duck, just like you always—" He stopped for a moment and looked at her. "Like you always do."

She swallowed. "And you had the General Tso's. Extra spicy, with dumplings." She wasn't sure if the memory was from last night, or one of the many she'd packed away, thinking she'd never open and hold again up to the light. She remembered coming back to the safe house after collecting her suitcase and weapon, and she vaguely remembered a shower, but in between... "And you saved me your fortune cookie...like you always did."

He gave her a soft smile, but his eyes looked worried. And a little sad. "I had the Szechuan Shrimp."

She sighed heavily, rubbing her eyes as if she could somehow scrape the memories out from behind them. "I don't need this right now."

Alex grinned and slapped her back cheerfully. "Ah, don't worry about it. Let's just go out for breakfast. Mills said if you took it easy, you'd be good as new in a couple of days." He pulled his keys out of his pocket and flipped off the lamp.

"I don't have a couple of days. If I don't have my wits about me when I meet Petrov, Ryan's dead."

The lamp came back on. "What do you mean, 'when you meet Petrov?'"

* * *

Raeanne bumped the door closed behind her with her hip. Her hands were full of grocery bags. After breakfast, Alex had gone crazy and had purchased enough food to feed a baseball team. But he'd been uncomfortably silent while doing it.

Probably because he hadn't believed her half-assed excuse about meeting with Petrov being a slip of the tongue.

"So Mr. Grand Gourmet," she said more playfully than she thought she'd be able to carry off, "can you really cook, or am I gonna have to order pizza later?"

Alex raised one eyebrow. "I'm going to cook you dinner later. You're going to sit at the table and enjoy it. A good time will be had by all. In the meantime, you will tell me all about this meeting with Petrov that you conveniently forgot to mention."

Crap. She busied herself unloading the groceries and tried to sound unconcerned. "It's no big deal. Petrov called, I answered. He wants me to join him—and Ryan—at the Blue Lagoon in DC Wednesday night. If I come alone, then Ryan goes free. Or so he said. It's probably a setup, but I don't have much choice. If I choose not to show up, or if I come with backup, Ryan will die. Simple as that."

"And you chose not to tell me this…why?"

"Because I didn't trust you."

He stopped with one hand halfway to the last grocery bag. "You didn't trust me? After all the years we've known each other…after everything I've done to help you over the last few days, you didn't trust me?" He gave an ironic bark of laughter, heavy with injured emotion. "Gee, thanks, Rae."

Her heart slid sideways, as if trying to hide in shame. "I'm sorry," she said.

He looked at her with that level expression that always used to make her wonder at his self-control.

"I was desperate; I thought you'd try to stop me again. If you remember, the last time we were here, you wouldn't even let me have any pajamas."

"That was to keep you from doing something stupid."

"Like flying to DC and meeting with Petrov without you?"

He didn't answer.

She stepped up to him and put a hand on his arm. "Look, Alex, I'm sorry. I'm telling you about it now, okay?"

He flashed her a look of glacial green ice. "Don't ever lie to me again."

"I didn't *lie*, I just didn't tell you—"

His mouth came down upon hers and bit off her words. She froze for an instant, then some other part of herself took over. Memory, habit, conditioning, she didn't know what, but passion flared within her and her mouth responded. She returned the kiss, pressing him back against the counter, her lips pressing harder into his, her mouth tasting, seeking, searching for something she knew was still there.

A soft moan escaped him. The sound drove directly into her soul and forced her blood to rush faster through her veins. His teeth nipped lightly at her lip, and she let herself go limp and liquid against his mouth.

His chest felt hard and solid pressed against her. And warm. She savored the mass and outline of firm chest and abdominal muscles, ran her hands over shoulders and arms, and a groan of pleasure escaped her, drawn forth by the strength and heat and force of him, sweet and dark and decadent like Swiss chocolate. She wanted him. She would have him.

His lips broke contact with hers, but before she could find them again, he was kissing the length of her neck. She shivered in ticklish delight. Reaching for him, she meant to bring his face up to hers, but he gently pushed her back against the counter. A grocery bag tipped over behind her, spilling its contents on the counter to clatter onto the floor. He tugged her blouse free of her jeans, ran a hand up the flat of her stomach until it came to rest over one of her breasts. She leaned her head back and enjoyed the sensation of his touch, his strength as it flowed into her, the familiar safety of being a part of him.

Then reality shook her awake. She was no longer a part of him, hadn't been for years. Probably never had been.

He looked down at her, tentative, questioning. "What?"

What... She asked herself the same thing, then gave up. What did it matter? He was with her now, the man she loved — the man she had always loved. She could no more turn away from him now than refuse to breathe.

Besides, by Wednesday night, she'd be dead.

"Nothing," she said. She grabbed his hand, kissed his palm, her lips hovering over the long scar that still crossed it. She remembered that scar and its mate across his thigh, souvenirs from December Ice. Time may have continued on without them, but some things would remain forever. No amount of time could completely erase who they were, what they'd seen together, what they'd done and been. He was still Alex. And he would always be hers.

She grabbed him around the neck and pulled him to her, then kissed him with everything she had.

* * *

Alex didn't resist. Ardent wasn't the word, nor passionate, although the drag of her mouth along his bottom lip was both of those. But there was something else there as well, an edge of something dangerous, something desperate, in the way she dug her fingers into the hair at his nape and bore down upon him, as if she were fighting for her life.

And he couldn't deny the same sharp, dire need for her as well. The need to join with her, as if in doing so, the rift between them of space and time could somehow be sealed and she could once again be a part of him. He opened her blouse without breaking the kiss. His breath tripped hastily from his mouth as his hand glided over her skin from her navel to one lace-covered breast and circled the nipple with his index finger. It responded to his touch, growing taut with pleasure, with the unthinking response to the truth between them, the essence that had bound them together years ago and which plainly still existed. He'd always known it. The tie between them wasn't something so easily severed by mere time or distance. Or even by Abe King.

And if she didn't realize that yet, he'd make sure she did before the night was out.

His lips brushed the velvety skin of her cheek, drawing from her an involuntary moan. *Yes. Don't think, just feel. Just remember.*

She opened her eyes then, and he could have sworn she

had just read his mind. *I do remember,* her eyes seemed to say, and her hands echoed the thought. She pushed the shirt up over his chest, slowly, never taking her eyes from his. His blood thrummed hot through his veins, his skin rippling with sensation, and every brush of her fingers felt like fire as she peeled the shirt over his head. He smiled, but she didn't smile back. Instead, she kissed him. She kissed him and ran her palms up and down his body, coming to a stop at the hard ridge of his cock behind his jeans and lingering there. He exhaled softly and pressed into her palm, felt her smile against his lips.

He smiled back against hers.

His hands slipped to her legs again, fumbled with the zipper, and tugged the jeans down. His fingers stroked across her thighs, across the flat slope of her belly, then trailed lower, and she gasped. A moment later he slid her panties downward and found her wet and ready. She slipped the button of his jeans, never taking her lips from his, simply ripping open the zipper and freeing his cock from the clothing that had become a wall between him and the warmth of her skin.

He pressed against her inner thigh, eager, needy, and she rocked backward to take him. He stepped on something, kicked a package of frozen something out of the way. She laughed and mumbled something about dinner, but wrapped her leg around his hips more tightly. She was hot when he entered her, like fire, like life itself, as if she clung to him just to stay alive.

They moved together against the counter, slowly at first, and it felt like coming home.

He felt her lose herself in her bliss, just as he was, in the heat and the touch and the ripples of pleasure singing through her body as she started to move in time with him. Pleasure he was stirring in her.

Remember, Rae. Please say you remember...

Their sighs intermingled into a hum of pure sensation. He

moved faster against her, and she matched him, pushing him forward with her hands on his ass. He could feel her responding, moving with him to each higher peak, each new level of sensation, and at each he pushed her further. There was so much he wanted to do, so much he wanted to give her, but this wasn't about moonlight and romance.

This was about possession, and submission, and the call of life and death.

He felt her climax around him and he followed her then, heard himself utter her name. She answered with kisses, soft, breathy kisses against his neck. He felt her tug him tighter against her, the way she always did.

She mumbled something hot and breathless beneath his ear.

"What, love?" he said.

"I said, 'I remember this so well.'"

Chapter Ten

Raeanne let herself relax against Alex's chest, knowing he'd hold her up. As she would him. It felt so good, the two of them holding each other. It had always felt good when he'd held her.

What on earth had seemed so important that it was worth giving up this?

"I love you," he whispered, his breath warm against the skin of her face, his words white fire in her heart. "I never once stopped. No matter what you thought—I want you to know that."

She pulled him closer. She could feel his heart beating fast in his chest, hear the rasp of his breath close to her ear. He smelled like Dial soap and gun oil, and she drew in another long gulp of air, as if trying to capture his very spirit with his scent. "I never forgot you, Alex. Never once. I tried to, but I couldn't."

His breath escaped in a gentle sigh. "Then…why? What happened to you, Rae?"

She turned her face up to him, up to those vibrant green eyes that had never looked so intense. "Please, Alex. Not now. I don't want to think about the past." She started to turn her head away, but he delicately caught her chin in one hand, turned her face back to him, and kissed her. Very softly, just a touch of his lips to hers.

Her mind tried to make her feel angry again, angry at him

for leaving, at what had happened. But she refused to feel the anger. The past was over. There were more important things than who did what to whom seven years ago. Like a little boy growing up without a father. Like a man, a good man, going the rest of his life without the love of his child.

Whatever blame he held seven years ago didn't justify that kind of penalty, and Ryan was the one who was losing the most.

Ryan. How could she have let herself forget for one moment that he was lost to her, maybe suffering, maybe already dead?

Her impulse was to push herself away from Alex and the pleasure they'd just shared, but instead, she felt herself cling to him more tightly. She needed this. She needed him.

When they got Ryan back, she'd tell Alex the truth. Hell, he'd probably figure it out on his own, anyway, once he saw those little green eyes, vivid as a hot tropical jungle in their frame of dark lashes, so much like his own.

You lose, Abe. She pulled Alex tighter and kissed him once more. *Whatever little game you were playing, you lose.*

* * *

The cell phone rang, jarring Alex from a glorious dream of sleeping tangled in Raeanne's long, naked legs. He glanced down at the glowing hands of his watch. 3:45 a.m.

Only the legs were no dream. Bare and pale in the darkness, they were smooth and warm against his own, as was the rest of the sleeping woman spooned up against his belly. His body jolted awake, hot and needy.

The phone rang again.

He snatched it from the bedside table before it could wake Raeanne and gently extricated himself from the musky warmth of their bed. He hoped to hell it wasn't Richardson calling to tell him the gig was up.

"Dante."

There was momentary silence, then a voice. "Dante? Not Major Alexander Dante of the United States Marines? Well, well. This *is* a surprise. I knew my lovely Raeanne was back under the wing of the American government, but I never in my wildest dreams thought she'd lead me straight to you."

The last of the sleep tore away in a rush of ice. Petrov. Alex took the phone from his ear and stared at it a moment, then cursed his own stupidity. It wasn't his phone—it was the dead man's.

"So it was you who came to her rescue," Petrov said. "I should have known. You always were her little guardian angel, no?"

"What do you want?" He glanced at Raeanne to make sure she was still asleep, then moved to the spare bedroom and sat down at the table. He jiggled the mouse plugged into the laptop and the screen came to life.

"You've been a difficult man to find, Major Dante. I've spent considerable resources over the years trying to locate you after you nearly ruined my operation. Imagine my glee to hear you simply answer the phone. Truly, the fates must be smiling upon me."

"Enough chatter, Petrov. What do you want?" One soft click brought up the CODA software. Alex entered the cell phone number, selected Trace, and sent the request to the main office.

A few seconds later, a popup message appeared on the screen. *Initializing trace… One moment please.*

"I seek resolution, Mr. Guardian Angel. And answers, now that you've stirred my curiosity. Who are you? Why are you helping my little Raeanne?"

Initialized. Trace in Progress. Do not disconnect. The blue progress bar began to inch to the right… *2% Complete. 8%… 14%…*

"No answers until you answer me first. Where's the boy?"

Alex stared at the screen, silently urging the network to work faster. *31% Complete...*

"Tsk, tsk, Major Dante. So cold. But I suppose a killer must be cold in order to do his job, no? And you did your job well yesterday. You and my little Raeanne have caused me quite a loss in personnel."

"If you didn't want them to die, you shouldn't have sent them. Now where's the boy?"

49% Complete...

"What a shame. So much anger in one so young. So much like my little Raeanne. And to think it isn't even your son that's missing."

"You touch one hair on that kid's head and I'll ram my gun down your throat. I don't like cowards who hide behind children."

A soft chuckle. "Such posturing, Mr. Guardian. The boy is quite safe. Do you think I would harm my own flesh and blood?"

Alex felt the bottom of his stomach drop.

"I see she never told you."

"Told me what?"

"About the boy. About my son."

"You're lying. Raeanne would never have touched a piece of filth like you."

Another chuckle. "Ah, so that's it. I thought so. You still carry a torch for her, after all these years. A pity you weren't able to hold on to her. But you know what they say. What woman would choose beer once she tasted champagne?"

Alex felt the blood thrumming at his temples. With anger. With fear. With the desire to see Petrov's limbs torn from his body. But he forced himself to remain calm. His anger would do nothing but compromise his position. As Petrov was well aware. "Nice try. But I know for a fact Raeanne never slept with you."

"Ah, facts. Such troublesome little things. And just how

did you come by these facts, Mr. Guardian?"

"Enough, Petrov. What do you want?"

"Perhaps, Mr. Guardian Angel, your little Raeanne chose to tell you only the facts she wanted you to know. Perhaps she thought her other lovers were none of your business."

Alex bit down the wrath that threatened to spew forth like blood. "You were never her lover, you were a target. She did what she did to get inside your organization and destroy it."

More laughter. "Oh, dear. I do extend you my deepest condolences. How terribly humiliating to learn you've been taken for a fool."

Alex clenched his teeth harder.

"Well, Mr. Guardian Angel, I do regret being the bearer of such ill news, but your precious Raeanne did indeed lie to you. The fact is the boy is my son. Whether she was genuine in her desire for me or not, she was quite…enthusiastic in trying to convince me she was. She's quite a good little spy. I've had many women in my life, Mr. Dante, but none quite as willing to throw herself into her work."

His head was spinning with confusion. Disbelief. Despair. It all made sense, but it made no sense at all. He'd done the math, but hadn't wanted to believe that the boy had been conceived during December Ice. But apparently, the math didn't lie.

"But I'm being insensitive. Perhaps I should give you some time to mourn the loss of your illusions before we discuss business."

"Enough games. I want the boy."

"As do I, Mr. Guardian."

"Come on, Petrov, you've got no use for a child."

"Well, to be perfectly honest, while it's been very diverting to finally meet the fruit of my loins, my lifestyle is not precisely what one would call 'conducive to child rearing'. As long as you cooperate, I have every intention of returning the boy to his mother. And as it just so happens, she has something I've wanted for a long time, as well."

"And what's that?"

"You, Mr. Guardian."

"I thought you wanted Raeanne."

"Ah, yes, how fickle of me. Until I heard your voice, I admit to suffering from a certain amount of frustrated desire. Women are notorious for making men suffer in such a manner, are they not?"

"Get to the point."

"Raeanne's betrayal hurt me, Mr. Guardian, I won't lie to you about that. But she was not responsible for the collapse of the entire Syndicate. That, my friend, was your doing. And before anything else, I am a businessman. Finally being able to repay the man who nearly ended my career—let alone my life—is far more important to me than getting the last word in a lover's quarrel. I want you, Mr. Guardian. I'll return the boy to his mother in exchange for you."

"Come on, Petrov. You know we don't negotiate with terrorists."

"Tsk, tsk. Let's not call names, Mr. Guardian, your mother should have taught you better manners. Still, it's unfortunate that your government prefers to do things the hard way. But I suppose they'll have plenty of trite sympathy for the boy's mother when they explain how they let her little boy die."

The trace... Alex glanced down at the laptop. The pop-up box was gone and in its place was a message reading, *Trace complete. Click Download Now.*

"I'm all yours. Where do you want me?" He clicked Download and waited for the number to appear.

And waited.

"I'll contact you tomorrow evening. Be prepared to come alone. We'll enjoy a nice dinner and reminisce about old times."

Alex jiggled the mouse. Nothing. He clicked the mouse buttons, jiggled it again, then pressed Enter. Still nothing. The damn laptop was frozen.

"Son of a bitch..." He jiggled the mouse again, but the arrow cursor on the screen remained still.

"Come now, Mr. Guardian. Didn't we just discuss the name calling?"

He hit Alt-Control-Delete to reboot and had to grit his teeth to prevent himself from flinging the computer across the room. The information from the trace was lost.

"Yeah, we'll see what else I call you tomorrow night." He flipped the phone shut and stood in the spare room, gritting his teeth with anger and frustration. It was only four a.m., but there was always someone on the agency comm desk. He went into the living room, picked up the secure line, and dialed the main office. Maybe the IT people could restore the failed download.

"Good Morning, West End Supply. How may I direct your call?"

"Dante for IT."

"One moment, please."

Alex waited while the laptop finally rebooted, then let out a sigh of resignation. As he'd expected, there was nothing on the screen to indicate that any downloads or programs had recently run. He checked the recent documents folder, but it too was empty, as he knew it would be. He didn't know why he'd bothered checking. The CODA field software automatically deleted its last activities on shutdown, but it was one of those things he had to check anyway, like making sure that the car door was really locked.

"Major Dante, this is Specialist Liz Dean. Can I help you?"

"I just ran a trace. Did it go through?"

"Let me check the server. Hold on."

Alex ground his teeth. His eyes drifted toward the door, toward the room where Raeanne slept. Raeanne...

He turned himself abruptly away.

"Yes, sir, I've got your trace."

"Do you have the location of the caller?"

"Yes, sir, I do. Do you require a download?"

"No, just tell me where he is."

"The number belongs to a cell phone. 555-316-4789. That number is consistent with one of several used by your objective."

"I know who it belongs to, what I want to know is where the hell he is."

"One moment."

Alex heard the clack of her keyboard over the phone.

"The call originated from the industrial district, about two blocks west of I-15... Number 2970 West Mountain Road."

"Good. Excellent." Alex snatched a pen and a pad of sticky notes from the table and scribbled the address.

"Do you require anything further or shall I transfer you back to —"

"No, that's it, thanks. You're a lifesaver." Alex snapped the phone shut, tossed it onto the table, and ran a hand over his tired, dry eyes. There wasn't much time. He had to get to the location of the call before Petrov moved out, if he wasn't on the move already.

He dressed silently, then strapped on his holsters and checked his weapons. Raeanne lay breathing heavily with the languor of deep sleep, and he was glad of it. Talking to her right now was the absolute last thing he wanted to do.

Petrov's *son*?

No wonder she'd left without a trace. No wonder Abe had bitterly refused to allow him a minute's mourning over her abrupt retirement and relocation. He'd known it all along. She'd gotten pregnant during the op and had retired to protect her son and raise him like a normal child. And she hadn't wanted Alex to know because...she'd lied to him? And to everyone at CODA about her involvement with Petrov? Why? She'd told them all in her debrief that her cover had never required her to actually sleep with him, but why would she lie about that? That kind of thing sometimes happened in the field—it wasn't like anyone would believe she'd actually have chosen to sleep with that snake.

The boy. It was to protect the boy. The entire thing was classified so that she could take advantage of CODA's help in relocating and not have to worry about anyone tracking her down.

Then why would she have come back?

Whatever her logic, she apparently never felt that he had a "need to know."

Abe King had lied to him when he told him he had no idea why Rae had chosen to retire. Abe had helped her disappear, and wherever she went, it wasn't Minnesota. That's why Abe had been so adamant that he needed to get over her and move on, and why he'd given him the op in Afghanistan, where he was so entrenched in the enemy that he couldn't spare a thought for anything else.

Damn them both.

Back in the other room, on the table by the computer, he found the sticky pad he'd used to jot down the location of the trace. The warehouse district. It was a good half hour away. Odds were they'd be on the move by the time he got there.

He jotted her a quick note telling her to stay put, which he fully expected her to ignore, but since she had no details of his whereabouts, there wasn't much she could do about it in any case. And if she were gone when he got back, well, maybe it would be better that way anyhow. He wasn't sure seeing her face-to-face was in either of their best interests at the moment, damn her hide. Damn her beautiful, lying hide.

He threw a handful of extra magazines into his duffel bag and headed for the door. If she was still there when he got back, she was going to tell him all about her dirty little secrets—and all about why she left him, and all about Petrov's son.

Chapter Eleven

At the faint click of the front door closing, Raeanne opened her eyes. The bastard. This was how he played fair? She brushed away the tears that had seeped past her self control as she lay there listening to him on the phone, trying to make out his words as he spoke to Petrov, then someone at the agency, planning to continue on without her. Just as she'd feared he would, even though her better self had told her not to be so suspicious and to trust him.

Trust him. Ha.

He'd said he loved her. Hadn't any of that even mattered?

She guessed he was right—she had no business trying to play CODA operative anymore. The Raeanne of seven years ago wouldn't have been reduced to tears. And she wouldn't have been fooled so easily by a man's pretty words. When had she gone so soft and stupid?

Maybe he was right. Maybe it was better that she just sit back and let him do his job.

Like hell.

She pushed back the covers and threw on her clothes, then raced into the other bedroom where the laptop was closed on the table. She laid her hand along the top of it. Still warm.

She booted it up and tried to find the files he'd most recently used. Nothing. The most recent document was saved three months ago.

Damned CODA software. She wasn't computer geek

enough to retrieve whatever data it had trashed.

She thought for a moment, trying to recall if there was anything in his conversation that would lead her to where he'd gone, but she hadn't been able to make out much. Just the name Petrov. And something about tracing his call.

Alex's handwriting leaped out at her from a yellow sticky pad on the table. She picked it up. "Went out for a while. Back soon." Then, squeezed between the last line and the edge of the page, like an afterthought: "Stay put."

"Right," she said and tossed the pad back onto the table. "As if I have a choice."

She paced the room a moment, trying to remember anything from his conversations that could indicate where he'd gone. She knew what he was up to, the damn fool. He was running off all alone to follow up on the trace.

Damn Alex Dante. He'd effectively shoved her right out of the way and carried on, as planned, without her. She'd never forgive him for this. And she'd never forgive him if he went and got himself killed.

She picked up the sticky pad once again and stared at his chicken scratch, which over the long years of their association had somehow grown legible to her. She ran her thumb over the cramped letters, hoping it wasn't going to be the last thing of Alex Dante she ever saw.

She felt ridges. Scratch marks, indentations on the paper. She held the pad up to the light filtering in through the dingy window, turned it so the light struck the paper side on.

Yes! It was the imprint of the pen, from whatever he'd written on the sticky note just before hers, engraved, so to speak, into the paper she held in her hand.

An address. 29-something. West…M-something. Was that Rd.? West Mountain Road? Yes, that was it. 29-something, looked like two more digits, the last looked like a zero, but maybe not.

"God bless control freaks with heavy handwriting." She

turned back to the laptop, launched the web browser, and typed in the URL for a map site. She typed in the address and a second later was looking at a map of the city, zeroed in on 2900 West Mountain Road. It was a long road, lined on both sides with huge industrial buildings and warehouses, just a couple of blocks off the highway.

She shut down the computer, strapped on her spare 9mm, and made sure her keys and wallet were in her suitcase. She fumbled around in her bag and found the box of 9mm rounds she'd tossed in from home, along with the extra magazine, and made sure it was loaded and good to go.

"See you soon, Alex. Whether you want me or not."

* * *

Alex drove past the large, industrial buildings on what he hoped was the right block. It was hard to read building numbers, and some of the large buildings didn't seem to be numbered at all, but this has to be it.

There were two huge warehouses set back from the road. They both looked quiet, their parking lots empty, the loading bay doors closed tight. Not that there would be a whole lot of shipping activity before dawn.

One building looked vacant, the other, though, while just as still, seemed slightly less desolate. There were shipping containers parked beside the loading bays, but even better, there were two Dumpsters along the edge of the wall. The trash people wouldn't leave Dumpsters hanging around if no one was paying for waste removal.

Alex circled the block. All quiet. He drove past the building once more, then pulled into the parking lot. A wave of discomfort skittered over his flesh.

The lot in the front of the building was wide open, not an inch of cover anywhere. If he were going to be ambushed, this would be it. A sniper from one of the top windows could pick him off like a toy duck at a shooting gallery.

He continued toward the building, waiting for the sound of his window shattering and the thump of a bullet entering his head. Each moment that nothing happened seemed almost unnatural, until finally his car was behind the building and pulled up beside the Dumpsters out by the back door.

The place was deadly quiet. Unfortunately, that could also mean he had the wrong building.

He got out of the car and looked around as he drew his Smith. Silently, he slipped past the Dumpsters toward the back door. Something hissed at him, a small calico cat with her fur standing on end. She arched her back and leaped sideways toward him, spitting a warning to keep away from her treasure — some half-eaten take-out in a foil container. Unless the local stray cat population had learned to dial out for Chinese, the place wasn't as deserted as it looked.

He peered into the small windows high on the double back doors, but they'd been painted over from inside. He tried the door. It was unlocked.

This was the place all right, but nothing said "ambush" like an open door. He let go of the knob. Careful to tread silently, he turned around and made his way around the building, looking for another way in.

* * *

Raeanne stepped out of the cab outside the ER of the US Army Hospital on East Sahara. She hoped coming here wasn't going to turn out to be a mistake, but she had no choice. She needed help, and this was the only way she could think of to get it.

The waiting room was empty. One obstacle down.

She stepped up to the window. The receptionist looked up from her book and slid back the glass.

Raeanne smiled at her. "I realize it's a little early to come looking for someone, but could you tell me if Dr. Mills is currently on duty?"

"Yes, he is. Do you have an emergency?"

Before she could answer, she heard that familiar, taunting voice. "Mrs. Dante. What a surprise."

Raeanne raised her eyes from the receptionist to the man standing behind her. Something about his expression said it wasn't a surprise at all to see her standing in the ER at four-thirty in the morning.

"Good morning, Dr. Mills. I have an urgent matter to discuss with you, if you have a moment."

"Buzz her in."

She pushed the door open and stepped into the wide hallway that ran the length of the ER. "Thank you, Captain. Can we talk in your office?"

"Why do I get the feeling this has nothing to do with your head?" He turned and led her into the small, neat office a few yards down the hall and closed the door. He leaned back against his desk and crossed his tanned arms over his chest. "So where's your gallant husband today, Mrs. Dante?"

"It's Springfield, and it's Ms.," she said, ignoring the two chairs in front of him and remaining on her feet. "And Alex Dante's whereabouts are precisely the reason for my visit."

He looked her over, as if assessing her credibility. "Okay, I'll bite. What's the problem?"

"How much did Alex tell you about our situation?"

"Not much. But I know Special Forces when I see them."

"So do I," she said pointedly.

He raised an eyebrow at her.

"Here's the deal, Captain. I no longer work for the same people Alex does, and they don't particularly like me underfoot. But the fact is, they're up against some very heavy hitters, currently under the leadership of a very ruthless man who Alex and I almost brought down seven years ago. Not only do these people have their own objectives, which Alex's people are handling, but they're also out for revenge. Against me." Emotion began to tighten her throat, but she swallowed it. "You were right about my son. They have him, and I believe Alex has gone off to try to get him back."

"You mean without the knowledge of the rest of his organization."

"That is correct."

"Now why would he do that? He struck me as a sane individual."

"I'm not sure. But he led the operation that took them down, and from the little I overheard from his phone conversation with them this morning, it sounded like they offered to let my son go in exchange for him."

"So why not alert his team? Have them send in some back up for him?"

"I can't. He disobeyed direct orders by allowing me to be involved. If they find out I'm not where I'm supposed to be, Alex will be in very big trouble. They could charge him with treason. I'm the only person who can help him, but I'm not functioning at 100% yet. I need help."

Mills leaned back against the desk and looked up at the ceiling, considering. "Sure sounds that way. So why are you wasting time jawing at me?"

"Because you're the only person I know who's likely to help me."

He guffawed loudly. "Me? What the hell makes you think I'd want to help you?" He gave her a wan smile. "Unless you're talking about psychiatric help, in which case, I can refer you to some good people."

"I'm very serious. I need your help."

"No."

"Please, Captain Mills. They have my son. And now Alex. I need your help."

He released a heavy sigh and stood to face her. "Look, Ms. Springfield, or whatever your name is, I'm just a small-town army doctor waiting for the next six months to hurry up and happen so I can sit back, collect my pension, and play golf for a living. I have no desire to play cowboy."

Raeanne pulled herself up a little straighter. "Bull. You've been lusting after some kind of action since they dumped you here."

"And what makes you say that?"

"Come on, Captain, don't insult my intelligence. This job bores you to tears. Look at you. You keep yourself in fighting shape, your hair's cut to regulation, and you're the only person in the whole place who's wearing boots instead of white sneakers."

"So?"

"So you grabbed my weapon out of my hand last week, Captain. I wouldn't call those the reflexes of a retiree."

He gazed at her, silently. Blankly. "You were incapacitated."

"The hell I was. Groggy, maybe, but that's a hell of a far cry from incapacitated. And besides, even sound asleep I'm still faster than 90% of the people out there."

"Modest, too."

"No, just honest." She nodded to the tall file cabinet beside him, on top of which sat a tactical holster and a set of headphone-shaped ear protectors. "Been to the range lately, Captain? Bet you've kept up your expert rating with that pistol, haven't you?"

"Look, go ask someone else to play. I'm sure you know plenty of Delta force-types who'd just love to spend the afternoon pumping lead into bad guys."

She sighed. "That's just it, Captain; I don't. I've been working the private sector too long. The only people I know who are capable of what I need are part of Alex's organization, and they're pretty much looking to lock me up."

"I wonder why."

"Please, Captain. You're the only person I know who has

the right background, the right training, and the right mindset for this. Please. Alex is going to get himself killed. And my son with him." She took a deep breath and gave him a long, hard look. "Please."

He stared at her hard, then sighed loudly and ran his hand through his cropped, salt and pepper hair. "I can't believe I'm doing this. If I end up court-marshaled six months short of retirement..."

"You won't. I promise."

"You promise. That's reassuring. I suppose you can wave your magic wand and make sure we don't all wind up dead, too."

She pulled herself up straighter. "I have no intention of winding up dead. You're not the only one with an expert pistol rating."

He gave her a small half smile. "You know, Ms. Springfield, you're good. You're very good. But you blew it on that one. Truth is, I'm only adequate with a pistol."

She smiled. "Adequate will do."

He went to his locker and opened it up. He drew out a black case, popped it open, and drew out a beautiful bolt-action M40 sniper rifle. "I'm much better with this."

He turned over the weapon, giving it the once over, then set it lovingly back in the case. "Scored first in my class in Sniper School. Spent the first half of my career sitting under a net in the desert."

The smile blossomed across Raeanne's face.

Mills lifted the magazine from its foam depression, checked its contents—loaded—and put it back. Then he pulled a box of rounds from his desk drawer, closed the case, and grabbed his sidearm in its khaki tactical holster from the top of the cabinet. "Let's go if we're going. Before I change my mind."

Raeanne couldn't keep the triumph out of her voice. "I knew I wasn't wrong about you."

He gave her a dark, defeated look. "If only I'd been wrong about *you*."

* * *

Alex stepped lightly across the roof jutting up over the small side door. Above it, the pane of glass he'd outlined with the glass cutter in his agency-issue pocketknife popped out with a dainty snap, and he set it gingerly down on the tar paper shingle beside him. Reaching into the small open space, he felt for alarm wires, found none, and offered a silent prayer of thanks to his friend St. Matthew the Apostle, the patron saint of security systems. He found the lock and flipped it, and within moments he'd opened the window and was lowering himself down onto the warehouse floor ten feet below.

The place was silent as death. There were no guards, not even by the unlocked door, which made his intuition twitch with unease. Around him, rows of huge shelves lifted their steel arms to the raftered ceiling, clutching fifty-five gallon drums in neat rows. A faint chemical odor permeated the air, but Alex couldn't identify it.

The windows were few and coated with grime, so without the glare of the huge overhead lights, the lighting was dim at best. Shadows pooled around the bases of the shelves and collected where the huge rows met and formed street-like aisles and intersections. To his left, two forklifts sat at rest by the closed loading bay doors, quiet and still. But beneath the silence, the place hummed with the latent energy of danger.

Alex kept along the wall, avoiding the puddles of greasy morning light and moving in and out of the shadows. From his circuit of the outside, he'd located the business offices and employee areas to the right, at the far end of the building opposite the loading bays. That would be where they'd be keeping Ryan. He hoped. His eyes followed the long rows of drums, each of them easily large enough to hold the body of a small boy.

He made it to the opposite end of the warehouse and found the offices. One room with glass windows running the width of the wall sat to the right of a short corridor, looking out into the warehouse. Some kind of supervisor's office. It appeared empty, the window looking out into the warehouse dark and still. A door with a frosted glass window opened into the hall. Down the short hallway, two more doors led to other offices, one on each side of corridor, and at the very end, under the red, lighted exit sign, stood a heavy steel door marked Authorized Personnel Only.

Keeping back from the doorway, he tried the knob to the supervisor's office. Locked. The door to the office beside it was not. He pushed it open with his foot, weapon up and ready, then swept the interior.

Empty. He moved in and proceeded to search for anything that would indicate the recent passage of Ryan Springfield.

"Drop your weapon! Down on the floor!"

From behind him came the clatter of a half dozen rifles chambering rounds.

Alex froze. He slowly held his gun out to the side, then lowered it to the ground. They hadn't killed him outright, which meant they wanted him for something. If so, they wouldn't shoot to kill. Or so he hoped. He moved as if to let the .45 fall, then spun and fired. He got three shots off before the sting of lead ripped the gun out of his hand and splattered blood from his forearm over his shirt. The next shot took him down.

Chapter Twelve

Raeanne sat in the passenger seat as Mills sped along the Interstate. Her eyes flitted to her side mirror.

"We being tailed?" Mills asked.

"I wouldn't rule it out. But I'd rather a tail than a cop. We don't have time for a ticket."

"So you going to tell me any more about this situation, or am I just expected to go AWOL from work and put myself in harm's way for no reason?"

She put her hand up to shield her eyes from the rays of the rising sun streaming over the horizon. "What else do you need to know? They're bad guys, they've got my son, and Alex Dante's walking right into their hands."

Mills flipped down his visor. "So why not let him? It's his call, I imagine. He didn't strike me as a fool."

Her pulse began to race, which made her head pound uncomfortably. She bit back the retort that was burning her tongue and made a distinct effort to keep her eyes on the road ahead of her. "I'd rather not discuss Alex Dante, if you don't mind."

"Oh, I get it. Had a tiff over who's running the op. He thinks he's protecting you by leaving you out, and you think you're protecting him by rushing in. Too bad that kind of nonsense will get you both killed."

"No one's going to get killed. Except Dmitriy Petrov. And perhaps a few of his goons, if they get in the way."

Mills gave a short bark of laughter.

Raeanne glanced briefly toward him. "So if you think I'm going to get us killed, why are you here?"

"Delusions of grandeur, I imagine. I keep thinking I can either help get your boy back or help keep you and Dante from getting under each other's feet. Either way, I'm sure it's a hopeless task."

"It's not hopeless."

"No, of course it's not."

He pulled the car off the exit ramp and headed for West Mountain Road.

Her head was pounding. "Look for the 2900s. I don't know the last two digits. Hopefully Alex's car will be around somewhere, a beat up GTO."

"And you think he'd just drive right up to the front door?" He made another sound of defeat.

"Just be quiet and look. He'll be around the area somewhere. If he's still here."

"How many hostiles?"

"Unknown."

"Great." He unstrapped his seat belt and reached back for his holster, keeping one hand on the wheel. "Is this the same location where they're keeping your son?"

"Unknown." She tried to breathe normally, but at each building, her heart raced with the expectation of finding something out if the ordinary. Such as Alex's car. Or the sound of gunfire. But at each turn, she was disappointed by the quiet regularity of the mundane.

"And Dante's objective?"

She sighed. "Unknown."

Mills sighed back. "Is there anything about this little soiree that you do know?"

"I know Alex received a call from Petrov, that they exchanged words which made Alex extremely angry, and that he traced the location to here. Then he went off without

Agency blessing and left me a note to stay put. I have no concrete proof, but I expect that yes, my son is here, and that from the sound of the call, Alex was taunted into coming to here to make an exchange—his life for my son's. And while I'm grateful for his dedication, I don't particularly like those terms."

"Because you're lovers."

"No. Yes." The warehouse on her left appeared deserted. "Pull over here." She glanced at him briefly, then back to the empty warehouse. "I want him to survive the mission for a number of reasons, not least of which is that he's a good man and a good operative and the world needs more men like him, not fewer."

"And because you're lovers."

She turned and stared him down.

"The boy his?"

"No."

"Liar."

She turned back to the building and rubbed at the knot of tension tightening at the base of her skull. The place looked desolate. Weeds grew up from the cracked pavement around the building. Broken windows gaped like missing teeth from the upper levels. "This may be it. Try the next one, just to make sure."

Mills pulled back out into traffic and passed the next building. It, too, was deserted—no, not completely. There were no cars in the parking lot to indicate there were any employees currently at work, but there were trucking containers by the loading bays and the building itself wasn't in poor repair. "Maybe it's this one."

"I'll circle around. Maybe there will be something out back." Mills turned the car up the side street adjacent to the second building and made a circuit around the block. "I don't see anything. Are you sure it's one of these two?"

"No."

He completed the block and pulled back onto West Mountain Road to make a second pass. "There's nothing here. It may be farther up."

"Yeah. Cover the entire area. The 2900's go on for a little way still." She tried to calm the flare of adrenaline that had quickened her pulse in expectation. "I just hope it won't be too late when we find him."

* * *

Alex closed his eyes and tried to not let the pain in his forearm and knee cloud his judgment. It was only pain. He was in no immediate danger. He'd gambled correctly—Petrov wanted him for something because he wasn't mortally wounded. But he wasn't about to let a little thing like a couple of nonfatal gunshot wounds keep him from getting the boy back. Or from breaking Petrov's neck.

"Open your eyes, Mr. Guardian. I asked you a question."

"Sorry, must have dozed off. Your conversation's beginning to bore me."

Petrov's three remaining gorillas had beaten him soundly with fists and boots, and he'd stopped straining against the ropes that kept him tied to the chair in what appeared to be Petrov's office. He'd killed three, but unfortunately, the three that were left weren't fools. They'd tied him effectively, wrists bound together tightly behind the back of the chair, ankles tight together and cross-tied between the chair legs. When he got out of here, his left knee was going to require a whole lot of surgery to repair both the damage done by the bullet and the work they were doing on it now.

"Sergei? Once more, if you please."

Petrov's huge, blond goon brought the length of copper pipe down across the damaged joint. Alex clenched his teeth a moment before impact to avoid biting his tongue and tried to let the pain pass through him. It would, eventually. It wasn't real. It was only a neurological reaction, just a chemical message sent to his brain to tell him about an injury he was already aware of. There was no immediate danger. The wound was not a threat to his life.

There was no immediate danger. The wound was not a threat to his life.

There was no —

"Once more, Mr. Dante. Which government agency employs you?"

Alex tried to keep his mind on his mantra, but it was difficult with Petrov's continual litany of questions, over and over and over, the same thing. What government agency was he from? Where was Senator Helmsan? What sort of resistance were they planning to counter his mission? Over and over and over, a thousand variations on the theme.

"All right. I see you'd rather not talk about your job. Let's discuss something more personal then, shall we?"

Alex focused his mind somewhere else. Bermuda. He'd always meant to go there, but hadn't gotten around to it. He wasn't sure why; there was just something about the idea of those little scooters and plaid Bermuda shorts and beaches with pink sand.

"How about our little Raeanne? Where do you think she is at this moment, Mr. Guardian?"

Raeanne. He kept his mind far away. He was expecting this, the use of someone he cared about to try to break him. It was standard operating procedure, and it wouldn't work. They'd tell him all sorts of lies about her, about having her there, about being ready to torture and kill her if he didn't cooperate, but it wasn't real. It was just more of the same. More games. And he was by far the better player.

Petrov sighed. "Such obstinacy. What a pity. Sergei?"

* * *

Raeanne sat forward in her seat. "Slow down, I think we're in the 3000's."

Mills slowed the car, and Raeanne craned her neck to see the building to their right. The number above the doorway read 3016.

"Damn, we're too far."

Mills pulled into the parking lot and turned back the way they'd come. "We must have missed something, then."

"Go back to those two empty buildings. I should have listened to my instincts when we were down there."

He drew up to the intersection before the block where the two empty properties sat huddled side by side, this time on their right. He drove through the intersection, passed the buildings, and Raeanne scoured the place again for anything that would indicate Alex's presence.

"What's that?" she asked.

"What?"

"It looked like a car, back behind the first building. Behind the row of Dumpsters."

They passed the second building and turned up the side street, pulling into a small, dingy office building behind the warehouse. Between the two properties, an aged stockade fence leaned drunkenly against the sky, poking spindly fingers up toward the rising sun. It was too light to hope for the cover of darkness, but still early enough, maybe, that there wouldn't be anyone around to see them.

Mills pulled close to the fence and Raeanne hopped out to peer through a gap in the boards. Alex's demolished GTO, sans windshield, riddled with bullet holes, sat empty beside the Dumpsters. A small calico cat lay curled up on the hood. "That's his car," she said.

Mills was out and beside her, peering through a second opening and strapping his holster to his thigh. "Guess you weren't kidding about the shootout," he said.

A lump formed in her throat, but she swallowed it. "No."

If his car was still there, that meant he hadn't yet completed his mission. There could be a number of reasons for that, none of them reassuring.

But he was here. And that meant maybe Ryan was, too.

But presumably, so were Petrov and his team.

"I don't know how much good a sniper will do you inside, unless we can get in undetected and locate them. And find me a decent vantage point so I can start taking them out."

"Okay, then, use your judgment. I don't have any comm devices, so once we get inside, we need to stick together until we locate Petrov. After that, I'll try to draw them out into your line of fire. Late as it is, we should assume Alex is down. Finding him and bringing him out is one objective. But retrieving my son is the primary."

"Roger that." Mills placed a hand on her forearm. "You sure you're feeling up to this? Your head okay?"

"Captain Mills, I haven't been this close to my son in three days. My head is dancing a jig."

They slid silently toward the building, past the row of Dumpsters toward the rear entrance. The windows were darkened; she couldn't see inside, but when she gingerly tried the knob, it slowly turned in her hand. She glanced sideways at Mills and nodded slightly, indicating that he take the right and she would take the left when they stepped through the door.

He nodded his understanding, secured the strap holding his rifle over his shoulder, and drew his sidearm from his holster.

She quietly pulled the door open and swept the area to the left. Beside her, Mills searched to the right. When she was satisfied that they'd entered undetected, she glanced at him. He reached back and shut the door soundlessly behind them.

Raeanne glanced at the high shelves holding rows and rows of fifty-five gallon drums. She sniffed the air—chemicals of some sort. She was no chemist, but it didn't smell like the kind of thing one ought to be inhaling for extended periods. The HAZMAT signs on the walls confirmed that thought. Flammable. Reactive. Corrosive.

Great. She wondered if the contents of those barrels had anything to do with the Ice Syndicate's import legislation. What exactly were they so hot to import these days, other than weapons? Or was this warehouse simply a convenient side business to launder the money? Or did they have the wrong place entirely? She stepped cautiously up to the first row of barrels. Letters were crudely stenciled with spray paint across the sides. In Arabic. And in Russian.

But all it said was "flammable."

Why in Arabic, though? Alex had said the Ice Syndicate had ties to Al-Qaeda and Hamas...but what did that have to do with trade legislation?

Mills nodded toward the end of the building on their right. His whisper was almost soundless. "I think there ought to be offices along that wall. If so, I could get a clear shot from the top of this shelving, up by the rafters."

"Okay. I'll go left, you go right. Secure the perimeter and meet me on the other side. From there we'll move on the offices. You can select your vantage point and I can check—"

From the other side of the warehouse, she heard a sharp cry of pain, quickly stifled.

Mills looked at her, her own fears reflected in his face. *Alex.*

"Go," she said.

* * *

Alex drew a deep breath and tried not to cry out again. He tasted blood that time, he'd bitten his tongue after all. His knee hummed with pain, and his vision had become close and speckled with black dots at the edges. It wouldn't be long before his brain would try to shut out the pain by passing out, an attempt to conserve the body's energy and focus it on staying alive.

"Yeah, yeah," he said, working to keep his voice as close to neutral as possible. "I know the drill. You have Raeanne in the other room, beating the crap out of her, and me talking to you is her only hope. I know the game."

Petrov eyed him coldly, a reptilian glint in his small, gray eyes. "A pity you're so impervious to emotional considerations, Mr. Guardian. Perhaps that was why your little Raeanne chose me instead of you. Women need tenderness, Major, not severity. They need love. Affection. Warmth."

"And you're the poster boy for warmth."

"Or perhaps it was just that you weren't virile enough for her. There are a thousand reasons why women chose one man over another, and often they have no logical reason at all."

Yeah, no joke. He forced down the rising tide of anger and despair and fear and love and swallowed the blood that was flooding his mouth. He wasn't going to let them do this to him.

"But one thing is certain, Major Dante. Your little Raeanne will not survive the dawn unless you cooperate. Immediately."

"Nice try, Petrov. But a.) I don't give a rat's ass about who Raeanne finds more *virile*, and b.) even if I did, I'm not stupid enough to fall for such a pathetic bluff. I know exactly where Raeanne is, and it's not here."

Petrov stared at him, an expression of disgust and rising impatience twisting his tight, lizard-like features. "Then you leave me no choice. Perhaps you'd enjoy hearing what that same pipe sounds like across the knees of a small boy." He lifted the walkie-talkie to his mouth. "Vladimir. Bring the child."

* * *

Raeanne's half of the perimeter was clear. Mills had been right — the offices were here, around the corner from where they'd entered. There was a short corridor, with four doors leading off it: a steel exit door at the end, two doors in the middle, probably offices, and the closest to the end leading into a glass-fronted office, its darkened windows facing out into the warehouse.

Ryan was in one of those four rooms, she just knew it.

A second later Mills appeared beside her and signaled all clear. Raeanne stepped closer to the wall, just to the left of the window looking out into the warehouse. Gingerly, she cupped her hand to the glass at the edge and peered in. All was in darkness. She looked back at Mills and shrugged.

He stepped up beside her and drew her away from the window. "Got a plan?"

"Maybe. How about we create a diversion at the far end of the warehouse to draw them out. You take your position up in the rafters and see how many you can take down. I'll wait here and take any you miss."

He gave her the most rudimentary twitch of the lips. "I don't miss."

"Good. Then I'll do my nails."

"You're sure you can recognize them? I don't want to shoot up the accounting department."

"Oh, yeah. I'll recognize them. And they'll be shouting in Russian."

"And after they're down?"

"I move in and bring out Alex and Ryan."

"And if they're not in any of these rooms?"

She hesitated a moment, wishing in vain for inspiration to strike. It didn't. "Then I'm open to suggestions."

He gave her a wary look. "I'm fresh out of those, so let's hope we won't need them."

Raeanne nodded toward the metal toolbox she'd found at the far end of the warehouse by the forklifts. "I brought this along. Ought to make a decent sound when you dump it onto the concrete floor from ten feet up."

"Nice work." Mills slung his rifle onto his shoulder by its strap and picked up the toolbox. "Give me two minutes to get up there and around the other side."

"Will do."

Raeanne reached 120 seconds just as she heard the crash of the metal box hitting the concrete and the metallic clank of tools bouncing and scattering over the floor. They had to have heard that. She kept to the cover of the shadows, just behind the first row of huge floor-to-ceiling shelves. Between the steel frame of the shelving and the drum in front of her, she had a clear line of fire to the corridor and to anyone who may decide to leave those offices. With any luck, whoever was sent to check out the noise wouldn't stop to inspect each row on their way to the source of the sound.

A light came on in the windowed room to the right. The face of a small boy appeared against the glass, peering out into the darkness.

* * *

Petrov frowned at the crash from the far end of the warehouse and paused to listen.

Alex grimaced with renewed energy. "Here they come, Petrov. Game's up." He tried to put as much bravado into his voice as he could muster with most of his vision grayed out at the edges. Whatever had made that sound—rats, aliens, whatever—at least the threat of attack would divert Petrov's attention from harming the boy. "In fact, is that a chopper I hear?"

With a glare of accusation at Alex, Petrov thumbed the button on his radio. "Vladimir, what's going on out there?"

"It sounds is if something fell over at the other end of the warehouse. Most probably those damned cats again. I've sent Mikaelivich to check it out."

"Go with him. I want the place searched top to bottom.

We need to make sure none of our little friends have come looking for their commander."

"Too late for that, Petrov," Alex said. "My men ought to be getting ready to take out Mikaelivich just about—"

The crack of a rifle punctuated his sentence—once, twice.

Huh? Alex knew he was losing the struggle to hold on to consciousness, but auditory hallucinations, now?

Petrov spun toward him, dropped his walkie-talkie, and grabbed him by the shirtfront. "Where are they? How many are there?"

Alex gaped at him for a second, then it registered. He hadn't hallucinated the gunshots.

Someone besides Petrov's men was out there.

He smiled and felt a surge of adrenaline clear some of the fog from his head. So they'd sent a team after him after all. Whoever that Specialist Liz Dean in IT was, he was going to give her a big fat kiss when he got back to the office.

Two more shots from the warehouse, this time a hand gun, probably a 9mm. And much closer.

He grinned into Petrov's tight, anxious eyes. "Sounds like at least two teams, wouldn't you say?"

The walkie-talkie crackled from the floor.

"Dmi...triy... Come in, Dmitriy." A woman's voice, purring through the static. *Raeanne.*

How the hell...?

Petrov's face contorted with disbelief. He stared at the walkie-talkie a moment before snatching it up off the floor. "Identify yourself!"

"What, no hello Dima? I'm hurt. After all we've been through together."

Petrov pulled Alex's .45 off the table and thrust it against Alex's temple. "Sergei. Bring her to me. Alive or dead, it matters not."

Blondie picked up the MP5 and headed for the door.

Raeanne's voice crackled over the radio again. "Let's

see…ten to one says you just sent one of your dogs to sniff me out. Care to guess the odds that we've got a sniper in the rafters with his scope trained right on your door?"

Blondie hesitated and looked back at Petrov.

"Are you a betting man, Dima? No one should come to Vegas without trying to woo Lady Luck." She laughed her deep, seductive laugh. "Come on. Take a chance. Send a man out." The clack of a round being chambered came through loud and clear.

Alex grinned through the hazy vision. She'd always had a flair for the dramatic.

Petrov spun toward his man. "She's bluffing! Go find her!"

The man obeyed.

A bead of sweat snaked its way down Petrov's left temple as he thumbed the button to talk. "Throw down your weapon and allow Sergei to bring you in, or I will kill both your boy and your Guardian Angel."

Sergei's MP5 roared and echoed in the warehouse, louder than thunder.

* * *

Raeanne hit the deck. Bullets whizzed past her and made Swiss cheese of one of the fifty-five gallon drums, which immediately began fountaining its contents onto the floor. From over her shoulder, Mills' rifle returned fire.

"Come on!" he called. "That stuff's flammable as hell!"

"Pun intended, I hope." She slid past the drum and searched the darkness for the Russian gunman.

"No, unfortunately. Didn't you see all the signs? Can't you smell it?"

"You're the doctor. I got a D in chemistry."

"That's because you probably spent too much time in the gym trying to outlift the guys." Mills tapped her arm and indicated she follow. He stopped at the end of the row, then stepped silently out into the aisle. "One target down at the far end of the warehouse."

"Another down just outside the main aisle. Got his radio, but they just sent another one out, the one who just shot at me. My son's in that right front office. From the way they dispersed, I think Petrov and Alex are in the room just behind it."

"How many more of them are there?"

"Unknown. I only saw the three that came out."

"That leaves just the new one with the MP5. Plus Petrov. If there were any more he'd have sent them out by now." Mills glanced around and shook his head. "So now we just have to play a round of Where's Waldo, then we can move in to get Alex and your boy."

"I say we get them now and screw Waldo."

"I'd rather not, but it's your op."

Mills' whisper was closer than she'd expected. For a doctor, he sure moved like a guerilla fighter. "Apparently, you're no stranger to this kind of thing either."

"I've led my share of search and rescue ops."

Raeanne glanced at him in the semidarkness. "You've led a very colorful life for a doctor." She turned to peer through the barrels toward the offices. The light in Ryan's room had gone out. Either someone had come in, or perhaps Ryan had heard the commotion and had gotten scared and turned off the light himself in an attempt to hide. Either way, she couldn't leave him there another moment.

"I'm going to get my son. Once I'm certain he's secured in that room, I'll move in on Alex and Petrov. I need you to cover my back."

"Roger that." Without a word of argument, he moved off to get a better vantage point. "Give me sixty seconds."

If only Alex listened to her as easily. If only Alex were there. She cut that line of thought before it could go any further. He was there, he was alive, and he was coming out with her within the next five minutes.

She glanced around once more. Where's Waldo? If only the gunman with the MP5 were wearing a goofy red and white cap, her life would be a lot easier.

The office window was still dark. She estimated the distance at thirty feet. If she sprinted, she should be able to make it even without Mills' diversion. A few seconds later, the thump of something on a drum on the far side of the aisle drew fire from the MP5.

She sprinted for the corridor, slid in, and pressed herself against the wall. All was quiet both out in the warehouse and from the office corridor. The door to Ryan's room was directly in front of her. Glancing down the corridor to her left, then out into the open area to her right, she darted across the hall.

The door was locked. She sighed and rapped very lightly on the glass.

Nothing. She glanced around her, her heartbeat pounding loudly in her ears. "Ryan!" she whispered and tapped lightly again on the glass.

"Mommy?" His voice was as loud as a gunshot against the silence.

"Shh. Stay very quiet. Are you alone?"

He pressed his hands against the frosted glass, trying to peer out. She barely made out his nod of assent.

"Can you open the door?"

He shook his head. The knob wiggled, but didn't turn.

"I'll be back to get you in five minutes. Stay very quiet. Lay down on the floor against the wall, right over here."

The shadowed face pressed closer to the glass for a moment, mumbling something she couldn't quite hear, then he moved away from the window. It took all her strength to not put her fist through the glass and pull him into her arms, but she knew that would only get them both riddled with bullets. She had to at least locate Alex before grabbing Ryan and making a run for it.

A shot rang out in the warehouse, Mills' rifle, and then a three round burst from the MP5. She waited for an answering shot from Mills, but none came.

Oh, God, don't be dead...

She tightened her grip on her 9mm and took a deep breath. Three doors remained: the two other office doors and the steel door under the exit sign at the very end of the corridor, marked, "Authorized Personnel Only." From that, she gathered it probably led through some kind of administrative offices, maybe a cube farm or a foyer, but the lighted exit sign meant it eventually led outside. It wasn't difficult to decide which door Petrov had taken.

If Mills were dead, she wouldn't have long before the gunman returned. She had to move now.

She took hold of the doorknob to the steel door and very gingerly tried to turn it. Locked.

Now what? Too bad she didn't have any of the toys from the safe house. The set of lock picks or a little C4 would come in handy right about now.

She turned to glance out into the warehouse. Yeah, with all that flammable stuff wafting through the air? Good thinking. Too bad she didn't just have some kind of battering ram to break down the door with.

But she did, sort of, on the other side of the warehouse. If she could make it past the gunman with the MP5 to get it.

Chapter Thirteen

Raeanne was halfway through the warehouse, keeping to the cover of shadows along the periphery. The gunman was nowhere in sight. Neither was Mills.

"You're too loud," he said, falling into step beside her.

"You're alive," she managed, after quelling the startle reflex.

"Yeah, but so's Waldo. What did you find out?"

"I found Ryan. He's waiting for us in the front office on the right. I couldn't get into the other door to locate Alex or Petrov, but I'm sure they're behind that steel door at the end of the corridor. Probably making a run for it."

"Got a plan yet?"

"Yep. Take cover up by the offices somewhere and be ready to move out when I get there."

"Will do."

"And if anyone goes into that windowed office other than Alex, shoot him."

She turned away and continued on alone, across the warehouse and over to the last row of shelves. Fifty feet away, across the open area surrounding the loading bays, two forklifts were parked beside the huge garage-type doors. She gave one more glance left and right. No one in sight. With a breath to steady her, she dashed out for the closest forklift.

The MP5 thundered behind her. She dove for the space between the two forklifts, arms outstretched, then hit the cement hands first and rolled amid the clink of spent casings hitting the concrete. She came up in a crouch between the forklifts, her pistol in both hands. Over the top of the padded seat, she scanned the shadows for the shooter.

There he was. In the corner of the warehouse beside one of the huge concrete support pylons.

Even as she drew a bead on him, the muzzle of the MP5 flashed bright as a firecracker. She felt a bullet whiz past her head, then heard the angry whine as it ricocheted off the steel support between two of the bay doors. She tried to make out her attacker, but the bright afterimage of the MP5's muzzle flare was dancing before her eyes like a drunken blue daisy. She fired blindly, the 9mm kicking in her hand and filling the air with its flat report, but she couldn't tell if she'd hit him, or if he was still waiting for her to raise her head.

From somewhere at the other end of the warehouse came the crack of Mills' rifle. The MP5 answered, farther off than it had been a moment ago. Now was the time to move.

She jumped into the seat of the forklift and glanced down at the controls, trying to make sense of them. There was a key in the ignition. She turned it and rammed down on the gas.

Nothing happened.

A gunshot rang out and a bullet struck the forklift's roll cage. If one of them hit the propane tank that powered it, she was toast.

She cursed and began to flip levers, keeping the pedal floored. The forks raised and titled wildly back and forth, then the forklift jumped forward. It surged out into the clear area with a high-pitched whine of gears as another burst of shots peppered the floor around her, dusting the air with concrete chips.

She tried to swerve, hoping to throw off the gunman's aim, but she oversteered. For a horrible moment, the forklift veered violently out of control toward one of the huge metal shelves stacked with fifty-five gallon drums. She regained control just as one of the forks kissed off a corner pylon, spitting sparks.

The gunman appeared from between the shelves and fired at her. She returned fire, her one-handed steering erratic, but good enough to aim the forklift straight at her attacker. He leaped back behind cover of the shelving as she shot past and accelerated up the aisle.

She sped down the length of the warehouse, gears screaming in protest as she pushed the machine to its limit. The MP5 continued to dog her, but she couldn't stop to return fire. She was almost to the offices and the locked steel door that separated her from her son.

She took her foot off the gas, and the forklift jerked to a stop, almost throwing her from the cage. She regained control, floored it again, and spun around the corner, straight for the office corridor. Straight for the locked steel door.

The steel door opened.

She took her foot off the accelerator, and the forklift lurched to a halt. Mills and Alex stepped through the door and ran toward her.

Or rather, Mills ran toward her, Alex slumped over slumped over Mills' shoulder, barely conscious.

"Petrov's gone," Mills said.

She wanted to ask what the hell had happened, but right now, it didn't matter. She darted to the door of Ryan's prison.

"He's gone too," Alex said.

It was still locked. She elbowed the frosted glass window, turning aside as the shards rained down onto the concrete with a musical crash and then reaching in and flipping the lock.

The floor beside the door, where she'd told Ryan to lie and wait, was empty. She turned to the other side and spun to take in the entire room.

"Ryan?" She ran to the far end of the office, moving to search the corners behind the desks and file cabinets and conference table. He had to be here, hiding somewhere, frightened by the sound of the commotion outside. "Ryan, it's Mommy! Come on, it's time to go!"

Her voice came out shrill and panicked, and the sound reinforced the terror that swept through her as she was greeted only by silence. "Ryan? Ryan!"

Mills was beside her, still supporting Alex with one arm. "He's gone. We've got to go before our friend with the MP5 shows up."

"He can't be gone! I left him right here!"

"Petrov took him and ran." It was Alex who spoke, although he looked incapable of putting one thought in front of the next. His face was ashen beneath the layer of blood and grime, and he was barely supporting his own weight. One leg in particular was a twisted, bloody mess. "I tried to follow him…"

She wanted to say something, but the thoughts were moving too fast. She couldn't believe what her eyes were telling her. Alex was half-dead. Ryan was gone. Nothing made sense, and she couldn't begin to separate all the sensations of horror and despair that were pummeling the air out of her lungs in short, involuntary spasms.

"Come on!" Mills' voice snapped through the haze of her disjointed consciousness. "We have to move! Now!"

Her body responded automatically to the order, and she was faintly surprised to find herself following him through the open steel door.

It led into a dingy outer office, at the other end of which stood the business's main entrance. Several outdated vinyl chairs sat along one grimy wall, adorned with cheap paintings and a hole in the plaster poorly hidden behind a dusty plastic palm. A desk and several wide lateral files took up much of the opposite wall, along with a couple of large metal bins full of assorted mechanical parts.

From behind them came the raucous chatter of the MP5, and the fronds of the fake palm exploded into green confetti.

"Keep moving!" Mills turned and fired back at the gunman with his handgun.

Raeanne took two running steps and threw herself behind the metal bins as more rounds struck the cement floor, shattered a window, and thumped into something beside her.

She crouched against the wall and slipped a fresh clip into her 9mm. So much for improvisation. She heard Mills fire again. Peering out from around the bins, she saw the last remaining Russian with the MP5, the huge blond gorilla, returning fire from the hallway where the forklift was still parked just outside the door.

The MP5 chattered again, answered by another shot from Mills. Petrov's goon started to run, firing back wildly over his shoulder. Bullets from his submachine gun riddled the forklift's propane tank.

There was an instant of hissing from escaping gas as the man continued to fire, then the tank exploded.

The shock wave slammed the stack of metal bins into her and she skidded across the floor in an avalanche of machine parts. Shrapnel cut through the air in all directions. The breath left her lungs with a whoosh and her teeth clamped together with a hard clack. She lay on the cool concrete for a moment, trying to get her breath back, aware that her palms and face were scraped raw and that her gun had gone skittering off somewhere.

Then fire blossomed all around her. Waves of heat beat against her, reflecting madly off the walls. With a grunt, she crawled out from beneath the toppled bins and forced herself to her feet. The heat was astounding; it made her skin feel too tight for her body and the flames were so bright she had to squint. Her 9mm had wound up a few yards off. She ran to snatch it up, and the grip was almost too hot to hold. She had a brief flash of fear that the ammunition inside might cook off, but she couldn't leave it. And she couldn't leave Mills and Alex.

Flames had spread to the walls. Windows exploded like gunshots, spraying shattered glass outward like mist and dragging a torrent of flame with it. Black smoke billowed along the high beams of the ceiling and boiled out through the empty windows.

The sprinklers erupted above her, icy water pounding into her overheated skin like nails.

"Alex!"

She saw him, lying motionless beside an overturned chair. She raced to him, knelt beside him, felt for a pulse.

"Raeanne! Get out!"

She turned toward the voice. Mills' legs were pinned beneath an overturned lateral file amid a heap of rubble and spilled file folders.

"Get out!" he said again. "This place is going to go up like a rocket!"

She thrust her fingers against Alex's throat, searching for the pulsing carotid. She fumbled for it, but found nothing.

"Alex?" She shook him, then slapped his grimed face. Nothing. "Alex!"

"Raeanne! Get out!"

She turned back to Mills, his position under the weight of the wide lateral file finally registering. He was trapped.

She ran to him. "Can you move?"

"No, now get out!"

She pushed against the huge file cabinet, but it wouldn't budge. The metal was warm, very warm. The smoke billowing around the rafters was lower now, black and thick, and she looked out at Mills through a dark haze. What was she supposed to do? She felt the panic rising and wasn't sure if she'd be able to force it down long enough to think of something.

The smoke made her cough as she assessed the possibilities. The top drawer of the cabinet came to the middle of Mills' back. It was slightly open, the drawer sliding forward out of the cabinet and pressing itself into Mills' spine. With both hands she shoved against it, as if to close it. It moved, ever so slightly. She let it go with a grunt.

"Can you slide out if I can push this drawer in again?"

"No," he said, "there's too much weight pressing against my legs. I think one of them is broken."

She began scooping away bits of paper, then began emptying the drawer and tossing folders anywhere they landed. Once the top drawer was empty, she pushed it closed. It stayed shut.

"What if I can empty the other drawers? Can you crawl out?"

"Maybe," Mills answered, but he didn't look convinced.

Two of the lower drawers were partially open as well, but not far enough to remove any of the side-facing folders. She tried to push them shut, but they were just too heavy.

"Forget it," Mills said, "Just get out of here before the whole place goes up."

She ignored him and instead flipped onto her back and slid as close to him as she could.

"What are you doing? Get the hell out of here!"

Despite the sprinklers, smoke was billowing out from the back of the warehouse. It caught in her throat and singed its way down to her lungs.

"Quiet," she said, coughing on the last breath of air. She propped her feet against the cabinet. "And consider yourself lucky I spent more time in the gym than in chemistry lab. And that I liked the leg press." She extended her legs as hard as she could, but instead of moving the cabinet, she just slid backward.

"That's not going to work!"

"Yes, it will!" She turned on an angle and propped her backside against Mills' shoulder. She shoved her feet against the cabinet, which was now at a less than perfect angle, but it was the best she could do. "Now push into me as hard as you can." She pressed again. This time, the cabinet slid back about an inch, then caught and levered upward slightly.

Mills squirmed forward, but his motion took Raeanne with him and her legs gave way. The cabinet slammed back down onto Mills' hips, and he groaned.

Raeanne let out the breath she'd been holding. She couldn't control the coughing, and it was hard to get enough air. "Once more," she said, then thought she heard something through the sounds of the blaze. She stopped and listened. Yes. Sirens.

She pushed back against Mills' side again, pressed her feet against the cabinet, and then straightened her legs with a grunt. This time, the cabinet slid back about a foot, dragging over Mills' hips. He swore, but tried to wriggle forward.

"That's it!" Raeanne said.

The cabinet was down just past his hips, pinning only his legs. It was too flat for her to get her legs under it for another press, so she stood and grasped the top of the cabinet and lifted.

"Come on!" she said, feeling lightheaded with exertion.

Her efforts bought them only a fraction of an inch, but it was just the fraction Mills needed. He slithered out, and Rae dropped the cabinet, letting it crash to the floor. She grabbed Mills' arm and hauled him up.

"Where's Alex?" he asked, sputtering to get his breath, almost collapsing as he tried to put weight on his left leg.

Raeanne stopped. She was vaguely aware that she knew the answer to that question, but somehow, she couldn't quite find it.

"Raeanne, where's Alex?" Mills asked again, coughing through his words. He grabbed her arms. "Did he get out?"

The answer came to her, slammed into her and took the last of her breath from her lungs, leaving a sick emptiness inside her.

"No," she said.

No, he didn't get out.

She couldn't make herself move. He wouldn't ever get out.

"Where is he?" Mills shouted, coughing.

"He's dead." She heard herself say it, but her voice sounded far away, as if it belonged to someone else. "Alex is dead."

A thickness grabbed her chest, squeezing out the last of the air. She lost even the desire to cough. Alex was dead.

Oh Alex, what have I done?

Hands grabbed her. Someone was speaking; she heard words, tried to focus on them, but they were too far away. She felt herself moving, being turned and tumbled, but it never occurred to her to struggle. Alex was dead. And she wasn't sure she wasn't dead with him.

* * *

Raeanne opened her eyes. She was breathing into a mask. Above her, tubes and lines danced side to side with the motion of the gurney. No, with the motion of the vehicle.

A face appeared above her. It spoke, but not to her. About her. Evidently, she wasn't dead after all—her BP was seventy-seven over forty-nine, but—*get that light out of my eyes!*—her pupils weren't doing something right. She turned her head to look around.

"Where's Alex?"

The face over her said something, but it wasn't very clear.

She tore the oxygen mask off her face. "Where's Alex!"

"Please keep still, you're going to pull out your IV." The face was attached to a body with hands, and they pushed her back down onto her back. The face was female, about forty, and had the worst haircut she'd ever seen. Either that or she'd leaned a little too close to the food processor.

"Funny," the woman said.

Raeanne gaped into her small, dark eyes. "Did I say that out loud?"

"Yep."

"Sorry. I didn't mean it. I have a concussion."

"No kidding."

"Where's Alex?" She felt the pressure building in her head, a combination of tears welling behind her eyes and a throbbing she wished would go away. "He was with us in the front room of the warehouse. Is he really…" She forced the last word out on a choked whisper. "Dead?"

"No one's dead, hon. Take it easy." The hands came forward again and placed the mask back over her mouth. "Keep this on, okay?"

"Okay." No one was dead. Alex was alive. Thank God.

"Where is he?"

"On the way to the hospital, same as you. You're both going to be fine."

She let out a deep breath and felt the tears slide past her lids. He was alive. And he was going to be fine. "What about Mills?"

"What about what?"

She pulled the mask down. "Mills. He was with us. I think his leg is broken."

"I told you, he's fine. Now try to relax."

"No, not Alex. Mills. Dan Mills."

The voice hesitated a second. "There was a third person with you in the building?"

"Yes. Didn't you get both of them out?"

The hand pressed the mask back over her mouth and reached for the radio at her belt. "Dispatch, this is Rescue Two, over."

"Go ahead, Rescue Two."

"Patient claims there was a third person in the building. Did we pull anyone else out?"

"That's a negative, Rescue Two. Are you sure you heard

right?"

The EMT turned to Raeanne. "Are you positive there was more than one man with you in the foyer?"

Raeanne nodded. The relief she'd felt leeched away like silt with the tide, leaving behind a black, hollow certainty that she'd been right all along. Alex was dead.

"That's affirmative," the woman said. "She says there was a third person in the front foyer of the warehouse."

"Rescue Two, this is Rescue Twelve. My patient confirms there was indeed another man besides himself at the scene. A Dan Mills."

"Alex?" Raeanne shouted, snatching the mask from her face and sitting up on the gurney. "Is that Alex?"

The EMT glanced at her and brought the radio up. "Rescue Twelve, do you have an ID on the patient you're transporting?"

There was a moment of silence, then voice on the other end squawked back, "Sorry, Rescue Two, my mistake. It's the patient who's Dan Mills."

"And you didn't see a second man at the scene?"

"Negative, Rescue Two. If there was a second man at the scene, I didn't see anyone bring him out."

Chapter Fourteen

Raeanne waited for the doctor to leave the curtained exam before getting up off the gurney and getting dressed. She was back in the ER of the Army hospital, the last place she'd wanted to be again. Her clothes reeked of smoke and were wet and black and greasy with residue from the fire. A small, filthy smudge remained on the stool where she'd deposited them. Something about it made her want to cry, but she didn't. She couldn't. There was nothing inside but emptiness.

Alex was dead. Ryan was gone. But at least Petrov got him out before the explosion.

How could things have gone so wrong so fast?

She struggled into the stiff, grimy clothes and told herself to ignore the smell. Or get used to it. She'd experienced fire before, back in the old days. Its effects always lingered for a long time—in her hair, on her skin, in her breath as her lungs healed themselves of the smoke damage. Even after it was gone, there would be times when the odor suddenly appeared, then disappeared, elusive as a ghost.

This time, the ghost would be Alex's.

God, why couldn't she cry? A sick, dry feeling made her feel heavy as lead, and the air around her seemed thick and oppressive. Dressed, and with as much steadiness as she could muster, she grabbed her page of discharge instructions and headed down the hall, wondering, now that Alex wasn't there to argue about the safe house, where she should go.

What was going to happen to Ryan? How was she going to find him now, with half her hair singed off and half of CODA probably parked outside her house waiting for her to walk in so they could arrest her?

"Raeanne."

She stopped and turned to the curtained exam area to her left. The small plate above it said Room 5. The face peering out at her from the gap in the ugly plaid curtain belonged to Mills.

He didn't look like he was going anywhere any time soon, still in the thin cotton gown and lying flat on his back on the gurney. They'd cleaned him up to stitch the long shrapnel cut across his cheek, but they'd stopped an inch before his hairline, so that his clean, white face stood out from the black grime like a mask, and the orange stain of disinfectant around the stitches and scrapes made him look grotesque and phantom-like.

"You all right?" he asked, pushing himself up on one elbow.

"Yeah. Sore throat, heavy chest, you know the drill. You? Your leg broken?"

He shook his head. "Nah, the knee's just sprained. An ace bandage and a beer, and I'm good to go."

She smiled, sort of. There was a lot she wanted to say, but nothing that really mattered. "I'm sorry," she finally said.

He nodded. "They told me about Alex."

She nodded too. Her head felt top-heavy, and it was hard to lift it to look back into Mills' eyes. She'd felt this emptiness before, when Alex had disappeared seven years ago. But this time, she wasn't only feeling sorry for herself for being dumped. This time, Alex was dead. And it was her fault.

"I have no idea what happened," Mills said. "When they took you out, I told them there was a man down in the foyer and possibly more in the warehouse. I just assumed they'd go back to look."

She nodded again. "It doesn't matter. Alex was...he was

gone before the EMTs even arrived."

"I'm sorry, Raeanne. I did my best."

Absurd laughter bubbled up from her throat. "You're sorry? Look at you. You look like a freaking Mardi Gras zombie. You almost got blown to pieces, all because I couldn't just sit still and trust Alex to…" She swallowed the lump that almost choked her as she spoke his name. "Trust Alex to do his job."

"Alex wasn't exactly winning the war when I found him. He was barely conscious. And you didn't have a gun to my head, either." he said. "Everything you said about me was absolutely true. I'm an adrenaline junkie. It's lost me two marriages, gotten me court-martialed, and has nearly gotten me killed more times than I care to remember. But I could no more have passed up the chance to help you, if it meant getting out of those four walls, than I could have passed up a million bucks."

"I had no business involving you."

"I had no business getting involved."

She tried to outstare him, but she just didn't have it in her.

"Look," he said, "we both did what we did. You had your reasons; I had mine. I'm sorry we didn't succeed, and I'm sorry about Alex. He was a good man and a good soldier."

"You barely even knew him."

"I knew him."

She looked into his dark eyes, etched around the corners with faint lines. "You knew him?"

"I was his CO for a while, a lot of years ago."

"Why didn't you say anything?"

"It took me a while to place him. His name wasn't Alex Dante back then."

It took a minute for his words to gel into meaning. "You mean Alex Dante isn't his real name?"

On one level it didn't surprise her; the agency was like that. Sometimes a new cover was needed, or an old operation

and all its personnel had to make a quick disappearance into
the realm of fiction. But even so, the knowledge that Alex had
never shared that with her made her feel oddly hurt. Hurt and
angry. As if the man she thought she knew didn't exist, and
the one she did know was someone else entirely. Someone
who'd never even trusted her with his name.

Her anger sputtered and died, dwindling into dark
tendrils of shame. Who was she to judge someone for their
secrets? She had her own secrets, her own lies. There was no
room to be angry with Alex. Not now.

"He was just a young pup back then," Mills said. "Cocky
as all hell. And a Marine, to boot. Told him he'd never make it
in the kind of work we were doing." He grinned at her,
looking like a singed jack-o-lantern. "He proved me wrong his
first time out. Brought home five men who'd been trapped
behind enemy lines — and took out the target on his way."

"Were you...who were you working for?"

"Oh, you know...no one glamorous. Nothing like you
folks are involved in now."

"So you weren't always a doctor, then."

He grinned again. "Oh, I was, I just couldn't stand the
boredom of private practice. Being in the Army was a hell of a
lot more fun, and when they found out I'd been a competitive
marksman during my undergrad days at Columbia, well, it got
even more fun."

She studied his face, wondering about the Alex he knew,
and how different he might have been from the Alex she knew.
Or rather, the Alex she had known.

"What was his name?" she asked. "You know. Before."
Somehow, not knowing his real name was like losing the last
piece of him she had.

Mills frowned. "I honestly don't remember."

Outside in the hallway, footsteps grew louder, then
stopped at the door behind her.

"Just the two people I was looking for."

Raeanne turned and looked up into Joe Richardson's angry dark eyes.

He'd changed since she'd seen him seven years ago. He was still tall and rangy, and probably still as fast on his feet. His hair had gone gray at the temples in the way men had that always made them look so stately and genteel. The heat in his gaze now was anything but.

"Yeah, I know," she said. "I'm under arrest on a dozen assorted charges. Just leave him out of it. I had a gun to his head."

Richardson released a long, impatient breath. "Raeanne, sit down."

"No, thanks, I'll stand. I'm either just leaving or about to get cuffed, so either way, it'll save us time."

"I said, sit down. That's an order."

She didn't have the energy to resist. Wordlessly, she pulled up the metal stool and sat.

"Where's Alex?" he asked.

She drew her brows together and scowled at him, knowing that if she opened her mouth to tell him to go to hell, she'd start crying.

"Cut the crap, Raeanne. I'm tired of playing games with you two. I've looked the other way while you and Dante played fast and loose with this operation because I trusted him, and I trusted you, but things are way out of control. Enough is enough. Either you tell me where he is, right now, or both of you will be spending your golden years in a cell."

"Try Heaven. Or maybe Hell. Who knows?"

"Damn it, Raeanne, I—"

"He's dead, Joe! Where the hell do you think he is?" The tears forced their way past her lashes and exploded onto her cheeks with a sob.

"He's not dead! You know it, and I know it. Now either you tell me where he is, or I will arrest you. Last chance."

She opened her mouth, but nothing came out. She had no

idea he could be such a cold, ruthless bastard.

"Are you saying Alex Dante's alive?" Mills asked.

Richardson tore his gaze from Raeanne and spun to face Mills. "Of course he's alive."

Raeanne's throat tightened with hope she was afraid to acknowledge. "But I saw him," she said instead. "He was dead before the fire even started."

"Well, it looks like you were mistaken. Both the fire department and our own people have searched the warehouse, inside and out. They found the bodies of several of Petrov's men, all of which have been positively ID'd, and other than those, the place was completely empty. Whatever happened to Alex Dante, he sure as hell did *not* die in that warehouse."

* * *

Alex Dante was not having a good day. He'd lost enough blood to make him woozy, which was starting to affect his driving. His right forearm was burning from the bullet wound that had stuck to his shirt, only to have the shirt ripped away...and then there was his knee. He was never more grateful to be driving a big old car with plenty of legroom and an automatic transmission. There was a very good chance he'd never walk on that knee again.

He leaned over to pop open the glove compartment and felt the car veer toward the sidewalk. He corrected, just in time to avoid the newspaper machine at the corner, and decided he'd better pull over. He managed to find a spot a few yards ahead, cut the engine, then grabbed the sat phone from the glove box.

A bead of sweat dripped into his eye as Raeanne's cell rang through to voice mail. Richardson's phone did the same.

McHugh answered from the safe house.

"Finally someone's home," Alex said.

"Dante, where the hell are you? Richardson is hot looking

for you."

"I'm about a half hour out. I had Petrov and the boy right in my sights, and I lost them. Have you heard from Raeanne?"

"No, but word has it she's at the hospital. Richardson's headed down there now—himself—to bring her in for a debrief, she and that ex-Delta guy she picked up. You'd better get your butt to the office if you want to have one left after today."

"Ex-Delta?" That was it! The missing piece that made the rest fall into place. Dan Mills—he knew the guy had looked familiar. But his name hadn't been Mills back then; it had been Flaherty. Kevin Flaherty. He'd been the biggest SOB. of a commanding officer Alex had ever had the misfortune to meet.

So who was he working for and why had they decided he needed a new identity?

Jesus, was he even a real doctor?

"If Richardson calls, tell him I'm on my way. I have a stop I have to make first."

* * *

Raeanne grabbed Richardson's arm. "Are you telling me they searched that warehouse, and Alex's body wasn't there?"

He stared at her a moment, the annoyance in his dark eyes giving way to sympathy. "You're serious—you think he died in that fire?"

She scrunched her nose to hold back the tears but it didn't work. "Please, Joe. Please just tell me he's alive."

"He's alive," Richardson said. "He'd called in a trace to that location, so we had to assume he went there. Believe me, I was as determined as you are to make sure that every single body had been pulled out of that warehouse, and that every single one had been positively ID'd. I assure you, none of them belonged to Alex Dante."

"So you don't actually know that he's alive. You just know

his body wasn't found at the scene."

Richardson didn't say anything for a few moments. "His car wasn't at the scene. So if he's gone, he's driving. Unless he was captured and they took his car. That's assuming he took his car in the first place."

She let out the breath that had been lodged in her throat. "Yes."

"So he's alive. You're certain you don't know where he might have gone?"

She looked up at the man who had been both her best hope of finding her son, and her biggest obstacle to doing so, and for the first time, she was too tired to maneuver. "Petrov escaped with Ryan just before the fire. I imagine he went after them."

"That's what I figured. I want you at the office first thing in the morning for a debrief. Unless you're being admitted?"

She shook her head. "I'm fine."

He turned to Mills. "Same goes for you. Have they told you when you're going to be discharged?"

"No, Sir. Not yet."

"Then sit tight. I'll send someone around to take your statement." He looked back down at Raeanne. "And you. Right now, you're the person who has the most information on the whereabouts of your son, of Alex Dante, and of Dmitriy Petrov. Eventually, Petrov is going to want to see you face to face. So as much as I dislike the idea—and I want you to know, Raeanne, that I *hate* the idea—I've decided it's in my best interest to reactivate you."

She gaped up at him, not believing what she was hearing. "Are you serious?"

"Yes, God help me. But there are going to be conditions. First, you will follow orders to the letter. I'll make you a member of the team, but I'm sure as hell not making you the commanding officer."

"Agreed," she said, the relief flowing off her in waves that she hoped weren't actually visible.

"Second, you will not go black on me when you decide you don't like the orders you're given."

"Agreed."

"And third," he said, softening his stance a bit, "I know you and Dante are close. I know you both feel a certain loyalty to each other. But it's getting in the way of this operation. From now on, your loyalty will lie first and foremost with your commanding officer, like it did back in the days when I knew I could trust you with my life and the lives of everyone else on the team. I know you're loyal enough and honorable enough to keep your word on this if you give it to me. And I'm asking you to give it to me, now."

Raeanne tried to smile, but she was sure it came out only a grimace. "You have my word. On one condition."

His brows shot up an inch. "You're giving me conditions?"

"Just one. You won't try to keep me strapped to some desk somewhere. I expect to be a real part of the team."

Richardson sighed. "If I could get Petrov to come visit you on your lunch break, I'd make you my new secretary. But I have a feeling it's going to be a little more complicated than that." The corner of his lip curled up in a wistful smile, and he held out his hand.

She took it and clasped it firmly, feeling all her ragged edges start to come together. Alex was alive. And she was going to be able to help find him and Ryan and bring them both home.

"Well, look who's here. Just like a high school reunion."

Raeanne turned to the door. "Alex!"

He stood in the doorway, propped up on one crutch, gritty with soot and two days' stubble and looking like the closest thing to heaven she'd ever seen. She leapt toward him and threw her arms around his neck, almost knocking the crutch out from under his arm.

His sharp intake of breath made her let go and leap back. Through the filth that covered most of his clothes, she saw the dark stain that stiffened the fabric of his torn sleeve. "You've been shot. Are you okay? You need to see a doctor."

He exhaled slowly, evidently in pain. "That would be one of the reasons I'm here."

"One of them?" Richardson asked.

Alex looked over at him, glanced briefly at Mills, then back. "One of them."

"Nice to see you again, too, Major," Mills said.

Raeanne glanced from one man to the other. A current of unease hummed between them, but she couldn't quite decipher it.

Richardson was still looking at Alex, but he wasn't smiling. "Dante, get yourself patched up. Raeanne, go wait for me outside."

"But I—"

"That's an order."

She cast a long glance at Alex, as if trying to reassure herself that he was actually there. She wanted to stay with him, wanted to find out what had happened, but Richardson was already heading through the door.

"You've got your orders," Alex said. He still wasn't smiling.

"You're okay? You're sure?"

"I'm sure."

She reached up and kissed him lightly on the cheek, but he didn't return the kiss. He didn't even move. When she looked up at him again, he turned and looked down at the floor, pointedly ignoring her.

With nothing else to do, she turned and followed Richardson into the hallway, wishing like hell she knew what was going on.

* * *

Alex pulled up a round swivel stool and sat, leaning his crutch against Mills' gurney. He hadn't been looking forward to confronting Mills on this kind of turf, but here they were. He adjusted his leg to take the pressure off his shredded knee and looked at the man he'd once wished fervently to meet in a dark alley, without witnesses. "Well. Don't you look like crap."

Mills raised what had once been an eyebrow before it had been singed off. The look in the narrowed eye beneath it said he wasn't looking forward to this, either. "Me? Another minute and you're going to slide right off that stool."

"May not take a whole minute." Alex let out a long, pent-up breath. What was done was done. "Thank you for taking care of her."

Mills barked a laugh. "I'd say no problem, except that it's turned into a very big problem."

An awkward silence fell, and Alex let it stretch on. He listened to the sounds of the hospital around him, nurses talking med-speak, pages coming over the PA system, rubber gurney wheels squelching over the tile floor. Hospitals had always made him uncomfortable, and so had the man on the gurney beside him.

"So are you going to say it, or should I?" Mills finally said.

Alex turned to face him, but remained silent.

"Okay, guess I go first. Long time no see, thought you were dead, yadda yadda. Your turn."

Alex wanted to smack the attitude out of him, but he kept his cool. He had other reasons for this conversation besides trading barbs. "Who're you working for?" he asked.

"No one. Other than the obvious, that is. Just a regular old Army doc tending sick people. You, on the other hand, are still having all the fun."

"Yeah, fun. Watching that creep snatch an innocent kid right out from under me. Twice. You know, it strikes me as odd how every time there's a mission that goes wrong, you show up."

Mills' dark eyes narrowed. "Are you accusing me of having something to do with the boy's kidnapping?"

"Me? Nah. Just thinking out loud. Reminiscing about the good old days." He adjusted himself on the stool, but comfort would be a long time coming. "Hey, how about that time in Nicaragua? That was a hoot, wasn't it? We had a damn good team, back before everyone got blown to hell. And now, here we are again. You, me, another operation going belly up... Small world, isn't it?"

Mills narrowed his eyes and glared at him. "I had nothing to do with that operation going bad, and you know it. The charges against me were dropped."

"Of course they were."

"I ought to kill you for even suggesting I'd do something to hurt a kid. Forget the idea of treason, do you actually think I'd let anything happen to Raeanne's kid?"

Something about the way he said it made Alex's blood go hot. "Got a reason to feel proprietary?"

"Got a reason to have a problem with it if I do?"

"Yeah. I do."

"Good. Then put that reason to good use and focus on finding the kid instead of badgering me. I'm one of the good guys, here."

Alex just glared at him.

"And when you're done, take your woman and kid home and help them try to feel safe again."

The words caught in his throat like broken glass. "He's not my kid."

Mills laughed, but his eyes were hot with disdain. "I always said you were too stupid to be in this business."

Alex felt the room tilt crazily around him. "When this is over, you'd better go somewhere far away, where I can't find you."

"If you can't find Leavenworth, you're stupider than I thought."

A nurse tapped him on the shoulder. "Major Dante? I've been looking all over for you. They're waiting for you in x-ray."

He grabbed his crutch and heaved himself off the stool. The room took an awkward twist, and he wanted desperately to slide back down. But he wanted Mills more. "If you want to live to *make it* to jail, you stay away from Raeanne."

"Now, you see?" Mills said, smiling his vague, half smile. "That's the kind of energy she needs from you, not that pathetic cold-shoulder crap, whatever that's all about. You've got a second chance, Dante, don't blow it."

Chapter Fifteen

The Main Office of the Counterintelligence Defense Agency was in a different building these days, but it was still in a medium rent district, still just a tad too shabby to look like anything out of the ordinary. Raeanne sat in the main waiting area across from the reception desk while the late afternoon sun streamed through the large front windows. It had always seemed odd to her that there would be an actual reception desk, like a law firm or a doctor's office, but there had always been some kind of legitimate business conducted there, not that she had any idea what the West End Supply Company supplied. Evidently their cover business was as covert as their real one.

These days, the desk was occupied by a cute blonde with round blue eyes and a short, flippy hairdo, who, if things were anything like they used to be, was probably a trained assassin with a fifth degree black belt and expert certification in every firearm in existence, even though her name plaque read, "Heidi Smith, Receptionist."

Several doors branched off the reception area, leading to the other departments deep in the heart of the Main Office. IT. Communications. Intel. Others. And, of course, Richardson's office, where he'd disappeared twenty minutes ago after offering her coffee and promptly forgetting about it.

She could have used the coffee, too. She crossed her legs and folded her hands around her knee in an attempt to contain her nervous jittering. Slow, easy breaths. It was ridiculous how she was cool as a cucumber in the field, but a blubbering mess when it came to meetings. Like a kid waiting outside the principal's office. She inhaled to a count of two and exhaled to four, coughed once, and tried to relax her shoulders when she realized they were scrunched up somewhere near her ears. Caffeine was actually the last thing she needed.

"Hi, I'm Heidi."

Raeanne jumped, then looked from the dainty, French-manicured hand that was stretched out toward her, up to the woman's round blue eyes, rimmed with white eye shadow.

"Sorry, didn't mean to startle you," Heidi said. Her smile was frosty pink, and she had entirely too many perfect, ice-white teeth.

Raeanne smiled back and took the hand that was stretched out toward her. "Raeanne Springfield."

"I know. Richardson's been on a rant for days about all the gray hairs you've been giving him."

"Uh-oh," Raeanne said, a little self-conscious about the state of her own teeth, which she wasn't sure she'd even brushed today. Or yesterday.

"He'll get over it. Word is you were one of the best field operatives the agency ever put out there."

"Uh…"

"Can I get you some coffee? It looks like Fearless Leader forgot. Which is typical."

"Uh, sure."

Heidi disappeared down the hallway and through one of the doors. That would be the supply office, then. They always kept the goodies in the supply office—coffee machine, microwave, fridge, gun racks. Raeanne made a mental note of it in case she needed to get her hands on another weapon on short notice.

Then she remembered the promise she made Richardson. She'd promised to be a good girl and do as she was told. She hoped she hadn't just sold her soul to the devil.

Heidi came back and handed her a paper cup of steaming black coffee. "I assumed you took it black," she said and sat down beside Raeanne with her own coffee, liberally creamed.

"Thanks," Raeanne said, taking the cup and putting it to her lips for a tentative sip. It was perfectly fresh, perfectly hot—it even burned her fingers a little through the cardboard—and again Raeanne was struck by how little things had changed. The agency had always had perfect coffee, no matter what time of day or night, as if there was some magnetic field around the coffeemaker. Or a bubbly receptionist with nothing else to do.

"Yeah, you field people are all black-coffee types," Heidi said. "Give me a grande low-fat sugar-free caramel mocha latte macchiato any day. That's why you won't catch me rappelling out of helicopters."

Raeanne paused. "Because they don't serve lattes on helicopters?"

"Well that, and because it's hell on the nails." Heidi gave a little grin. "And it's gotta be damned dangerous jumping out of a moving helicopter. You field people are all nuts, if you ask me." She blew on her coffee, her pouty pink lips forming a little O, then she took a sip.

"We're crazy?" Raeanne took another sip of her own. "Must be from all the undiluted caffeine."

"Seriously."

Raeanne took another sip and wondered if Richardson was planning on leaving her out here all afternoon. He didn't appear to be worried about her taking off. Or maybe that was what Heidi was for. There was no way she was as dumb as she looked. Not only wouldn't CODA have hired her, but she wouldn't have survived to adulthood.

"So. You've been assigned the odious task of being my keeper, huh?"

"No way. Hernandez drew that straw. I told Richardson if

he made me babysit you, I'd quit." She smiled at Raeanne, and Raeanne couldn't help but smile back.

"Figured I might do something that would ruin your manicure, huh?"

"Well, yeah... Ever get an acrylic nail yanked off wrestling with someone? Hurts like a bitch. Then you're trapped in the house 'til you can get an appointment to get it fixed."

Raeanne smiled into her cup. "So where's Hernandez? Getting his nails trimmed before the wrestling begins?"

"Nah, he's in 'a meeting' with the rest of the field team. Don't ask me what about; I don't know. I don't have top secret clearance, just regular secret. All I know is that it has to do with the op in DC." Her eyes lit up, and she halted Raeanne with her hand. "Ooh. Which reminds me. Don't go anywhere."

"Wouldn't dream of it."

Heidi stood and clicked to the desk in her strappy heels, which made her long showgirl legs seem even longer as they stretched from beneath her pinstripe mini. "I have your things for your trip."

"My trip?"

"Uh-huh. To DC Richardson said to pack three days' worth for you." From behind the reception desk, she lugged a three-piece set of brown luggage. She plopped the overnight bag on top of the larger suitcase and wheeled the whole thing closer. Raeanne made out the Louis Vuitton logo printed over every square inch.

"Loaning me your luggage?" Raeanne asked with a grin.

"Ha! If Only! I love Richardson, but he's —" She put her hand to her mouth as if to hide her whisper from unseen observers. "*Cheap.*"

Raeanne couldn't help laughing. "I was kidding. I just meant that they looked more your style than mine. Maybe we should trade."

Heidi's eyes bugged. "Me? I'm not going, I'm just the grunt slave labor who does all the *real* work around here for little or no monetary reward. I told you — you field people are a bunch of wackos." She put the suitcase on the floor and daintily crouched to open it. Inside were all the things Raeanne had taken from home, including the little red cocktail dress. Plus about three quarters of everything else she owned.

"Three days, huh? Wow, I forgot I even had those shoes." She grabbed the overnight bag and unzipped it, and found it filled with typical travel things. Wallet and passport, gum, crumpled tissues. "Eww, have these been used?"

Heidi's face lit up with a huge grin. Unsurprisingly, she had a perfect matched set of dimples. "Don't worry, I just crunched them up a little and ran the glue stick between them here and there. Looks real, though, huh? It's like, the perfect cover."

As someone with a cold? Raeanne smiled at her. "You have…quite a talent. You packed all this yourself?"

"Mm-hmm."

"Did you manage to conjure my Glock that McHugh and Briggs confiscated?"

"Inside compartment."

Raeanne did a double take, ending on Heidi's guileless, white-lined baby-blues. "You're kidding."

"Nope, honest. Inside compartment. You'll need to clean it, though; I don't do guns, I'm a vegetarian. Besides, it was mad filthy. Like, Shootout-at-the-OK-Corral filthy." She shuddered as if a goose had walked over her grave.

Raeanne unzipped the center compartment and pulled out her missing .40 caliber. "Well, whaddaya know."

"Your cover is a federal air marshal, which is how you're getting on the plane with the gun. All your paperwork and badge and whatnot's in the front zipper compartment. There's a video on deportment in the media room, all cued up and ready to go. Requisite frumpy blue suit's in the suitcase. You're a size eight, right?

"You mean we're taking a regular airline? Why aren't we

flying into Andrews?"

"You were supposed to. But you can't now that the Russians know you're coming."

The blood froze in Raeanne's veins. "What?"

Everything around her seemed to telescope in, until all she saw were those big, blue eyes. What the hell had happened? Petrov had sworn that if he so much as smelled Agency backup, Ryan was dead.

"What what?" Heidi asked. "Haven't you heard?"

"Evidently not. What haven't I heard?" The blood throbbing in her head was revving up her heartbeat, and she could feel the makings of another headache.

"The operation's been compromised. They think from inside."

* * *

Alex laid his head back against the pillow and stared up into the acoustic tiles of the hospital ceiling. He'd moved his hand too quickly, forgetting the IV catheter that was taped into his vein, and it was bleeding a little, turning the fluid in his IV line pink. It hurt, too. But nothing like his knee.

They said he'd never walk again without a cane. If he was lucky, that is, and the series of surgeries they'd proposed for the next two years were all successful.

So much for keeping his promise to Raeanne to get her boy back.

He sighed, resigned.

Maybe that was the lingering effect of anesthesia in his brain, because resignation wasn't something he normally gave in to that easily. Maybe he'd always suffered from an over-inflated ego. Maybe Raeanne had been right when she'd say he was the most stubborn thing God ever created, second only to the rock. Maybe he was just plain ornery and didn't like it when life told him no. Whatever it was, he was never one to just bow out gracefully when something needed doing.

So maybe this was a lesson. Maybe he should learn to resign himself to the idea that he wasn't superman. That he couldn't always make things work out the way he wanted them to.

The last seven years should have taught him that.

Hell, that was definitely the anesthetic in his brain. Yeah, so he'd hated the last seven years without Raeanne, so what? People got screwed every day. Whining about it had never been his style, and it sure as hell wasn't going to be now. Besides, she certainly hadn't spent her time whining over him. She'd been too busy having Petrov's ba—

A sick, sinking feeling slid through his slightly woozy stomach. Why on earth had she lied to everyone about that? It made no sense. None at all.

But a niggling little thought gnawed at the edges of his thoughts, nipping away at his confidence. What would he have done if she had told him? If she'd just up and told him that her cover had required her to sleep with Petrov, and that she'd gotten pregnant? And that she was going to go through with it? That she was going to give up her career with CODA—God knows you couldn't take a baby into the field— give up everything she knew and everything she was and everything she had always wanted? What then?

The niggling little thought grew fangs.

He wanted, God he really wanted, to say that it would have made no difference to him. But would it have?

What would he have said? Hell, did he even know what he'd say right now?

Yes. Yes, he did. The last seven years had been the emptiest, most meaningless years of his life. If he could have her right now, have her walk through that door and tell him she wanted to stay with him forever, he would damn well let her—babies, secrets, and everything else be damned. He wanted her, damn him. Petrov's kid and all.

He felt the air leave his lungs in a soft exhalation of relief. Or maybe it was renewed resolve. Mills was right, the bastard. He still had a chance. And this time, he wasn't going to blow it.

But first, he had to get the hell out of this hospital.

Yeah, right. First he had to get the hell out of this bed.

He glanced at the door, and through the narrow window that ran the length of it, he saw that he still had company. Two uniformed MPs with M-16s, standing guard. Not agency issue, either. Not guys he knew.

Some days, it just wasn't worth getting out of bed.

* * *

"What do you mean the op's been compromised?" Raeanne couldn't quite grasp what Heidi was saying. She heard the words clearly enough, but her brain refused to accept them. It dawned on her that she'd never known the details of the operation; she'd been so focused on her own myopic goal of getting Ryan back. "Is my son safe?"

"Yep. He's in DC But they can't go in and get him until they're ready to move on the rest of the operation, and those are the plans they had to change."

"To what? What are they planning to do?"

"I have no idea. I told you, I don't have TS clearance."

Raeanne took a breath to steady her patience. "Tell me who does know."

"Who knows what?" Richardson asked. He stepped out of the hallway and handed Raeanne a paper cup. Her overdue cup of coffee. It was cold.

"The status of the operation. Of my son." Raeanne stood. "Heidi tells me Petrov knows you're coming."

"Why don't you follow me," he said. Raeanne tried to read what he knew through his eyes, but they were closed tight against her tired, unpracticed radar. "I was just coming to ask you to debrief the field team. We're going over that information right now."

A little surprised not to hear him argue, she followed him down the hall. For a second, her blood raced in anticipation — or fear, she wasn't sure which — and she wished she'd remembered to grab the overnight bag containing her .40 caliber.

She followed him through one of the doorways, which opened into a large conference room. A dozen people looked up at her from their seats around the oval table in the center. On the far wall, a screen revealed a series of grainy satellite photos, real-time recon shots of the target. What she saw was a boat, more specifically, a yacht. Petrov's yacht, the *Lady Rake*.

It was like stepping back in time. She'd spent a lot of time aboard that yacht during December Ice. Small, by luxury standards, only 155 feet, but she was a gorgeous vessel, with a catamaran, two jet skis, and a powerboat for zipping back and forth to shore. She was exquisitely appointed, all teak and brass, with artwork and furnishings from all over the world and a gorgeous open flybridge where Raeanne had spent many sunny afternoons sipping frozen margaritas and watching the lazy Caribbean coastlines drift by.

She didn't need a close up to recognize that flybridge now, or the small boy curled up on the chaise. Her heart tripped in her chest and her throat tightened. He was curled on his side, one arm pillowed under his head, the other draped bonelessly over the edge, sound asleep. Her baby. Was it only ten hours ago that she'd seen him? Stood close enough to touch him? She should have just smashed that damned window and been done with it...

On a chair beside him, a man sat reading a newspaper with an assault rifle lying casually across his knees.

The shot advanced to the next in the series. The yacht had moved, turned almost away from her now so that only the edge of the lounge chair was visible from behind the starboard side of the pilothouse. The arm hanging over the edge of the chaise had moved, too.

He was awake.

"Where are they?" she asked, trying to keep her voice neutral.

"About four miles off the coast of Maryland," Richardson answered.

Raeanne looked away from the screen to the faces staring back at her. No one spoke. They sat, watching her, waiting silently for whatever it was they expected her to say.

Some of them were familiar, people she'd worked with, some she'd even considered friends before Abe King had shown up one Sunday evening with her belongings in a cardboard box and told not to come in the next morning. She'd been told not to contact them. None of them had contacted her.

She suddenly wondered what exactly they'd been told. None of them had jumped out of their chairs to greet her.

She looked them each in the eye, wondering what they were thinking. Four of them were strangers, two men, two women. The others she knew: Clay Henderson, the demolitions expert. Jimmy Hernandez, her supposed babysitter. The two Bobs, Russell and O'Rourke, both ex-CIA. Rosa Tate. Rosa looked exactly the same, dark and mysterious, and she was gazing at Raeanne with genuine, unmasked sympathy.

If she had ever thought Abe King was a total hardcore bastard, it was now.

"Raeanne, meet the rest of your team," Richardson said. "Matthew and Katrina Martin, Kyra Powell, Connor Frey. You know the rest."

The four strangers around the table nodded politely, but Raeanne felt their undisguised disapproval. She couldn't blame them, really. God knows what Abe had said about her and her disappearing act all those years ago. And worse, about her chaotic re-entry into their disciplined, well-ordered world.

Jimmy Hernandez and Bob O'Rourke finally smiled. And

Rosa got out of her seat and came around the table.

"Welcome back, girl," she whispered and wrapped Raeanne in a tight hug.

But over Rosa's shoulder, Raeanne saw Bob Russell and Clay Henderson watching her silently, the way a cat watches a mouse.

"Raeanne, if you'd like to take a seat, we'll catch you up on the details." Richardson took an empty chair and motioned for her to take the one beside him. She did. She discovered that she was still holding two cups of cold coffee.

"I'd like to know how the operation was compromised," she said.

The facial expressions of the team ranged from disbelief to confusion to outright anger.

"Maybe we should be asking you that," Clay said, leaning his linebacker bulk forward over the table. "Seems your boy Mills had some less than exemplary comments in his files. Did you know he was tried for espionage and treason about ten years ago?"

Raeanne glanced around the room, trying to gauge everyone's reaction. No one looked as if Clay's words were a surprise. Her heart sank into her chest. "You're not suggesting that Dan Mills had something to do with the operation being compromised," she said, trying to sound more certain of herself than she was.

"I'm not suggesting anything," Clay said, "Just wondering if you'd bothered to do any checking up on the people you've been leaking information to."

"Shut up, Henderson," Bob-O said from the other side of the table. "In three days, she and Alex located and took out Petrov's main warehouse, which you've been trying to locate for three months."

"And it's a lot easier when you're fraternizing with the enemy, now isn't it?"

"That's enough," Richardson said quietly.

Raeanne took a sip of cold coffee. So taking out the warehouse had been an objective until now? Nice of Richardson to tell her. "I suspect people have their own opinions about things, and I suppose that's fair. But if anyone truly believes that Dan Mills had anything to do with compromising this mission, he or she is misinformed."

No one answered. No one looked at her. In fact, everyone worked painfully hard to make sure they were engrossed in something going on in another direction.

She let out a heavy sigh. Her head was pounding, and she was feeling lightheaded in the extreme. "Let's just get on with it."

Richardson stood and began recapping the details of the warehouse incident for the team. She tried to focus on his words, but all she could think of was Dan Mills, and how he'd just happened to appear at the right place at the right time.

* * *

With a heavy sigh, Raeanne lay her sore body back into the bed she and Alex had made love in the night before. The pillows still smelled of him, the sheets still held the scent of their passion. The clock beside her glowed 11:15 p.m., not terribly late, but given the day's events, late enough. She'd been "assigned" to the Hyacinth Street apartment until the next day, when the team would scatter on its way to DC. Except for Alex. Alex was still in the hospital, and when he was discharged tomorrow, he was officially on desk duty, assisting the accounting people, which was as close to the field as Richardson was going to let him get. By the time he was up and walking, the operation would be completed, one way or another. Either she'd have gotten Ryan back and would be on her way to safety, or…she wouldn't.

And either way, it looked as if her days with Alex Dante were over.

Or whatever his name was.

She turned over and pulled the second pillow closer. The scent of him was so alive, so present, that it was hard for her to believe she'd probably never see him again. He'd made his thoughts on that perfectly clear when he'd shown up in the ER earlier. The way he'd looked at her, she'd have thought he was ready to flay her alive. It certainly hadn't been the joyous homecoming she'd imagined. What had happened? Was it because she'd shown up at the warehouse?

Never mind. He was alive. That was more than she'd hoped for.

But she still couldn't help but wonder about his name.

It didn't matter. There was nothing between them anymore, anyway.

Except for Ryan. Whoever Alex Dante had been born, whatever he felt for her now after the mess she'd made of everything, he still had a right to know he had a son. And Ryan should have a father. Should have had one all along.

The dead man's cell phone twittered from the bedside table.

Raeanne stared at it as a cold sweat broke out over her skin. Richardson had made her keep it "in case Petrov called." In case. As if there had been any doubt.

It twittered again and she took a deep breath, sat up, and picked up the phone. Flipped it open. Put it to her ear as gingerly as a sliver of broken glass.

"What," she said, barely audibly.

"Ah, my dear, why the dejection? I thought after your very colorful destruction of my warehouse, that you'd be more upbeat."

"Where's my son?"

Petrov sighed. "Perhaps if your Guardian Angel had not disobeyed my orders and had come alone, as I'd requested, you would be sitting at home with your little boy as we speak. I had every intention of letting the boy go. Now? Who knows."

"What do you want, Petrov? Me? You want revenge? Then take it. My life for my son's. Name the place."

"Ah, my beloved, it's no longer quite that simple. Who is going to pay for my warehouse? For all my inventory? Your interference has cost me millions, my beloved. *Millions.* And that's not even taking into account the value I had placed on finally having my revenge on Alex Dante. So you see, you owe me much more than just your pitiful little life. Especially when you add the boy into the bargain."

"Then what do you want?"

"Sadly, I shall never have what I want. So the question then becomes, what will I settle for instead? Watching your face as you lose everything you've ever loved? As I did?"

Her hand tightened around the phone, as if it were Petrov's throat.

The sound of the front door *snicking* shut brought her head around in the dark.

"I've decided I'd rather not wait until Wednesday to meet you," he said.

She strained to hear another sound in the apartment. With her free hand, she reached silently under her pillow for her Glock. Slowly, careful not to squeak the bedsprings, she sat up and got to her feet.

"Where?" she breathed.

"Aboard my yacht. Surely you remember the Lady Rake? It will give us the opportunity to get reacquainted. I'll send a boat around to collect you from the Chesapeake Marina. I use slip B-33. Be there at six p.m. We can enjoy the sunset over dinner on the deck, the way we used to."

"Fine." She edged her way to the door and kept her back to the wall.

"Oh, and don't forget to wear something red. How I loved you in red."

She snapped the phone shut and tossed it onto the bed. The air was cool against the bare skin of her thighs below the tank top and panties she'd gone to bed in, but she ignored the goose bumps that peppered her skin. A light came on down the hall. Keys jingled onto a tabletop, something thumped into the kitchen, banged into a table leg, and swore colorfully.

She sighed and lowered her weapon, trying to contain the wash of relief and excitement at hearing that voice. At the doorway to the kitchen, she flipped on the safety. She wanted to run to him and cry into his shoulder, but she didn't.

Not after the way he'd acted at the hospital.

"Hi, Alex," she said instead, as coolly as she could with her heart lunging against her ribs in response to Petrov's threats and tears pressing against the backs of her eyes.

He jumped, spun around, banged a crutch into the refrigerator, and dropped his soda.

Raeanne couldn't help the wide smile that spread across her face. He could be as mad as he wanted with her, but he was alive, and he was here, and she knew that whatever became of them, he would still be there for Ryan.

"God damn it, you scared the hell out of me. What are you doing here?" It was clear he didn't know whether to gape at her or try to stop the river of soda pouring over his foot. His eyes settled somewhere around the patch of bare midriff below the bottom edge of her tank top.

She put her weapon down on the table and reached for the dish towel by the sink. "Let me get that. Sit down."

He sat.

She knelt and began soaking up soda. "What are you doing here? You're not supposed to be out of the hospital until tomorrow."

"I left. And you?"

"Richardson told me to stay here until we leave for DC in the morning."

"Funny. He didn't mention that to me."

She raised her eyes to his. "Did you talk to him?"

"I just left him."

Rae tossed the towel into the sink and pulled out a chair across from Alex's leg, stretched out like a padded, strapped-up blue log in its immobilizer. "Are you supposed to be up? Is your leg okay?"

"It's good enough. I had to get out of there, MPs or no."

"MPs?"

He studied her eyes a moment, as if evaluating the sincerity of her response.

"MPs, Alex?"

"Yeah. You know, guys in camo with M-16s and little arm bands with the letters *MP* on them? Someone had them posted outside my door."

"Who? Richardson? Why would he post guards?"

"He didn't. When I got to the office and told him I wasn't happy about it, he was as surprised as I was."

Raeanne looked at him, studied his harsh features sharpened by lack of sleep, the circles under his bloodshot green eyes, the deep vertical crease between his dark brows. Two days' growth stubbled his jaw, and for the first time since she'd known him, she noticed the glints of silver in the sides of his cropped hair. "Then who?

The anger-muscle clenched in his jaw. "Seen Mills lately?"

"No, not since we saw him at the ER earlier." A hard feeling settled in the pit of her stomach. "You don't think he had anything to do with it, do you?"

"I don't know. But I don't trust him."

"Why not?"

"I just don't."

"Does it have anything to do with the animosity between you?"

He looked up at her, searching her face. "What do you mean?"

"I mean the looks you two were exchanging in the ER."

Alex let out a long, deep breath, and it made Raeanne tired to watch it. Whatever it was that was between him and

Mills, it wasn't something she wanted to think about. Mills had helped her, unquestioningly, and without reservation, risking his own life to help her rescue Ryan and Alex. There was no way she'd believe he was responsible for compromising the operation. Besides, word from Heidi was that the op was compromised from the inside, and from the discussion earlier at the office, it was clear that Mills was no insider.

"The looks we were exchanging in the ER had nothing to do with this operation," Alex said.

"No. I suppose they were old baggage from when you two worked together."

"He told you about that?"

"Some of it. Not much." She was dying to say the rest, that he'd also told her about Alex's new name, but she couldn't get the words past the lump in her throat.

Alex smiled. "Guess the cat's out of the bag then. Dan Mills is the biggest jerk I've ever met."

"Funny. He had only the nicest things to say about you."

Alex gave a wry snort of amusement. "I'll bet."

Rae smiled at him. "Guess we all make mistakes."

He smiled back at her, but it was a melancholy smile, as if afraid to commit itself to being happy. "The question is, are we going to keep making them?"

She sat quietly, watching him, watching those vivid, green eyes, and seeing everything she'd ever felt for him looking back out at her. "I don't want to keep making them," she said.

"Neither do I."

She stood and went to him, took his hands in hers, lifted him. He stood, watching her, as if waiting for her to change her mind, but she didn't. She couldn't. Not when he looked at her like that, his green eyes tearing into her with heat and hunger and fear and longing of their own. And questions. So many questions.

The questions remained unasked. Questions could wait. Healing couldn't.

They came together softly, quietly, with a gentle insistence that couldn't be stemmed, like the slow lapping of the incoming tide. Rae kissed him all the way into the room where they'd slept the night before, pressed him back into the rumpled sheets that still smelled of their last joining, and careful of his injuries, made love to him until sleep took them both.

Chapter Sixteen

Raeanne's stomach was churning—nerves, hunger, too much coffee—and she wished she'd eaten the cardboard airport breakfast, after all. The tactical team had assembled around the conference table reviewing the last minute details. On one wall of the nondescript room near Maryland's Chesapeake Marina, just before noon, Richardson's laptop projected satellite photos of the marina and the surrounding waters.

"We have a Mark V combat boat in range and a Nighthawk chopper setting up," he said. "The boat has made visual contact with Petrov's yacht about three miles off shore, and they're standing by to make sure it doesn't leave its current location without our knowledge."

"Who's on the boat?" Raeanne asked.

"Henderson, Tate, and Connor Frey, the new kid from NSW. Underwater demolitions expert. He and Henderson will be going down to wire the yacht from below. Tate has her spotter scope trained on the yacht, but so far, there's been no movement. Her shotgun mikes have picked up a number of voices inside speaking Russian. A number of individuals are unknown, but we've confirmed voice IDs on Petrov and several of his known lieutenants."

Raeanne let out a deep breath, feeling more confident by the minute. One of the agency's directional shotgun mikes could pick up a whispered conversation a football field away.

With the world's most sophisticated equipment, and Rosa Tate, one of the world's best acoustical engineers at the keyboard to filter out the sounds of water and wind, they might as well be right there on the deck.

"And Ryan?"

"Tate has confirmed that one voice is definitely that of a child."

Raeanne's heart flipped in her chest.

"This is a schematic of the yacht," Richardson went on, pressing a key on his laptop and advancing to the next slide. "She's called the Lady Rake, home port Monaco. She's 155 feet long, with six staterooms and a master suite. There's an enclosed bridge, with an open flybridge at the stern, plus two smaller decks, fore and aft. The first is in the bow, between the second and third levels. Contains patio furniture, a bar, that sort of thing. The other's in the stern, the lowest level. It's unfurnished and houses docking facilities for her leisure craft. It's here we'll insert the assault team."

"Can I get the chopper close enough without cutting down her antennas?" Bob O'Rourke asked. He was going to be flying the Nighthawk, which made Raeanne rest just a shade easier. Bob-O could drop a man onto a rubber raft in a hurricane. Drunk. She'd seen him do it.

"That's a negative. And she may very well be on the move, so you'll have to keep moving with her." Richardson glanced around the table for further questions, then continued. "She carries with her a power boat, a catamaran, and two jet skis. She has crew quarters for five, but she's currently being crewed by Syndicate personnel, so you don't have to worry about civilians. Other than the boy, of course."

"And Raeanne," Clay Henderson said.

Raeanne turned to him, but he wouldn't look at her, the bastard.

Richardson spoke up. "Raeanne is to be considered a full member of this team, with all the rights and responsibilities that entails. May I continue?"

Clay said nothing else. Neither did anyone.

"Raeanne will be on the boat when you get there. Petrov contacted her yesterday and she's to meet his agents at the Chesapeake Marina at eighteen hundred hours. His objective is to get her aboard the yacht, where we believe he will kill the boy, and then Raeanne, in revenge for her actions during December Ice, which you've all been briefed on. You are to consider both Raeanne and the boy in lethal danger. Getting them out is the primary objective.

"Team Alpha, in the assault boat, will send a diver to set the explosives under the yacht after sunset, which is about nineteen hundred hours, when visibility will be poor and they can get close without being seen. Team Bravo, in the chopper—you'll move in at twenty-two hundred. Four of you will drop onto the aft deck, or wherever you can find a position. Your first priority is to find and extract the boy. Your second priority is to find and extract Raeanne. Then, once they're both out, you hightail it out of there. Once you're out, Alpha Team will detonate the vessel."

Raeanne gazed up at the blueprints, feeling the enormity of the task ahead pressing down on her. It all sounded so easy. Fly in, rappel down, grab Ryan, and go. But she knew it would be like every other mission she'd ever worked. Too dangerous, too sensitive, too hard to contain.

"But they're not going to make it easy for you," Richardson continued. "Tate has printed twelve distinct voices, not including the boy, and one questionable. That means at least twelve, possibly thirteen hostiles, perhaps more. Presumably these will all be armed personnel."

"Great," she said. "So they're lifting my son out by helicopter?"

"Correct," Richardson answered.

"While the yacht may be moving?"

"Correct."

Raeanne frowned. "Bob-O, you feel confident you can do that?"

"Piece of cake. I'd suggest keeping someone back in case he panics and needs to be carried up."

"Done," Richardson agreed. "After that, once we've got the boy and Raeanne out of range, Henderson and James will detonate the yacht."

"And Petrov?"

Richardson looked over at Raeanne. "On paper, the objective is kill-or-capture."

"And what about not on paper?" she asked.

Richardson smiled. "There are no instructions to airlift the bastard out of the water."

* * *

Alex leaned back in his chair and tossed the last invoice into the out-box for accounting. His knee was killing him. Even so, there was nothing quite as maddening to him as being grounded. Even as a kid he'd hated being grounded. Maybe that was where he's gotten his start in covert operations. There wasn't a bedroom window in existence that could keep him in if he felt he had somewhere else to be.

He wondered if Raeanne's son was a hellion, or—he was going to say 'more like his mother,' but he was pretty sure she'd been a hellion, herself. His next thought ran automatically to the boy's father, but the sick, dark feeling that came with it made him push the whole topic aside. They'd wasted seven years apart, seven years that they could never get back. The boy's father didn't matter. Raeanne's past didn't matter.

The present mattered. Raeanne and the boy mattered. That was all.

He closed the accounting program and grabbed his crutch—one was easier to move around on than two—then hobbled out of Richardson's office and down the hall to the supply room for more coffee. It was eerie how empty the place seemed when Richardson wasn't there. The support staff was still there, of course, but they kept mostly to the IT center or the administrative offices, "the sweatshop," as they lovingly put it, down the hall and out of sight of anyone that may be in the office for other reasons. Out front here, it was just Heidi, the Receptionist from Hell, and him, the unrepentant sinner damned to suffer her torment for all eternity, or for the duration of the operation, whichever came first.

It sure as hell was starting to feel like eternity. Heidi was driving him nuts. If she straightened up his desk or offered him coffee one more time, he was going to throw her out the window. He didn't know how Richardson could stand her. Granted, the man had always liked them long, blonde, and stupid, but there wasn't a woman long enough or blonde enough to make up for being that...vapid. The woman was a walking blonde joke.

"Oh, here, I told you not to get up, you bad boy. Let me get that for you."

Slim, perfectly artificial Heidi squeezed in between him and the coffee machine and took the mug from his hand.

He bit back his temper and smiled. "No, really. I can manage."

"Of course you can manage, I mean, duh, you're a field operative. You could probably manage to snap my neck like a straw while you're at it, and not even spill any. But that's just the reason why you shouldn't have to." She turned to face him, held out his cup, but didn't let it go.

"Excuse me?"

She was standing way too close for social correctness, and her big blue eyes were gazing up at him, meaningfully. Very meaningfully. They had little tan rings around the pupils, and her lashes were way too black. "Because if you killed the receptionist, Richardson would have a fit, and then you'd have to work the comm desk for the op. And I'm not supposed to tell you where they are, so then he'd kill *me*. Better for everyone if you just let me run for your coffee." She raised up on her toes and for a minute, it seemed like she was going to kiss him.

Uh, yeah. Like that.

Alex darted back, Heidi fell forward, and the coffee burned a path down his shirt and pants like hellfire.

"Oh my God! I am so sorry!"

"Ah, hell!" Alex pulled the burning wet fabric away from the sensitive skin of his lower abdomen and then reached for the legs of his trousers.

"Are you okay?" Heidi asked, grabbing a stack of paper napkins off the counter and blotting the shirt back against his burned flesh.

"Ah! All right, that's fine, thanks," Alex said, grabbing her wrists and pushing her as far away as his arms could reach. "Thank you. Really. Thank you."

"I'm so sorry, Alex. I feel terrible. Here, let me get you another cup of coffee."

"Uh, no, that's fine. Really. I'm about coffeed out." He hobbled toward the closet, with Heidi somehow still attached and dabbing at his shirt. "Uh, excuse me a minute while I grab some fresh clothes."

"Oh," she said, looking up at him, biting her frosty-pink bottom lip. "We don't keep them there anymore. I put them back in IT. This closet was overflowing with junk."

"Spare clothes in the supply closet are considered junk?"

"Yeah, and the riot gear, too. That's all back in IT now."

Alex pressed past her and opened the closet. It was neat, he'd give her that. But it was also nearly empty, save for paper goods and miscellaneous...junk.

She reached in and pulled out a stack of napkins. "Here. You dry off and I'll go get you some dry clothes."

"No really, I can..."

"Khaki, camo or black?"

Alex sighed and took the napkins. Sometimes it just wasn't worth the fight. "Whatever is fine."

"Be back in two seconds." She smiled a contrite smile and backed out of the supply room.

Alex sighed again. It just wasn't worth it. Not even for those legs. He'd have to get Richardson on the Victoria's Secret mailing list and have him hire an old, matronly secretary, like they always used to have. One who stayed at her desk and didn't follow him around and...

It hit him all at once, how big of an idiot he was. She was spying on him. That lying bastard Richardson set her to spy on him to make sure he wasn't making any plans to jump back into the fray.

Alex let his eyes wander to the door. The one she'd closed behind her. No one ever closed the supply room door.

So what was going on elsewhere in the office that was so important, that she had to come up with this stupid diversion to keep him here?

The comm desk. She'd said she was working it for the operation. There must be something going on that she wasn't supposed to let him know about.

He was going to kill Richardson when he got back.

He opened the door silently, peered out, and very softly, slowly, crutched to the corner of the hallway where the reception area opened out. He heard her talking, on the phone, it sounded like. He didn't put his head out, he knew she'd probably be watching for him. Instead, he pressed himself as close to the wall as he could and strained to listen.

She was speaking quietly, but not quietly enough. He could just make out the distinct, rough consonants.

She was speaking Russian.

"*Yes, that's affirmative. The operation is a go. At sundown, a Mark V combat boat will insert two underwater demolitions personnel to wire the yacht, then at twenty-two hundred, a*

Nighthawk helicopter will drop an assault team to extract the boy and the woman. They plan to detonate the yacht with Petrov and whoever is with him still aboard... Yes, that's correct. Yes. Yes."

Alex's blood ran like ice. Whoever she was talking to, it wasn't Richardson. And whatever she was spying on him for, it wasn't his obedience to desk duty.

He pulled his weapon and from the nylon shoulder holster he'd taken to wearing now that he needed his hands free for his crutches, and leaned the crutch against the wall. With a deep indrawn breath for support, stepped around the corner on his good leg.

He knew it was a precarious position, and if she'd been waiting for him, she could have knocked him down with one hot-pink fingernail. But she wasn't waiting for him.

She was behind the reception desk, facing out into the room, her back to the hallway. She was digging through drawers, looking for something, frantic, from the look of her.

Whatever it was she was looking for in her desk drawers, it certainly wasn't a set of khakis for him.

She was only three steps away, but they were the most agonizing three steps he'd ever taken on that knee.

He caught her in a headlock and pressed the muzzle of his Smith to her right temple. "Say goodbye, Sweetheart."

She froze. "Yes," she said, still in Russian, trying to glance back at him out of the corner of her round, blue eye. There was caution there, but no fear. "I have to go."

Slowly, she hung up the phone.

"Whatever you're thinking of doing, forget about it," Alex said. "I have no qualms at all about shooting a woman. Especially a Russian spy who has the balls to commit treason right in my own office."

"Alex, it's not how it looks."

"Of course it's not." He took his arm from around her neck and patted her down. It didn't take much; her skirt was microscopic and her neckline plunged to her knees. There wasn't much area to conceal a weapon, except maybe high on her thigh—

Yep, right there. He pulled the little snub nose .38, warm from its resting place between said thighs, out of its holster.

"Honest, Alex, it's not how it looks. I'm not a Russian spy."

He tucked the little gun into the small of his back, then pressed his big .45 between her shoulder blades. Hard. "Clasp your hands behind your head and walk."

She obeyed him, clasping her hands behind her head and stepping forward slowly. "Please Alex, you have to let me make another call. The team is in danger."

"No kidding. Now that you've just told Petrov they're on their way to blow him up."

"No, that's not it at all. I don't work for Petrov."

"Then who do you work for?"

"I can't tell you that. But I swear to you, we're on the same side."

He twisted his hand into her hair at the back of her head and pushed her into the hallway, down toward the last door. It was marked "Janitor."

The agency didn't employ a janitor.

He shoved her into the darkened room, not pausing to turn on a light. Around them, shelves of janitorial supplies looked as natural as could be. But they weren't janitorial supplies.

The closet at the other end of the room wasn't a closet, either.

It did a good impression of one, at first, because inside, it was small and dark. But at the back, there was another door.

Alex had to let go of Heidi's hair. "If you move a muscle I will shoot you in the head. Is that clear?"

"I won't move. Please, Alex, you have to listen to me."

Alex finished entering the alphanumeric code and the lock *snicked* open. He grabbed her hair again and pushed her through the door.

The room that opened before them was dim and utilitarian. Several doors branched off to interrogation rooms. To the left was the security area, separated by barred doors on a sliding mechanism, like those found at a maximum-security prison.

Alex entered the code and the first barred door slid open. He shoved Heidi ahead of him, his pulse racing at his temples. If Raeanne were hurt because of this woman's treason, there would be nothing left of her to stand trial.

When the door clanged shut behind them, he entered the second code. The door ahead of them slid open, leading into a wide hallway, the agency's detention facility.

Surveillance cameras lined the ceiling. Four steel doors opened off the hallway, marked with numbers 1-4, each fitted with 4x4-inch viewing windows, covered with small steel shutters that opened from the hall, allowing the guards to look in on the prisoners. There were no guards now, though.

The first door on the left, number one, was closed. The other three yawned open, only darkness within.

Alex pushed Heidi into the last door on the right and slammed the steel door. The lock automatically engaged with the clang of metal slamming home.

He opened the viewing window and pressed the intercom. "Who did you call in Petrov's organization?" His knee was on fire, and his vision was starting to gray out at the edges. But there was no way he was going to pass out in here.

Heidi's composure was finally starting to crack. "Alex, listen to me. The team is in danger. I was calling one of my contacts."

Alex turned to her. "In Russian? I hate to tell you this, but in this light, the Russians look like the bad guys."

"We have a mole inside Petrov's organization. They can make sure Petrov gets whatever misinformation you want. All you have to do is let me call them back."

"Hmm. Moles. Seem to be a problem for everyone, these days. Well, at least they like small dark places. You should be perfectly comfortable down here for a few days." Alex gazed at her big blue eyes, gone wide now with the realization that she was in deep trouble. But still not panicking. Right now, those eyes were burning with a cold, hard intelligence that actually unnerved him. He wondered how he'd ever thought she was stupid.

Damn Richardson for a fool.

"At least I feel better about why this mission went to hell. You were the one who put all that bogus information into Raeanne's dossier, weren't you?"

"No, I didn't change anything, I only took out the information about her son."

"Brave woman, dropping an innocent kid into the hands of a nut like Petrov."

"That was an accident. I never meant to endanger her or her little boy, I swear. I took some of the information out to copy it, and Richardson came snooping around my desk like he always does and just took Raeanne's folder without asking me. By the time he'd read it and contacted the team and begun planning the operation, it was too late to put anything back, he would have noticed it and wondered what I was doing."

"Like I'm wondering right now?"

"Honest, I swear I had no intention of taking that information out of the files for good. I was just copying it and was going to put it back. Getting Raeanne's son involved was not part of the operation. It was an accident."

Alex glared at her, feeling his leg trembling beneath him. She was almost in tears, but Alex didn't believe those, either.

"Please, you have to let me call my contacts. Otherwise, the whole team is doomed."

"Who do you work for?"

"I can't tell you that."

"Then enjoy your stay."

He started to close the viewing window, but gave her a split second to reconsider.

"Wait!" she said.

He pulled it open again. He hoped she'd be quick about it. Much longer and he'd be crawling out.

"I'll tell you who I work for, but you have to promise to back me up at my trial, because if I tell you, I will be tried for treason."

"I doubt terrorists are much concerned with trials. They'll probably just shoot you. After raping you repeatedly. That is, if I don't lose my patience and shoot you first."

"I don't work for the Ice Syndicate." She took a deep breath and gazed directly into his eyes. "I work for the CIA."

Alex laughed. "Oh yeah? Where, the Moscow office?"

"No, I told you, that was one of my contacts in Petrov's syndicate. It's a long story. But you're in no shape to stand there and listen to the whole thing. Please, sit down before you fall down. And please, please let me call my contact in Washington and have them send a fixer team out to salvage the agency's operation. Otherwise, they're as good as dead."

Alex felt the blood rise in his temples, pounding with the anger that was threatening to burst the bounds of his control. It scared him. He never let his self-control slip like this. "You had better hope that nothing happens to anyone from this office, because I'm the only one who knows you're in here. If we all die in the field, then...well, you'll be in for a long, hungry stay."

He slammed the viewing window shut, and it was all he could do not to punch the steel door.

CIA, his ass. If he had a dime for every two-bit hood who claimed to work for the CIA...

He stepped across the hall to the other cell and entered the code. The lock disengaged and Alex pulled the door open. "Come on. I've got a couple of questions for you."

Dan Mills stood up and looked at him with distrust in his

dark, hawk-like eyes, but nonetheless, followed him out of the cell, through the cage and back to Alex's office.

* * *

Raeanne stood in the ladies' room of the cheap motel they'd stationed themselves in, and dabbed the tissue under her lip, trying to get the red lipstick the same on both sides of her mouth. God, she hated wearing makeup. She looked like a corpse at a wake. She sighed with frustration and went over her bottom lip again. Now she looked like the corpse of a clown.

A tap on the door, and Richardson walked in. "Almost ready?"

"Yeah, I guess so. I look ridiculous."

"You look gorgeous." He reached out to give her shoulder a reassuring squeeze, then held out his hand, palm up.

"Uh, there's really not much room in here for dancing," Raeanne said.

"Look again."

She looked closer and saw it, nestled in his palm, almost lost in the creases of his skin. It looked like a tiny pink seashell, no bigger than an eyeglass screw.

"What is that?"

"That's your comm device. Be very gentle with it. It's worth about 1.5 mil."

"Yikes." She picked it up and held it up to her eyes. "Where does it go?"

"In your ear. It will slide down into the ear canal a short distance and be completely invisible, while enabling you to hear and speak to us."

She tried not to make a face, but she couldn't help it. "How do I get it out?"

"Gentle suction with a bulb syringe, nothing painful. You'll be fine. Believe me, I'm more worried about it than you.

It's on loan to me from a buddy of mine in Cambridge, part of a new project he's working on for the Department of Defense. I have to get it back to him tomorrow otherwise we're both in deep trouble."

"Great. No pressure or anything."

"You'll be fine. Tip your head sideways."

In the wide mirror over the row of sinks, she saw him pull a pair of tweezers from the top pocket of his black field shirt. Raeanne tipped her head to the side and closed her eyes. There were some things she just didn't need to see over and over again in her dreams.

"Tate will be on the other end, receiving your communications and filtering out the sounds of your blood pumping and other ambient noise. In turn, you'll be able to hear our communications to you without anyone else overhearing anything, so we can keep up a stream of chatter if we need to without any security risks."

"What about water? This is a seagoing mission, remember."

"Just don't go swimming," Richardson said. "You're not dressed for it, anyway."

"The yacht has a hot tub. What if after dinner he wants to, uh…frolic?"

"Then frolic all he wants with your head above water."

"Thanks," she said. She turned her head to see her ear in the mirror. Nothing was visible, of course, and she couldn't feel a thing, but just knowing something was in there gave her the creeps.

Richardson pulled his sat phone from his belt and called in. "She's ready. Send her a test."

Very softly, almost as if she were dreaming it, Rosa Tate's voice spoke in her head. "Hi, Raeanne. Can you hear me?"

Rae turned to Richardson. "Can she hear me?"

"Yes," he and Rosa Tate answered together. If *that* wasn't weirdest thing she'd ever heard.

"I hear you," she said to Tate. "Can you bring up the volume just a tad, or is it fixed as is?"

"How's this?" Rosa asked, louder by the requested tad.

"Perfect. Can you hear me if I whisper?" Rae whispered.

"Yep. Don't worry, this thing's amazing. Just go get that bastard and let me worry about the earpiece."

"Will do." She turned to Richardson again and smiled. "I guess it's time to go get that bastard."

Chapter Seventeen

Alex fell into the cushioned leather executive chair in Richardson's office. His office, until the end of the operation. Mills dropped more gently into a leather chair on the other side of the desk.

"Don't move," Alex told him. He reached for the secure phone on Richardson's desk and started to punch numbers. "I am not having a good day and I would love the excuse to shoot someone right now—anyone—just to vent. So don't make it be you."

Mills let a small laugh pass his lips. "Roger that."

Richardson's cell went to voice mail.

"Damn." Alex waited for the beep. "Call me as soon as you get this. We have a major problem. We need to abort. And when we have time, I have some questions about the misinformation Abe King stuffed into Raeanne's dossier. But that's for another day. Call me."

"Why don't you just have one of the techies in the back contact them?"

Alex put the phone down and rubbed his tired eyes. "Because none of the techies are cleared to know where they are. You've heard of security, I imagine."

"They're in the field and no one knows how to reach them?"

"The person on the comm desk does, but I just locked her up."

Mills' eyebrow went up inquisitively, but Alex didn't say anything, just stretched out his bad knee and rubbed it.

"Who's Abe King?"

Alex heaved a great sigh, stretching his other leg out in front of him and closing his eyes. He was getting too old for this crap. "The bastard who ruined the best thing I ever had. Leave it alone. We have more important problems to deal with right now. What do you know about Heidi Smith?"

"That she's sure as hell not the kind of secretary I'm used to."

"Yeah, no kidding."

"If I may," Mills began, "is there a reason you decided to talk to me up here instead of down in your own private Alcatraz?"

"What else do you know about Heidi Smith?"

"Nothing. But I bet she's your leak."

Alex perked up at that. "And you know that, how?"

"Because you're suddenly more interested in what I know about her than in what I know about Petrov." He studied Alex a moment and seemed to relax his guard a bit. "And there was just something about her, like she was somehow always outside the moment. Not a natural part of the scenery, so to speak."

Alex nodded. It had been exactly what he'd been thinking. "Are you working with her?"

Mills made a face suggesting that Alex was an idiot.

"Look, Mills, I'm tired, my leg is killing me, and I'm really not in the mood for any crap."

"No," Mills said, "I am not in any way working with Heidi Smith."

"Good. Then that means you're working for me."

Mills laughed out loud this time. "What makes you think I'm interested in working with you? I mean, given the fact that you guys interrogated me like a common terrorist then tossed me behind bars. Not that I'm the kind of guy to hold a grudge."

"Because Raeanne needs you."

"Right. And I'm supposed to believe that you trust me all of a sudden?"

"Believe whatever you want. But I need you, and Raeanne needs you. Besides, she trusted you."

Mills let out another huff of amusement. "That's it? Because she trusted me? Not because you believe me, or that you could drive a tank through the holes in your people's accusations?"

"Look, I had nothing to do with your interrogation or with the decision to incarcerate you. I do, however, have evidence that Heidi Smith has been leaking information to Petrov's organization. I heard her myself. So that makes two things that I know: one, that Heidi Smith compromised this operation and has put the team at risk, and two, that Raeanne was ready to go to her grave defending your loyalty. That makes you my new best friend."

Mills gazed at him wordlessly a moment. "Thanks, I guess."

"I don't want your thanks; I want your help."

And that drew a sigh. "No can do," Mills said. "This isn't my business. I was supposed to retire in a few months, now I'm facing a court-martial. If you want to throw me back in the brig, fine, but I'm not getting myself in any deeper."

Alex felt his knee throbbing like a live lightning bolt, and something inside him started vibrating with the same hot, unpleasant energy. "So now you decide to be sensible? Funny how you weren't so concerned with being sensible when Raeanne came to you asking you to play cowboy."

"That was different."

"I'll say. Some woman you don't know comes up to you and asks you to help her kill some random bad guys? And you just said, 'Sure, lady, I don't know you, or who you work for, but let me get my rifle and I'll go shoot up a warehouse with you.' I guess you could call that 'different.'"

"Look, are you going to throw me back behind bars or am I free to go?"

"You must have had some reason for agreeing to help her." Alex felt his blood pressure starting to hammer at his temples. He'd seen how the guy looked at Raeanne, and he wanted him to admit it so he could threaten to feed him his liver if he ever looked at her again, and get this over with.

"I told you my reasons. I was bored. It was action. I couldn't have said no if I'd wanted to."

"Yeah, I know. Not many men can say no to Raeanne Springfield when she turns on the charm."

Mills laughed. "It wasn't like that at all."

Alex took a breath and swallowed. "Then what was it like?"

Mills let out a sharp breath. "Call it stupid sentimentality. As much as I don't like you, Major, I couldn't stand by and let you get yourself killed."

Alex opened his mouth, then shut it again. It was not the answer he'd been waiting for.

"You would have done the same for me," Mills added.

"Not if I could help it," Alex said.

"If it were you sitting there listening to Raeanne call every one of your bluffs and disarm every one of your arguments, you couldn't have helped it, either."

Alex sighed and rubbed his leg. "Now, that I might believe." He looked at the man across the desk from him, unshaven, a long line of stitches punctuating the angry red tear down his cheek, his dark eyes glaring back without fear. "On one condition."

"What's that?"

"Two conditions, actually. The first is that you get the bottle of Scotch out of the cabinet over there."

"And the second?"

"You're coming with me to DC"

Another sigh. "Why do I hear a third in there somewhere?"

"And third, the operation's been compromised. Petrov knows they're coming. If they move in on his yacht as planned, they'll be walking right into an ambush. And I can't reach Richardson to tell him to abort."

"So what are you planning to do about it?"

"*We* are planning to go down there and find him. I can't wait around for a callback that may never come. I promised Raeanne I'd get her son back. I can't let her walk into an ambush."

"Jesus, here we go again."

"Yep. And once we get to DC, if I still can't find them, you're going to fly me in to extract the boy myself."

"Fly?" Mills' calm finally crumbled, leaving him wide-eyed "You mean a helicopter?"

"You can still fly, can't you?"

"Hell, no! I haven't flown in ten years, and even back then I wasn't any good. Why do you think you found me in a hospital and not an airfield? I don't even have a license."

"Where we're going, no one's going to ask for your license."

"But my knee is all screwed up. You can't fly with a bad knee, you know that…"

"I know you're stalling, and that makes me wonder if it was a mistake letting you out of that cell."

Mills gazed at him a moment longer, as if considering his options, then stood and limped across the elegant office to the mahogany cabinet. From within he grabbed a bottle of Richardson's imported single malt Scotch and two crystal glasses, then brought them back to the desk. He poured for them both, doubles, then grabbed his glass and tossed it back. "What do you want, Dante. To be a hero? To fly in there and save the day?"

"Petrov knows they're coming. He's threatened to kill the

boy, and he doesn't make empty threats, I promise you."

"So why can't the field team take care of things? This organization of yours, whoever they are, strikes me as a very competent bunch."

"You know how to reach them?"

Mills was silent, glaring back at him with nothing to say.

"Neither do I," Alex said. "If I sit around and wait for a call-back, I may never get one. Richardson may already be dead. Either I go in there and warn them, now, or I can wait for some of my team to die. For maybe Raeanne and her boy to die. I won't let that happen."

"Have you considered the fact that maybe your CO put you on desk detail for a reason? Because he didn't want you screwing with the operation?"

"I'm sure that's exactly the reason. But that was before I knew Heidi Smith was working for Petrov."

Mills made a sound of disgust and poured himself another drink. "Ten minutes ago, you thought I was working for Petrov."

"Yeah, well I've changed my mind."

Mills took another swallow, then drained the glass. "The answer's still no. I can't fly a helicopter in this condition, and even if I could, I sure as hell was never good enough to insert someone onto a moving boat and lift out a little boy. A little boy? He won't know how to use the equipment, he'll be scared to death—probably so scared he won't even be able to move, let alone follow directions and be lifted into a moving chopper…while we take God knows how much fire? I'm sorry Alex, I'm just not your man."

"You're going to have to be; you're the only man I've got."

Mills groaned.

Alex downed his Scotch, giving himself time to thoroughly appreciate the heat rising up the back of his throat. He let it clear his sinuses, then burn its way down to his stomach before he set his glass down and spoke. "Look, I'm sorry you got involved. But you're involved now, and now I need you. You wanted to play cowboy? Then fine. Get your boots on and mount up."

Mills glared at him through narrowed eyes. "You're making a grave mistake, Dante. I'm not up to this. You want a sharpshooter, I'm all over it, but I'm telling you, I am not qualified to fly this kind of mission. I will get you and that poor kid killed."

"Then you'd better practice what you'll say to Raeanne when she finds you."

* * *

The marina was beautiful. Meticulously tended shrubs and flowerbeds wound in graceful, artfully lighted curves down past the main building and down toward the docks. "Heading down to the slip," she barely said.

"Copy," Tate said in her ear.

She found the "B" area and kept walking until she found the sign to slips for 31-36.

"Two men beside a small powerboat, looks like them," she said softly.

"Copy."

The two men looked up from their smokes. She didn't recognize either of them, which made her smile. Guess they'd gone through Petrov's A team and were playing against his bench. The taller one tossed his cigarette out into the water; the other took one more quick drag and ground the butt under his shoe.

"You are early," the taller one said, his dark eyes moving over her with unrestrained lust. "Illych, help the lady to embark."

The shorter man held out a hand, and she took it gracefully, allowing him to help her into the small powerboat bobbing at the end of the line.

The taller one followed, evidently the one with rank, and took a seat at the wheel. He started the engine while Illych untied the line and pushed off the piling with his foot. Raeanne sat on the contoured seat along the edge of the boat as the small craft moved smoothly out of its slip and toward open water.

"Raeanne, this is Tate," she heard in her ear. She looked out at the trees moving past on the shore, trying to listen unobtrusively. "I hear a motor," Rosa continued. "If you're aboard the boat and moving toward the yacht, clear your throat."

"A-hem."

The short one looked over at her. She gazed at him expressionlessly until he looked away.

"Good," Rosa said. "I'm here if you need me."

The urge to acknowledge bubbled up in her throat, but she remained silent. She watched the two men speaking softly in Russian. She tried to make out their words, but they were talking just a hair too quietly, and her Russian was just a hair too rusty.

The shore was moving away at a good clip now, and the wind was pulling her hair out of the clasp at her nape. She wondered why they hadn't stopped to search her, and wondered whether she ought to pull the little Derringer out of its hiding place high on her thigh and blow the two of them away while she had the chance. Before they turned into bigger problems later. Rosa could direct her to the yacht through the earpiece.

She let out a long breath. If Petrov saw her pull up sans bodyguards, that wouldn't bode well for the rest of the negotiations. Besides, she'd promised Richardson she'd follow orders.

She wished Alex were here. Somehow, moving along with this operation without him, she felt vulnerable, exposed. She didn't know what it was about him that made her feel so much safer and stronger and more capable than she did now, alone. Maybe that was what it was like to be in love with someone.

They were a good ways out to sea when she spotted the yacht.

The tall one picked up the radio and announced their arrival, and that they'd brought the stupid American cow with them. Apparently, he didn't know she spoke Russian.

Or maybe he did.

And speaking of stupid, they weren't really going to let her go aboard with a gun up her leg, were they?

The tall one cut the engine. There were two men waiting for them on the lower aft deck, where the boats and jet skis were stored. One of them tossed a line to the short one, who snapped it to its bolt on the bow and was winched up into its docking hatch. When the small boat was completely aboard and settled, the short one came over to her. "Stand up and turn around," he said in English.

Apparently they weren't quite as stupid as they looked. She stood, turning precariously on the uneven bottom of the boat in her stiletto sandals.

"Lift up your arms," he said in English.

She obeyed and didn't flinch when he used the opportunity to grope for more than a concealed weapon. When he got to her legs he found the revolver. "She's carrying a gun," he told his partner in Russian.

"Of course she is, the stupid cow, just take it off her and hurry up."

He unfastened the Velcro closure of her holster, letting his palm linger over the skin of her inner thigh and glancing up to make predatory eye contact with her.

She turned away and looked out at the water.

"She's a pretty little cow, though," the short one said, still speaking Russian, trailing a finger down her back. "At least the boss has good taste. I'd hate to see him go to all this trouble for an ugly woman."

"Too small, too skinny," the tall one said. "And look at her cowering there. She'd snap like a twig before you even got warmed up."

Raeanne kept her eyes looking toward the water. Let them think she was helpless. They'd soon find out differently.

"Perhaps before the boss kills you," he whispered to her in English, "he'll allow me to see for myself." He laughed and nudged her forward, to where another man held out a hand and helped her off the small boat and onto the yacht.

* * *

One of the men put a gun to her back and nudged her forward, heading her down a paneled passageway and into main salon of the Lady Rake. The place looked the same as it had back when she'd seen it last—all gleaming teak and brass, with gorgeous overstuffed furniture in rich, oxblood leather. The wide windows overlooking the bow were curtained now, but she remembered how the lights of the coast would glimmer at night through them, as if they were sailing through the night sky. Opposite the windows, the walls were lined with books, kept in their shelves with delicate, carved rails to prevent them from tumbling out in rough seas, although she didn't remember the seas ever getting that rough.

Beneath her feet, the dark Persian carpet was the real thing. So was the bastard who sat in the wing chair straight ahead.

"My dear Raeanne. How good it is to finally see you." He stood, all hundred and thirty pounds, soaking wet, of him. He'd aged considerably in the last seven years, his light hair having gone almost completely gray and his eyes seeming to bulge from his skinny face like a chameleon's. He'd always reminded her of a reptile, bony, grim-looking, and now with the lines around his mouth making tightly hung jowls of his flesh, and his eyes even more prevalent in their sockets, he looked as though at any moment his tongue would dart out of his mouth and catch a fly.

She knew she was supposed to be nice, to play along with him and make him feel as though she was still at his beck and call, but the bile was burning its way up her throat. "Where's my son?" she said, nearly spitting the words at him.

"Tsk, tsk. What way is that for old lovers to greet one another?" He took her elbows and pulled her forward to place a moist kiss on each cheek. Raeanne stepped back as soon as he pulled away.

"I want my son, and I want him now."

"And just what are you planning to do with him, my beloved? Swim him to shore? I think not. Why don't you rest a moment." He opened his arm toward the leather sofa, inviting her to sit. "Relax. Visit with me a while."

Reluctantly, she sat.

In her ear, she heard Rosa Tate. "Raeanne, the explosives will be set very soon, then you'll only have a few hours to go before the next phase. I want you to relax and let Petrov lead the conversation. Be pleasant. Be sweet. Chew off your own tongue if you have to, but do not, under any circumstances, force a confrontation."

She cleared her throat.

"Good girl," Rosa said. "I know you're dying inside, honey. Just keep it cool. I'll tell you when the chopper is in range."

She cleared her throat again in acknowledgement.

"Forgive me, you must be parched," Petrov said, standing and moving to the sideboard, where he poured her a drink from a crystal decanter. "The salt spray can be so drying to one's throat."

She forced herself down into that calm place, feeling herself remember how easy it had been back then, back when she was...

She almost said, *with Alex*.

Somehow, that calmed her. She could feel him, almost. She could almost hear him telling her not to worry, that he'd be right behind her.

"Thank you," she said, blinking the idea away. Alex was in Vegas. He was far, far from "right behind her." But she felt his presence, anyway, deep inside, where it mattered. She took the glass from Petrov's spindly fingers. Vodka. Petrov and his vodka.

She hated vodka, and the bastard knew it.

She downed it in one gulp.

"Thanks." She smiled at him as sweetly as she could through the fumes burning up her throat and choking her.

"Please, my beloved, sit down. We have a great deal to discuss."

* * *

Alex climbed into the cockpit of the chopper beside Dan Mills and strapped himself in. "Ready?"

"No."

"Good. Then let's get out of here before we attract attention."

Mills stared at the control panel for a moment. "I'm not even sure I can start this thing."

Alex reached over and pressed the starter. The engine whirred to life and the rotor began to turn, gradually moving more and more quickly until the thump-thump-thump of the air around them drowned out the sound of Mills' complaints.

Mills flipped a switch and Alex heard him over his headset. "This is your last chance to come to your senses before we die."

"Just fly."

Mills shook his head, grabbed hold of the cyclic, and lifted them into the air.

Alex pulled out his satellite phone. He'd tried half a dozen times since landing in Maryland to reach Richardson's cell, but he wasn't picking up. No surprise there. Anyone authorized to be contacting them in the middle of a black op wouldn't be calling on the phone.

Before they'd left, he'd searched Heidi's computer for anything he could use to reach Richardson, but as he'd expected, all he got was standard office programs and an unfinished game of solitaire. He'd considered going down to ask her how to reach them, but he was afraid that she'd be just clever enough to trick him into letting her out. And if he did, he was absolutely sure that she'd kill him. And in his condition, he wouldn't be able to stop her.

He prayed to God he'd be able to do this.

"Where's the boat?"

He turned his attention back to Mills. "Somewhere off shore, past the marina."

"Great," Mills said. "So we fly blind and look for a big boat, and try not to drop into the *wrong* big boat."

"Keep your ear on the radio and see if you can pick up any chatter. Maybe we'll get lucky." He felt an unaccustomed sense of foreboding as the water seethed by beneath them. Mills was right. This was crazy. How the hell was he supposed to rappel out of the chopper, evade enemy fire, locate Rae and the boy, and then get them back up to Mills all by himself—while hopping on one foot?

* * *

Raeanne leaned back against the leather chair and pretended to be interested in Petrov's prattle. Knowing that Ryan was somewhere on board was killing her. It was seven o'clock. Not long until Henderson and the new kid wired the boat, and another two-and-a-half hours or so until the chopper came for them. She had no idea how she was going to remain sane for that long.

Speaking of choppers...if she hadn't just downed her second shot of vodka, she'd have sworn she just heard one.

No, that was definitely a chopper. Change of plans? She glanced at Petrov, but he was engaged in rapt conversation with her breasts beneath the clingy red dress.

The sound moved off. Silence. Trying a different approach? Why wasn't Rosa coming on to give her any information?

"Shall we go up to the deck?" she asked. "I'm starting to get hungry for that dinner you promised me. And the sun's supposed to be setting soon, isn't it?"

Rosa chuckled. "Soon, Raeanne. Henderson and James are getting suited up as we speak."

Petrov smiled his thin, reptilian smile and stood, offering her his arm. "I'm so glad you've decided to do the intelligent thing and accede to my request," he said. "Can I get you another drink?"

She took his arm and giggled. It killed her, but she actually giggled. "Please, Dmitriy, you know I can't hold my vodka."

"Dmitriy? No more Dima?"

"Dima," she said, purring over the pet name like she used to. She wondered if he truly believed she could actually love him, or if he was just toying with her, or if he'd finally lost his mind.

He took her arm, hesitated, and then pulled her close and kissed her.

He tasted of vodka and bad teeth, and his collar smelled of one too many days between washings. But she kissed him anyway.

It was brief, thankfully, and then he smiled at her, wrapped her hand back over his arm, and led her to the companionway.

On the way out, she grabbed the vodka.

Petrov stopped and grinned at her.

"Changed your mind, my beloved?"

"Yes. The night is young, and ever since you mentioned it, I really have missed watching sunsets from the deck."

He chuckled and let her precede him with a hand to the small of her back.

The sun was sinking toward the waterline, etching the world in golden twilight. The breeze was cooler than she would have liked in her thin dress, but she just needed to make sure the chopper she'd heard earlier was truly just a coincidence. They weren't supposed to be here for another three hours.

It was no coincidence. She heard it coming around again.

She stretched her senses out, trying to determine which direction it was coming from, when Petrov led her to the chaise lounges and indicated she sit.

The deck of the flybridge was decorated for a garden party, as usual, with gaily colored striped patio furniture, a small, two-seat wet bar under a matching awning, and a circular Jacuzzi off by the starboard rail. Tall potted palms rippled faintly with the breeze, and a faint steam swirled up off the tub into the crisp evening.

"It's not too cool for you, my dear?"

"No. I like the ocean at sunset." She smiled at him. There. To her left. That was it, coming in from…the west?

Then, from behind her, "Mommy!"

She spun around and found Ryan running toward her, not ten feet away. A split second later, feet pounded onto the deck behind him.

Ryan threw himself into her arms before the two goons with the submachine guns could catch him.

"Mommy, I want to go home!"

Raeanne hugged him at tightly as she could, unable to think, unable to move. He was okay, he was here, right here, in her arms. Everything stood still, ceased to exist, except for the warm weight of him pressed up against her, his small arms tight around her neck and his downy hair pressed into her face, smelling of sun and salt and little boy.

One of the guards grabbed her and tore Ryan out of her grasp. She spun and punched the man in the nose, splattering blood over the deck. Then she pulled Ryan back into her arms.

"Let him go," Petrov said.

Raeanne looked over at him. The small gray eyes peering out at her from behind the round steel-rimmed lenses were directed solely at her, cold and uncompromising. The solicitous lover was gone, the deadly viper was back.

"Tell your men to keep their hands off my son, and I'll let your man keep his hands."

He laughed at that. "Well said, my beloved." He told them in Russian to leave them, and they acknowledged, stepping back and leaving Ryan where he was.

The chopper sounds became more insistent. This time, she wasn't the only one who noticed them. All heads turned to the left to see the helicopter bearing down on them. Not a Nighthawk, though, some tiny thing. Who the heck was flying that?

* * *

"When you get down there," Mills began, "secure the deck then go find Raeanne and the boy, because if they start shooting, I can't return fire."

"Roger that," Alex said. Mills' words replayed themselves, about the boy being too young and scared to use the line to be pulled to safety, but he pushed them aside. If he had to, he'd just have to grab the kid and pull him, kicking and screaming, into the chopper, and hope to hell the kid had his mother's gumption.

He wiped his hands on his black jump suit, feeling too heavy in all the gear. Kevlar vest and helmet, extra ammunition and flash-bangs slung around him, his sidearm, his rifle—it all seemed like too much to carry when he was going to be hopping on one leg most of the way, possibly with a flailing kid in his arms.

"I still can't believe you're doing this," Mills said.

"Just fly." Alex said.

Two minutes later, he saw it off in the distance. A vessel. It grew and took on realistic proportions. There were people on the deck. He grabbed his binoculars and zoomed in on them in the shadowy light of the sun, low on the horizon.

Men with submachine guns. Raeanne. The boy.

"That's them. Circle back for another pass." He unstrapped from the seat and took his position on the edge of the bay door, then connected his rappel lines. The wind roared past outside, pushing at him. The familiar rush of pre-jump adrenaline lit his veins. "And whatever you do, don't drop me too hard. If I break this knee again, it's all over. For everyone."

Mills groaned. "You'll be lucky if I don't put you down into the damn ocean. Or crash us into the damn boat."

They skimmed along the waterline, low to the surface. The setting sun was behind them, gilding the water with warm gold and dappling the yacht in shadow.

"Can you get close enough to put me down with all those people there?" he asked.

"If they're stupid enough to stand in the path of an oncoming chopper, they deserve what they get." Mills pushed toward the yacht, the wind from the chopper's rotors tossing up whitecaps and pressing Raeanne's dress against her legs as she looked up at them, shading her eyes with her hand. Then she grabbed the boy and shoved him toward the pilothouse, pressing him to the deck and covering him with her body. Petrov and the others pressed back, trying to get out of the way. From somewhere, the sound of automatic weapons fire crackled around him, pinging off the fuselage of the chopper.

Mills climbed and veered off.

"Where are you going? Get back there!" Alex shouted.

"Are you nuts? I can't put you down under fire like that, we're not armored! Besides, they're moving too fast; I can't keep us over the deck!"

"Yes, you can, and that's an order! Now turn back!"

Around both sides of the pilothouse came more Russians with automatic rifles. Alex saw Raeanne raise her arm and start shooting with some sort of sidearm. Men fell around her. Alex raised his rifle and took aim, but the chopper was bucking too erratically, trying to get in close without crashing.

"You see Petrov?" he asked Mills.

"Negative! Just get down there before I crash this thing into the damn pilothouse!"

Alex threw down the line and secured his clip. Below him, the deck moved in and out of view as Mills fought to hold them above it, now and then falling back over dark, angry water.

Alex jumped, anticipating their line of motion to bring them once again over the deck. Shots tore the air around him, ricocheting off the chopper, one tearing through the leg of his pants above his boot top and out the other side. Air raced past his face as he dropped, then a moment later he made his quick stop at the end.

The deck came up to meet him. He lunged hard to his good side, but his bad leg still took a jolt, it couldn't be helped. He swallowed a grunt of pain, then unclipped his rappel line and let the momentum of his landing slide him into the rail. Rounds went whizzing in every direction. He came up hard against the edge of the boat, scrambled behind the dubious cover of an overturned lounge chair, and pulled his rifle from the strap over his shoulder.

He was at the aft end of the deck, the pilothouse at his twelve, with Rae and the boy. He found Petrov, finally, crouched about three o'clock behind the edge of the hot tub, his gunmen hunkered down at intervals around the periphery. More shots dinged into the deck and the furniture. He swiveled his head around. Nothing behind him but water. That was good.

Mills was having a hard time with the chopper, letting it fall back to evade fire, then picking up speed to come back into range for the extraction, rolling side to side in his attempt to keep himself over the moving deck. Motion ahead caught his eye. Raeanne, racing across the deck toward him with the boy in one arm and her weapon raised in the other, shooting at everything and nothing to cover her travel. She slid into him like home plate, pushing the boy ahead of her, until they all slammed back into the rail.

"Give me your rifle!" she yelled.

He tossed it to her, and she immediately turned and began spraying the area to cover them.

Alex grabbed the boy. Mills must have been paying attention, because when he turned, the line was right there. He grabbed it, snapped the hook to his harness, and before he even signaled, they were moving upward and falling back, until they were over the water.

"Mommy!" The boy's voice was shrill and panicked, and very close to Alex's ear.

Raeanne continued to fire with one hand and raised the other to wave briefly at Ryan, but if she said anything, her words were lost under the whir of the chopper engine and the rhythmic thump of the rotors overhead. The boy reached out to her, pulling away from Alex, but he dragged him back against his chest. One of the Russians stood and raised his rifle at them, but below, Raeanne put both hands back on her weapon and took him down.

"Mommy!" the boy yelled again, panicking and tightening his little arm like a vise around Alex's neck as they gained altitude. His foot flailed out and kicked Alex's bad knee. Fire erupted in it, and for a second Alex thought he was shot, but then the winch stopped and they were at the open bay doors, and he couldn't stop to worry about it. He took a deep breath to clear the stars from his vision, then heaved himself upward, but the boy was in his way, his body trapped between Alex and the hatchway.

There was no one to haul the boy in, and the boy seemed to have every intention of garroting Alex with his wiry arms. Alex grabbed the boy's wrist, but as soon as he got it free, the other found Alex's neck and dug in for dear life.

"Let go!" he shouted. "Get in!"

"I can't!" the boy yelled.

"It's okay; you won't fall. I've got you!"

The boy stared at the open hatch, not loosening his hold on Alex's neck. Finally, he let go with one hand and reached tentatively for the hatch. Then he thought better of it and wrapped it back around Alex's neck.

Bullets struck the fuselage just beside them. Mills banked the chopper around and moved out of range.

The force of the turn swung them away from the hatch. The boy clawed Alex's neck again, and Alex dug in, wrapped his arms around the boy, and hoped they both didn't end up in the water.

The air was cold and fast moving, and it was hard to breathe. The boy was clinging to him, too scared to cry, his face a rictus of sheer horror. Alex tried once more to shove him up through the hatch, and this time, luck was with them. The boy grabbed on to something inside and Alex shoved him in. He scrambled in behind him, pressed him to the deck to keep him from rolling back out, then pushed him over to the opposite side, got him into a seat, and strapped him in.

He sat beside him and heaved a huge sigh of relief.

Mills turned to give him a thumbs up, then banked again and headed for home.

"I know you," the boy said in a soft, very small voice.

Alex glanced down at him. He really was a tiny little kid. Were all seven-year-olds that small? "What did you say?"

"I know you," the boy said again. "You're the man in the

picture."

"Oh, yeah? What picture is that?"

"The picture of my daddy."

Alex blinked, caught in a rush of foreboding. Then it registered. "You've seen a picture of me and your daddy?"

"No, my mommy."

Huh? "A picture of me, and your daddy, and your mommy?"

The boy rolled his eyes and heaved a dramatic sigh. Alex felt his breath catch in his throat; he'd seen that mannerism about a million times on Raeanne.

"No-o-o-o," the boy said, obviously annoyed at having to explain something so simple to such an imbecile. "Just you and my mommy. Sitting by the fountain with the mermaids. The one on the bureau."

His breath caught completely, like a bullet to the chest. The picture of Raeanne and him at the fountain outside the Paris Hotel down on the Strip, the picture he'd seen in her room when he'd caught up with her there, sitting right there on her bureau.

The picture of my daddy.

Oh, God…

And there it was. He didn't need to think about it, wonder about it, question it. It just was, as if it were something he'd always known, had always been. The boy sitting next to him, his baby-fine dark hair plastered to his face, gazing impatiently up at him with those green, green eyes. *His* face. *His* eyes.

His son.

"Yeah," he said, or tried to, but nothing came out. He cleared his throat. "Yeah, buddy. That's me."

Then the thoughts came, a thousand of them. How he could have missed it, how he could have not known. Why his fear and anger and sense of betrayal and loss had overcome common sense and made him think this boy could have been someone else's. Anyone else's. Especially…

But none of those thoughts lingered for more than a heartbeat. None of them mattered. All he could do was look into the small round face, into those eyes, and see himself. And Raeanne. And everything that did matter in the whole of the world.

"My-name-is-Ryan-A.-Springfield-it's-a-pleasure-to-meet-you," the boy recited, then thrust out his hand. The wrong one.

Something in Alex's throat caught as he reached out his own left and awkwardly shook the small, cold hand. "Alex Dante. And the pleasure's all mine."

* * *

Raeanne grabbed the MP5 that skittered across the deck from the hands of the fallen gunman. She could hear the chopper beating its way into the distance, carrying Ryan away from Petrov and this mess that had suddenly erupted all around her. With Alex Dante. What the hell had that been all about?

"Raeanne, acknowledge!" Rosa Tate shouted in her ear. She'd been chattering at her for the last few minutes, ever since the shooting started and the sounds of the helicopter's rotors became too loud to miss. But Raeanne couldn't answer; there was too much going on, too many bullets flying.

Finally, she got her feet under her and spoke. "Sorry about that. All hell's broken loose."

"Who's shooting? Whose chopper was that?"

"Everybody's shooting," she said, firing a three round burst at the oncoming Russian. Where were they all coming from? There were at least a half dozen bodies scattered over the deck, two had been knocked overboard somehow, when the chopper had come close to taking out the pilot house and only by some miracle had managed to remain upright instead of cartwheeling over into the water. That was when she'd seen Alex Dante rise up from the rubble around the deck, take Ryan practically out of her arms and launch them both at the line dangling out of the helicopter. After that, she'd taken up shooting everything that moved.

"Raeanne, who was in that chopper?" Rosa said again.

"Alex Dante."

There was a moment of stunned silence, then, "Come again, Raeanne?"

Another body darkened the pilothouse doorway. It was the short one who'd patted her down before boarding. He raised his submachine gun, but Rae's came up faster. There was only a moment of fire before her magazine was empty, but by then, Shorty was no longer a threat.

"Raeanne, acknowledge!"

She crawled out of her hiding place and reached for the assault rifle the dead man had dropped. "Yeah. I'm taking a lot of fire here; I could use a little help if you could send someone around."

"We've got the chopper in the air, ETA about seven minutes. Just hang in there."

"I'm hanging."

"Raeanne, did you say Alex Dante was in that chopper?"

"That's affirmative. He has Ryan, and they appear to have gotten off safely. Now I just need you to get me the hell out of here."

"We're on the way," Rosa said. "Just play it smart."

Another figure shadowed the doorway.

Petrov.

His shirt was torn and bloody, and he held the assault rifle casually in his right hand, pointing downward. His glasses were askew on his face, and it made him look crazed and desperate. And very, very angry.

"Drop the weapon," he said. "Now." He swung the muzzle of the rifle up and thrust it into her face.

A sense of recklessness overcame her as she stared up into those cold, reptilian eyes, and she toyed with the idea of just shooting him. But her weapon was lowered, pointing toward the deck, and in the time it would take to raise it, he would have killed her twice.

She put the recklessness aside and tossed down the submachine gun. Ryan was safe, and he needed a mother. Vengeance was nothing compared to that.

"Stand up and put your hands behind your head," he said.

She stood.

"Who were you talking to?" he asked.

"No one."

He swung the rifle and the muzzle connected with the side of her head. Pain shot through her temple and she spun into the bulkhead, losing all sense of equilibrium as she fell, until the deck slammed up into her face.

"I heard you talking, reporting about the helicopter and Alex Dante, and requesting your people come to extract you. Now where are they?"

"You're crazy," she said, feeling her gorge rise. She was going to be sick. Her hand brushed her hair and came away sticky with blood.

Petrov hit her again, and this time, everything went black.

* * *

Raeanne came to in darkness. She felt terrible, and her head was spinning. Just what she needed, another head injury. Her hair clip was gone, and her hair hung in her face, tacky with drying blood. She was tied hand and foot, around some sort of pipes. Engine room?

"Rosa, are you reading me?" she whispered.

Nothing.

"Rosa, acknowledge," she said, louder.

Nothing.

Crap. The blow to the head must have sent the earpiece to

electronics hell. Either that, or it was embedded somewhere in her brain. She tugged at the ties binding her wrists. Tight. Felt like nylon rope, boating line of some kind. She tested her feet. Just as tight. But tied up was better than dead.

She wondered how long she'd been unconscious. Rosa had said the team was only about seven minutes out, so either they'd be there any minute, or she'd been out for a long time and they'd come and gone. She listened, trying to identify any sounds that might be audible around her, but all she heard was the rumble of the engine.

A door opened, letting in a shaft of light. Petrov stood haloed in amber.

"What a shame you've deceived me, my beloved," he said. He flipped a switch and the lights came on, then he moved inside and took a seat at the console across from her. "I've worked very hard over the last few years to raise my organization from the shambles you made of it seven years ago, you and your friend Alex Dante. Now you have cost me my warehouse, and many of my most loyal troops, and now the Lady Rake."

"Yeah, well, you win a few, you lose a—"

"Silence!" He was bathed in sweat and a large vein bulged at his temple. A distant, half-crazed look in his eyes told her he was miles away from his normal, icy calm. "You have destroyed me," he said. "You, to whom I would have given the world."

"I didn't want the world," she said. "I just wanted my son back. It was you who forced the confrontation."

"Yes." He grabbed her hair and pulled her toward his face. The scent of him was stronger up close, pungent with old sweat and vodka and fear. "But that wasn't how I wanted it to end."

It was all she could do to not retch or turn away. "What are you talking about, Petrov?"

"I'm talking about us, my beloved. And about how

brightly we could have shone together, like stars in the evening sky." He caresses her cheek with one trembling finger. "But never mind. The engine room will burn brightly enough on its own."

He pushed her away, popped open the cabinetry that covered much of the mechanical workings of the vessel, raised his rifle, and fired a loud burst into the engine area, sending forth a rain of sparks and wood chips.

She heard it a moment before she smelled it. Gasoline, pouring out of a torn hose and splashing onto the floor.

"I would have married you all those years ago, my beloved," he said. "I would have cherished you above all else. Now, you leave me with nothing. Nothing." With a brief glance about the room, he stood, pulled a book of matches from his pants pocket, and struck one.

* * *

"Alex, I've picked up some radio chatter, sounds like your team," Mills said.

"What about?"

"They're sending in a boat and a chopper, seems someone was taking heavy fire, and now they're lost communication. Sounds like they're talking about Raeanne."

Alex's blood ran ice cold. "Turn us around," Alex said.

"But the boy..."

"I said turn us around, now, and that's an order!"

"Whatever you say," Mills said and made a sharp bank in the sky.

Petrov tossed the match toward the engine compartment. It landed on the floor, beside a spreading puddle of gasoline, but just as the puddle came close, the match guttered out, leaving only a small tendril of smoke wafting halfheartedly into the air.

"Fate mocks me," he said, "even down to the minutest detail."

Raeanne watched him, trying to still the erratic slamming of her heart in her chest.

"Very well, then," he said. "If fate is determined to control my destiny, then we shall let it." He bent down and untied her wrists, then her ankles. "Come with me."

She made herself go calm. No panic, no fear, just calm deliberation. She stood, resisted the urge to rub her chaffed wrists, and followed him, hoping to God that Fate wouldn't chose that moment to blow them to smithereens.

He led her through the passageway toward the staterooms, and she noticed he was limping slightly. She could take him. He was small for a man, not much larger than she was, and much older. All she'd need would be to get one good shot to his face, shatter his nose, and it would be all over.

At the end of the passageway, he turned into the forward-most stateroom. The master suite. He bent and pulled a revolver out of the nightstand beside the bed.

Crap.

He pointed the gun in her face. "Take off your clothes."

"I thought you liked me in red," she said, trying to smile.

"I'll like you better dead. Take off the dress."

She reached behind her and grabbed the zipper, then thought better of it. "Here, I need your help." She turned her back toward him and used both hands to lift up her hair.

Nothing happened for a moment, then finally, she felt the zipper being tugged downward.

With both hands holding up her hair, she took a breath and spun around, elbow first.

Her elbow connected with Petrov's head. He recoiled, but he didn't drop the gun. Raeanne slammed her foot down onto his instep and spun with the other elbow, down low. This time, he grunted, taking the elbow in the gut. She turned and grabbed his gun hand, twisting it.

"Ah, you little demon! I will kill you!" He grabbed her arm and got a hand into her hair, twisting her head back. Somehow, he still had the gun, and now it was at her head.

Raeanne spun in his grasp and got her arm around Petrov's throat. A fist to the temple and he went down like a rock. The gun fell from his hand and spun off across the floor.

He grappled for it.

She stomped on his fingers. His other arm reached out, longer than hers, and grabbed her leg. She went down atop of him and his arm snaked out to wrap around her throat.

She scissored her legs around him and flipped them both over, pinning him to the floor. He grabbed for the gun, but she was faster. Her fingers closed around the grip as he flailed beneath her, trying to throw her off.

She thumbed back the hammer and rammed the gun against his temple. "Now who's going to kill whom?" she said and pulled the trigger.

The hammer clicked harmlessly against the empty chamber.

She pulled the trigger twice more. Nothing.

"You lucky bastard," she said then she ran.

She ran to the deck, not sure where she was going to go, but hoping she'd stumble upon another of the dead men's guns. There were none. Bodies still littered the deck, but there wasn't a weapon in sight.

She found herself at the aft rail, overlooking the lower deck where the leisure craft were kept. The jet skis, the catamaran. *The power boat.* The wind ripped at the unzipped back of her dress, making goose bumps rise on her bare skin.

Then she heard the chopper. She waved her hands wildly overhead as it made a beeline for the yacht.

A gunshot rang out from behind her. She turned to see Petrov with the revolver, evidently reloaded, stumbling toward her out of the companionway. The thrumming of the choppers rotors overhead was getting closer, but they weren't as close as Petrov's gun. She feinted left, then ran right, dodging his last shot as she raced across the deck to where the starboard rail overlooked the icy black water below, then, without a backward glance, she vaulted over the side.

A huge burst of light exploded behind her, a bright orange fireball that glowed across the water and filled the air with billowing black smoke. The sound came a split second later, a boom that nearly deafened her. Then the blast hit her, the exploding mass of hot, moving air that swept over the ocean, blowing her through the air and slamming her onto the surface of the water.

Somewhere in her peripheral vision she saw the helicopter tossed into the sky like a toy, the hot orange fireball pressing it upward and outward, but that was all she saw before she hit the water again and was propelled through it like a plowshare, unable to think or move or breathe until the force that drove her through the rough wall of water exhausted itself and she came to a stop and started to sink. She took a second to get her bearings, then flailed madly for the surface, gasping and choking on mouthfuls of saltwater, and became vaguely aware that she'd lost her dress and her right shoe in the explosion, and that she was going to die wearing only a white lace thong and one dangling, broken sandal.

* * *

Alex's breath was swallowed in the furious roar of the explosion. Hot air pushed him out through the open bay door, and he hit the water hard, so hard the wind was knocked out of him as the cold water closed over his head. His lungs shrieked for air as he twisted in the dark water, trying to find his way to the surface again. Wreckage sank down around him in a strange rain of wood, melted plastic, and odd things—a tin cup, an unbroken ceramic figurine of a salty sea captain, and a charred, half-melted television with a shattered screen that toppled end over end as it sank on his right.

Above him the world burned. He could see the flames dancing above him, oddly distant through the surface of the dark water. It seemed like the entire sky was afire. And in this shifting, angry orange and red light, he thought of Raeanne.

And his son. He broke the surface just as his lungs were about to suck in seawater. It took him a few minutes to catch his breath, and while he breathed, he looked up into the sky, hoping to see the helicopter.

Please don't let them be dead…

Then he heard them. *Them*, plural. There was more than one chopper overhead somewhere. He turned himself in the water, but he couldn't see them.

A blast of heat greeted him. The entire stern of the yacht had been blown to pieces and thrown everywhere. The bow remained somewhat intact, though the flames were quickly devouring it. Floating debris was everywhere in the water, some of it still on fire. The gutted ship was listing, seconds from sinking and perhaps pulling them all down in the undertow.

He treaded water perilously close to it, ignoring the waves of heat that washed against him, ignoring the debris that knocked into him. The air reeked of smoke and the harsh stench of burning plastic. Greasy smoke curled up to cast a veil across the setting sun.

Yes, there. The chopper. The Nighthawk. He spun in the water, looking up into the dark sky. The other one, Mills', was beating the air behind him.

Please let the boy be all right…

He waved and called out, but he knew they couldn't hear him over the sound of the rotors. The Nighthawk was moving away, shining its searchlight over the dark surface of the water, but Mills' smaller chopper circled around. Alex saw a line snake out, but not to him. It splashed down about a hundred yards off. A form appeared at the waterline, on the rope, and he could barely see it being lifted out.

He swam toward them, coughing the nasty cough of fire and smoke—again—and when he kicked his bad leg, the pain nearly sunk him. He turned onto his back to let himself float, took a few deep breaths, and hoped he wouldn't pass out in the water.

Something hit him. He opened his eyes, not realizing he'd closed them. The chopper was hovering directly overhead, and someone was leaning out of the bay waving at him, a dark silhouette against the red light of the setting sun. He shouted, but his words were swallowed by rotor noise. The waving arm was definitely female; Kyra Knight, maybe? Mills must have fished her out of the water, too…

He glanced around and saw the line she'd tossed down. He grabbed it, wrapped his good leg around it, and let Mills winch him up, facing blindly into the sun, his insides twisting with the fear of not finding Ryan when he got to the top.

He got to the dark chasm of the bay doors, blinded by the sudden darkness, and felt her hands grabbing at him. "Where's Raeanne?" he asked. "Where's the boy?"

"He's fine!" she shouted over the throb of the rotors. "Now help me get you in!" She grabbed his left arm and pulled, and he felt himself sliding upward. Then his knee slammed against the fuselage. There was a sudden surge of white, hot agony, and he knew he was going to pass out. But before he did, he caught a flash of Ryan's small, grinning face across the bay, and…Raeanne? Darkness closed around him, but he could have sworn it was Raeanne leaning over him, smiling, wet, and…naked?

* * *

A cool hand brushed his cheek, pulling him back to consciousness.

"Hey, Alex," she said. "Alex!"

He came fully alert at the sound of his name. "Raeanne?"

It *was* Raeanne, looking down into his eyes, looking worried. When he brought her into focus, she smiled.

"Hey," she said.

"Hey," he said back. She was soaked, her hair plastered back from her face in a wet tangle, black eye makeup smeared around her eyes like a raccoon, hugging herself under a wool blanket and shivering.

She *was* naked.

"Alex! Alex!" Beyond Raeanne's right shoulder, Ryan was bouncing in his seat restraint, trying to get his attention. His *son*.

"Hey, buddy," Alex said.

"I'm still in my seat," he announced, proudly. Alex noticed he was missing a front tooth.

"You done good, buddy," he said. Laughter bubbled out of him, and it hurt—broken rib, somewhere—but he didn't care.

"So did you, buddy," Raeanne said and caressed his cheek again with her hand. The blanket gaped a bit as she moved, and her bare shoulder looked very…bare.

Gagging noises started coming from the seat where Ryan was sitting. "E-e-e-w," he said to Mills, "I bet they're gonna *kiss*."

"Yeah," Mills said, grinning back at them like a demented insect in his helmet and goggles. "Gro-o-o-ss!"

"Gro-o-o-ss," Raeanne whispered, her eyes bright as the blanket gaped a little wider, and then she bent forward and kissed him. Right on the lips, too.

Epilogue

Raeanne lay back and let the sun melt into her skin. Her toes dug a little deeper into the warm sand, her left hand brought the cool glass to her lips and she sipped the frozen margarita with her eyes closed. Overhead, gulls cried against the rhythmic music of the surf, and Alex's hand was warm in her right. She toyed idly with the band around his finger, the thick gold one that she'd slid onto it the day before, before God and her battered CODA teammates and Diane Helmsan, who showed up way overdressed to be her matron of honor at the Canterbury Wedding Chapel at the Excalibur Hotel back in Vegas.

It felt strange.

So did the ring.

But being married felt even stranger, and being married to Alex felt stranger, still. Like something from a movie. She almost expected him to disappear, or that she'd wake up and find out that it was, sadly, all a dream.

"What are you thinking?" Alex asked.

"After two margaritas and all this sun?" she said, not opening her eyes. "Nothing intelligent."

"Good. Because when you're quiet too long, that's when you get dangerous," he said.

She blew him a raspberry. It was starting to become a bad habit, but ever since Ryan's comment on the chopper, they'd been behaving like seven-year-olds.

"Just thinking about how weird it is to be married to you," she said.

"Uh, yeah. Thanks."

She squeezed his hand. "You need anything?"

"Nope."

"You ready to go back to the hotel?"

"Ryan's still building that sand...thing. Thank heaven there are no shrinks on this beach. He said it was a castle, but it looks like a giant, 3-D inkblot."

Rae smiled. "Must be crazy like his father."

"Yeah, he must, because I certainly can't think of one sane thing I've done in the last two weeks."

"Ha. You married me." She sat up, opened her eyes, and grinned at him.

He grinned back. "Like I said..." He leaned over and kissed her, and she let herself slide into the warmth of his lips.

It was truly paradise. The sun, the surf, the blue, blue water. It was only California, only a pre-honeymoon, a two-day stop at the beach to unwind, to spend a couple of days playing with Ryan and a couple of nights making love before Alex went back into the hospital to have his leg put back together. Again. He was in an immobilizer—again—and he was actually wearing it, which told her that it was bothering him more than he admitted. But they were together, at last, the three of them, and anywhere that took place would be paradise in her book.

"Do you think Richardson will offer Dan Mills a job?" she asked.

"He already did. I spoke to him this morning when you were out buying the bathing suit for Ryan."

"He changed his mind about him then, after the op?"

"After rescuing half the team from the water? Yeah, I'd say Dan Mills is pretty much everyone's new best friend."

"Good. He'll make a good operative."

"Better than you, at any rate."

Raeanne sat up abruptly and gaped at him, open-mouthed, like a fish. "Excuse me?"

Alex grinned. "*He* follows orders."

"Hrmph. Like you should talk."

Alex laughed and brought her hand to his lips.

She snatched it away and left him kissing air. "And don't even try to kiss me again until you tell me your real name."

"I told you, it's Engelbert Van der Krupkowitz."

"Give me break. That's not a real name. That's not even a real nationality." She leaned back into her chair and closed her eyes.

"Richardson also said he was sending Mills off to find the incredible disappearing Heidi."

She sat back up. "Mills? Why him?"

"Who knows. I think part of it's a test. I think he's still got a nagging feeling that Mills was involved with her somehow, ridiculous at that sounds. I think he wants to see if he's really going to bring her in."

"Does Mills have those kind of skills? To track someone who doesn't want to be tracked?"

"I guess we'll find out."

Raeanne was silent a moment. "I can't believe Heidi was a Russian spy. She was just so…normal."

Alex looked over at her with one eyebrow raised. "Normal? Uh, no."

"Well, I mean, ordinary. Like any typical twenty-something you'd find shopping for Coach bags." Raeanne sat up and finished her margarita, then looked over at Ryan and his sand…thing.

"I hope he catches her and brings her back and they hang her sorry ass for treason."

"Just how did she get out, anyway? Has anyone ever escaped from the agency detention area?"

"Nope. Someone let her out. Question is, who?"

"Well, Mills will get her. And then I'll be the first in line to testify at her trial." Raeanne felt the blood begin to pound through her veins. It was Heidi, after all, who'd taken the information about Ryan out of her folder, and caused him to be left unguarded.

She watched him dribbling wet sand on the big lump of dribbled sand that looked, as Alex had said, very much like a 3-D inkblot. He must have felt her eyes on him, because he looked up and waved.

She waved back, and felt a momentary tug at her throat, as if she were going to cry.

"I love you," Alex said. "Only next time you have my babies, let me know, okay?"

The tension bubbled out of her in a burst of laughter. "That joke is starting to get a little ragged around the edges, Mr. Van der…whatever."

He grinned his feral grin. "Van der Kripkowitz."

"Ha! I knew you were lying! Last time, it was *Krup*kowitz!"

"No, it wasn't."

"Yes, it was!"

He grinned at her. "See how nervous you make me, with all that talk about having more babies? Makes a man forget his own name."

She felt her blood begin to race again. "Alex, if you want to change your mind, it's okay, I'll understand…"

"About having babies?"

She swallowed. "Or about retiring from field work. I know the agency is your life, and I really don't believe you'd ever be happy behind a desk…"

He laughed out loud. "Rae, how long do you think it's going to be before I can walk again? Let alone walk without a brace? Babe, my days of jumping out of choppers are long gone, whether I like it or not. Besides, the last seven years the agency got out of me were more than they deserved for what they did."

"Not the agency, just Abe. And he was only doing what he thought was best."

"And look how well it turned out."

She glanced around her, at the warm sandy beach, the gulls squawking overhead, the frozen margarita sweating in her hand, the gold band glinting madly in the sun. "Looks good from where I'm sitting."

He sighed. "But it could have looked like this years ago. Ryan and I could have had all his life together. He could have avoided that whole ordeal. He almost got killed, Raeanne."

Her grin faded. Her throat tightened, and she got up out of her chair to move beside Alex. "We can't play that game — would've/could've/should've. A lot of things may or may not have happened. We don't know what might have happened. Any alternate past histories are just as unknown to us as the future. All we can do is be grateful for where we are right now. Here. Together. Safe."

He sighed again, resigned. "But I hate paperwork."

She slapped his arm. "Suck it up, Dante, Richardson promised you a non-paperwork-related position. Consulting."

"*Consulting*. Right." He smiled at her again. "I guess it's better than flipping burgers."

She laughed and wrapped her arms around his neck. "Besides, if you had a real job, how would we make all those babies?"

He kissed her, and she felt herself warming to his touch. Her blood started to race again, only this time, for a much better reason.

"Good point," he said.

She kissed him again, and a cold, wet, gritty glop fell on her head.

"Arrrgh!"

Maniacal, seven-year-old laughter bubbled around her as she leapt involuntarily out of her chair, wet sand running down her face. And her back. And the front of her bathing suit.

"Prepare to get very wet, you little beast!" And she chased him to the water's edge.

* * *

Alex watched her tear after the boy, catch him at the shoreline, and lift him, squealing with childish delight, high in her arms. She ran into the oncoming waves until she was hip high, then tossed the writhing mass of little boy into the water with a resounding splash.

He smiled. He'd been doing that a lot the last few days, smiling.

Hell, if she was willing, he'd give her a dozen kids. If that was what she wanted. But either way, his days as a field operative were completely, irrevocably, over. And he was ready for them to be. It was time to lay around on the beach...*consulting*...and let the new kids take the beatings.

From the bottom of the canvas beach bag, his cell phone rang.

What the hell had she brought that for? And she gave him a hard time about work?

It rang again, went to voice mail.

Good. What kind of idiot would bother them on their honeymoon, anyway?

It rang again, immediately, with that ominous ring of something very, very wrong.

He leaned over to Rae's bag and fished through it until he got the phone. "Dante."

"Alex, we have a problem." It was Kyle McHugh. "You have to come back. Richardson's dead."

"What?"

"He's been murdered."

Alex felt the bottom drop out of his stomach. "When?"

"This morning. He left some documents regarding protocol in case something happened to him. Apparently, he was expecting this."

"Who's running the agency?"

"That's what he left in those documents. You are."

Alex's blood froze. "No, that's not possible. I just spoke to him this morning. I'm supposed to be just consulting. I'm retired."

"Alex, please, after all this gets settled down, you can appoint someone to replace you. But right now we need you. His letter indicated that if anything happened to him, to look for Heidi Smith."

"Aw, hell," Alex said.

"And on top of that, Heidi's escape has left a huge security breach, and the place is crawling with friggin' CIA. Please, Alex. Just help us deal with the brass and help organize the investigation into Richardson's murder. Everyone's coming apart without a director."

Alex looked out toward the shore and almost jumped out of his chair to find Raeanne and Ryan standing right over him, grinning, and shaking water on him like a couple of wet dogs. She must have seen it in his face, because her expression sobered. *What*? she silently mouthed.

"Please, Alex," Kyle said again.

Ales heaved a huge sigh. "I'm on my way," he said and snapped the phone shut.

"What's wrong?" Raeanne asked.

"Richardson's been murdered." He didn't give her time to speak. "Seems he left documents implicating Heidi Smith. The place is crawling with CIA and everyone's a mess."

"And...?"

"And apparently he appointed me acting director. But only until the mess gets cleaned up."

She looked at him with defeat. "I guess we should get packed, then."

"I'm sorry," he said.

She took his hand and gave it a squeeze. "Don't be. The

team needs you. Richardson chose you for a reason, same as I did."

"Thanks," he said. "But I really don't know what they expect me to do that they're not already doing. Damn it, I hate the CIA."

She smiled again and planted a kiss on his lips, cool and wet and tasting of salt and sunshine. "I'm sure when we get there, you'll figure something out." And then she stepped back and started shoving toys into the tote bag, and he knew that no matter what they found when they got back to the office, he'd already gotten the most important things figured out. She was there, so was he, and Ryan, and nothing on earth could trump a hand like that.

~ About the Author ~

Kendal Flynn was born on a mountaintop in Tennessee before going on to sail with Long John Silver and slay dragons with Beowulf. It took her a while to realize that girls weren't supposed to be getting dirty with the boys, but she never quite found the fun in standing around and wringing her hands, waiting for some stuck-up dandy to ask her to dance.

She'd have been more likely to take the dandy at sword point and tell him to dance with her, or else.

Of course, in real life, she's a very ordinary administrative assistant, who's never taken anyone at sword point and who can't dance anyway. She lives in Southeastern Massachusetts with her husband, three children, and two amazingly spoiled Chihuahuas, which she admits are not the wisest choice for an action/adventure author looking to build an image.

You can find out more about Kendal at:
www.kendalflynn.com
www.kendalflynn.wordpress.com
http://twitter.com/kendalflynn
http://www.facebook.com/kendalflynn